Staying with Relations

Staying with Relations
A NOVEL BY
Rose Macaulay

THE ECCO PRESS
NEW YORK

First published in 1930 by Collins Ltd., London
First United States edition copyright © 1987 by
the Estate of Rose Macaulay

Published in 1987 by The Ecco Press
26 West 17th Street, New York, N.Y. 10011
Published simultaneously in Canada by
Penguin Books Canada Ltd., Ontario

PRINTED IN THE UNITED STATES OF AMERICA

Library of Congress Cataloging-in-Publication Data
Macaulay, Rose, Dame.
Staying with relations.
Reprint. Originally published: London : W. Collins Sons, c1930.
I. Title.
PR6025.A16S7   1987   823'.912   87-6759
ISBN 0-88001-148-3

*Publication of this book was made possible in part by a
grant from the National Endowment for the Arts*

Has the sea form ? It breaks, it drifts,
  Encountering with the steepy sands.
Has water shape ? It slips and shifts,
  Thinner than dreams, between thy hands.

Sly, dubious ghost, the blind mist slides
  At cockshut up the wasty fell.
The pale, the Protean cloud-shape glides
  Through a hundred forms, most mutable.

Shifting as mist, men's secret selves
  Slip like water, and drift like waves,
Flow shadow-wise, and peer like elves
  Mocking and strange, from the deep caves.

The brook runs bound within its hollow ;
  The cuckoo needs must cry cuckoo.
As swallows skim, so skims the swallow ;
  The wild deer does as wild deer do.

Grasp at the wind ; aye, bind the mist ;
  Read the bright riddling of the skies.
But the soul, like slippery eel, will twist
  Quick from thy clutch, and trick thine eyes.

It bears no form ; it breaks, it drifts,
  Encountering with the steepy world.
It holds no shape ; it slips and shifts,
  Thinner than tunes on the wind skirled.

CONTENTS

CHAPTER I

I

CATHERINE GREY, a young female, and, like so many young females, a novelist, went to America one autumn and lectured to its inhabitants on the Creation of Character in Fiction. Catherine was twenty-seven, but had, nevertheless, so far only published three novels, for though diligent, she wrote slowly and at some length. If anyone should desire to know whether or not she also wrote well, I can but reply that her novels pleased some tastes and not others, and that it is impossible to say more or other than this of any writings, since philosophers have unfortunately failed, down the ages, to arrive at any fixed standards of merit in art. Catherine's novels were probably quite averagely readable, as novels go.

Catherine wrote about people ; it was character that engaged her interest and attention. People, their temperaments, habits, and reactions to one another— these seemed to her, and very properly, to be the very stuff of fiction. She had always perceived between one person and another those little differences which it takes the observant and careful eye to remark. People stimulated and absorbed this young woman ; they were her hobby. " You're so clever," said the in-

9

habitants of Much Potton, South Devonshire, where
Catherine's father had a vicarage. "We're all frightened
of you, lest you put us in a book." At this Catherine
would smile, scarcely liking to say either that she
would put them in a book, which might seem impertinent, or that she would not put them in a book,
which might seem neglectful ; and, indeed, she scarcely
knew whether they desired her to put them in a book
or not. But in any case she had lived much too long
in Much Potton, South Devonshire, and before that in
Prior's Combe, North Devonshire, and before that in
Little Morton, Oxon, not to know that, whether she
put them in a book or left them out of a book, they
would believe she had put them in a book, as indeed
they did.

As to London, where Catherine lived in a flat, only
going to Much Potton for visits, London seemed less concerned about her books, and not at all concerned about
being put in them. The fact is that in London there are
so many novelists, male and female, young and old,
for ever putting other Londoners into books, and often
quite unkindly, that one more or less is scarcely
noticeable.

When Catherine lectured on the Creation of Character
in Fiction, she spoke so pleasantly and intelligently, and
with such interest in her subject, her reading of contemporary and past fiction (English, French, Russian
and American), was so wide, and her appearance and
manner so likeable, kind, and well-bred, that her
audiences were delighted with her, particularly as her
mother had been a Philadelphian. She was a nice-
looking young woman, with a pleasant oval face of an

agreeable olive pallor, dark straight hair sleekly parted
and coiled in the neat new manner, kind, candid brown
eyes, some sense of humour, and quite a lot of culture.
She was among the few novelists (anyhow the few
female novelists) who are not bored by writing novels.
Indeed, she was not bored by anything. Female
creatures are sadly often bored by their own work, and
fail to take it seriously ; as a sex it seems certain that
they lack that concentration and application so
necessary for sound results. When gentlemen, as they
so frequently and so justly do, refer to the inferiority
of the work of ladies in practically every department
of life, this, one fears, is one of the reasons which must
be offered for it. The other is, of course, one which
gentlemen will readily supply for themselves, that
ladies possess, as a rule, and as human beings go, sadly
small capability and intelligence.

Catherine lectured in late November, and early in
December she had a letter from her mother's sister, the
widow of an Iowa oil king who had bought an old
Spanish plantation in a Guatemala forest, and the
recently-wedded wife of an English judge interested in
archæology.

The letter was headed : " Hacienda del Capitan,
Perdido, Guat, C.A." " Do come right on here," it said,
" and pay our little home a visit before you cross over
to Europe. You'll just come in for the dry season, only
there's no real dry season here, as we lie in a valley in
thick forest, and it's rather steamy sometimes, even in
the verano. But I'd love to have you see the villa, which
is just on finishing, and looks fine ; your Uncle Heck
would scarcely know it again. We'll be quite a party

for the winter—your Uncle Dickie and myself, Isie and
her husband (he's been designing the additions to the
villa, you know ; he's just quite full of the cutest
fancies) and your uncle's four, Claudia, Benet, Julia and
little Meg (who is not keeping school this winter owing
to Infant Paralysis—I mean the school has it, not little
Meg). So you see you will find quite a family party as
well as Piper, our manager, a nice man, though quiet, and
though the society round is very small but for Indians
and ladinos, only a planter or two for miles, and the
very clergyman is a half-breed, and has three wives,
which for a Catholic clergyman is three too many, still,
what with dancing in the ballroom Adrian has made
(gold and pink it is) and riding, and having picnic
excursions to all these ruined old Indian towns they
find about the woods, quite remarkable they are, I'd
like to have you see them, you could put them in a
book, what with one thing and another we have quite
a gay time. It's been a real nice holiday for Isie and
Adrian, and they'll stay on till March, when we'll all
break up. Your Uncle Dickie is busy all day with these
ruins he finds, he just loves to pore over the peculiar
carvings those old Indians did on their stones (we've
got the cunningest old gate-posts by the by, great frogs
holding men's heads in their mouths, and cute bits all
over the house). Isie rides and shoots and fishes quite a
lot, with little Meg, but Claudia and Benet and Julia are
more interested in the way the house is turning out, and
keep on suggesting ideas to Adrian. They're quite full
of ideas, those three, they're travelled Europe over and
seen everything, but mostly palaces, it seems, and they
will have it that one room is to be like some big re-

ception room they've seen somewhere in Germany, and another like a ballroom they saw in Prague, and the little old mounds in the park they want turned into artificial ruins and called a Hermitage—I don't know why they want them artificial, seeing that they're real ruins all the time, but Claudia and Benet and Julia say they prefer things artificial. However, your Uncle Dickie won't have the old mounds built up, as he is going to dig into them. The way the Spanish monks built their convent on top of that old Indian palace shocks him to death. Your Uncle Heck used to think it inconvenient, too, but Dickie's children think it amusing, and I must say the old stone apartments look fine now they're done up. Well, now listen, Catherine, you come right along here at once. You take a passage from New Orleans to Livingstone, and the light railroad runs inland from there as far as the little lake, and from the lake our motor boat takes you down the river quite a way, as far as San Pedro, and there we'll have mules and mozos and the little buggy meet you and bring you right along to Perdido and the Hacienda ; why, it's only two days' ride from San Pedro, and you'll love every mile of the trip through those romantic old woods. But we'll write you all about the journey the moment you write us you'll come. Dickie's so pleased with his ruins and inscriptions, I know I'll have quite a job getting him away at the end of the season. I like to see a man, and specially a judge, so busy and so happy, and so quiet. Why, he won't want a thing all day. Now, your Uncle Heck. . . ."

But Catherine's Uncle Heck belongs to a past not included in this narrative.

2

Certainly, thought Catherine, she would visit her aunt, her new uncle by marriage, and her step-cousins, at the Hacienda del Capitan, Perdido, Guat, C.A. She loved her little Philadelphian aunt, and she was fascinated by the idea of the old Spanish monastery built after the Conquest out of a Maya palace in a tropical jungle, and now so glorified by the measureless wealth of its owner and the architectural conceits of Adrian Rickaby. Further, she was attracted by her aunt's step-children, whom she had met several times in London. What a setting, she thought, for a novel ! Those highly finished products of a modern civilisation so fantastically decorating the ruins of a vast primeval culture with their rococo European art ; those elegant creatures of the world tripping, fastidious and unafraid, about primitive forests, among ghosts, savages, and denizens of the wild. . . . For Catherine remembered the young Cradocks as somewhat sophisticated worldlings. Claudia, perhaps two years older than herself, ironic, amused, passionless, detached, elegantly celibate and virgin in a world where neither state is either usual or commended, a travelled European, a bland mocker, a rather mincing young gentlewoman. And Benedict, called Benet (his father having been educated at Corpus Christi College, Cambridge), five years his sister's junior, her male counterpart, a fastidious, amused, mincing young gentleman, and more usual, therefore, in his generation than his sister, for in these days it was quite the mode, among young men of intelligence and fashion, to mince. There was something finicking, spinsterish, bachelorish, about these two, a lack of that hearty co-operation with the ends of nature (as their step-mother had said, they did not care about nature) which is so necessary, it is said, for successful married life. Then there was Julia, a lounging girl of twenty-one, with heavy blue eyes that rolled lazily in a small white face, and a ridiculous flow of words. Catherine placed Julia as a flirt, a minx, even a rake. She, unlike Claudia and Benet, seemed not to be of the celibate or virgin type.

As to her young cousin, Isie, so recently married to Adrian Rickaby, Catherine knew her scarcely better than she knew her aunt's step-children; she was twenty years of age, of a very handsome appearance, ingenuous speech, delivered in young American slang that her mother deplored, and robust, jolly outdoor tastes. She would, no doubt, be happy enough in a forest, provided she could ramble about it and pursue its fauna, though ruined Indian buildings she would view with unquickened pulse, seeing them, as her mother did, as little old mounds in the park.

" I shall love to come and stay," Catherine wrote to her aunt.

Then she caught a train to Wigton, Pa, where she was to speak next day at a Woman's Luncheon Club on Fictional Types.

CHAPTER II

TRAVELLING

I

THE light railway ran, leapingly, fifty miles back from Livingstone port, among forests, mangrove swamps, coffee plantations, maize patches, sugar canes, valleys and mountains, and ended at the little lake, which was called Salvador. It had taken the little train four hours to reach the little lake, and it was now noon. The travellers leaped thankfully from the little train and went their several ways, some taking to mules along forest paths, some to various kinds of craft on the lake, others to their homes in the minute pablo of Ceniza, which stood like a brown toadstool patch festooned with scarlet creepers at the lake's head.

For Catherine there waited at a little jetty a white and scarlet motor launch. To this vehicle she was conducted by her cousin Isie, by Benet Cradock, and by an Indian mozo, for these had come to meet her train and convey her up the little lake and the river Merces to San Pedro, where the mule journey would begin. Catherine's luggage was disposed by the mozo in the launch's hold, and the party embarked. A half-breed priest meanwhile talked to them from the jetty in bad Spanish about how he, too, would, if it should be no inconvenience to them, make the journey up to

San Pedro in their launch. Benet, in Spanish nearly as fluent as his and more correct, apologised for not being able to take another passenger, owing to the great weight of Catherine's luggage. They continued the conversation until the launch was some way down the lake and the noise of its locomotion drowned that of the clergyman's voice.

"We could have taken him quite well really," Catherine said. "However, I suppose you don't like him."

Isie and Benet agreed that this was the case, Isie adding that the clergyman was a pain where it hurt the most.

"He is the parish priest in our village," Benet said. "If we let him come on the launch we should have him with us all the way through the forest. Talking. He always talks when he's drunk. When he's sober he's silent, and rather morose. To-day he's drunk, naturally, after a week in Livingstone."

"What does he talk about ? "

"Oh, parish shop, I suppose, but we don't really know, because we've never listened. . . . Do you find the scenery agreeable ? "

"Remarkably beautiful."

"I suppose in its way," Benet critically allowed, " it is. A shade too barbaric, do you think ? "

"Quit it," said Isie. "He's terribly affected, Catherine. So's Claudia. Always picking on nature. The scenery's all right. It's fine. I'm crazy on nature."

How handsome and sensible Isie was, thought Catherine, looking at the brown, strong, beautiful girl beside the fair, fragile-looking youth. A young Diana

S.W.R.   B

beautiful as a forest morning. She had been fishing in
the lake before the train came in, and her rod lay by
her like a dropped lance. In the creel beside it were
six alligator's eggs.

The lovely lake narrowed to its reedy end, and the
launch sped up the mouth of the river Merces. And
now they were indeed in a dense forest, which came
down closely to the river's either side, tree interlocked
with tree ; trees of all kinds and shapes, their boughs
vine-bound and rubber-twined, and linked together by
trailing lianas above a riot of white lilies, scarlet salvias
and convolvulus, giant purple and orange dahlias, little
sunflowers, heliotrope, banksias, orchids, and immense
tree-ferns.

It was now excessively hot and moist, after a storm
in the night, and felt quite tropical and disagreeable.
Wild animals crashed and made their appropriate
noises a few yards off within the jungle, and several
alligators swam after the launch with open mouths.

" The mother of the eggs," Benet said of one of these.
" She will probably pursue us all the way to San Pedro."

A small brown animal like a beaver dived from the
bank into the river, barking, and Catherine was informed that here was a nutria, and was pleased and
surprised to encounter this little animal, which had so
often provided her with fur trimmings, and which she
had hitherto ignorantly conceived to be one of those
mythical creatures imagined by the fur trade, like the
foxaline, the pony-seal, and the rabbit-skunk. But it
seemed that in Guatemala all the animals both of
mythology and of the natural history books pressed
about her with their gifts of wearing apparel, the snakes

and crocodiles offering her shoes, the nutria a fur coat, the birds feathered toques of all the colours of the rainbow.

Squealings and tramplings came from the forest on the left. Isie said, " Plenty of pig in there." And Catherine surmised, from her use of the singular number, that she would fain pursue these animals and take their lives. Animals seen as sport become to the mind meat, and cease to be individual creatures, so that you may feed fishes, but catch fish, ride elephants, but hunt elephant, fatten turkeys and pigs, but chase turkey and pig, throw bread to ducks, but shoot duck, admire moths, but seek to exterminate moth ; and some creatures, whom God would seem to have created merely for the chase, such as grouse and snipe, require no plural forms at all. And even as few as two pigs become pig if hunted.

" Peccary, I suppose," said Catherine, retaining the form preferred by her cousin.

The river wound round sudden corners, and each reach was most surprising, most lovely, and most strange, for now it was very narrow and overhung with rich and steaming vegetation that, almost shutting out the sky, turned the river into a green and shadowed lane, and now it widened out into a broad and shallow luminousness, a rippled mirror that held the gaudy noon. Now ravines, gorges, and mountains, pine-clad, could be seen distantly on either side, and Benet would say, " Oh, my dear, how shockingly Swiss," and avert his eyes from such a reminder of that small mid-European republic which he detested ; but in the next reach the forest would run lumbering up to the river's brink, and over the travellers' heads tropical trees arched, alligator pears and other delicious fruits dangled, blue jays chattered, humming birds exquisitely darted, monkeys swung by their tails, and a riot of every imaginable sweetness assailed the senses, drifting mingled on the swooning air.

Then the forest would recede a little, and small clearings and plantations made themselves apparent—coffee, maize, sugar, vanilla, or cocoa, with groups of palm huts dumped among them like bee-hives, and round the huts blossomed cottage gardens of brilliant colours, roses and lilies and trumpet orchids and tropical flowers of practically every description, of which the names are so little known to me that I cannot even mention them.

Neither could Benet. But Isie, rightly or wrongly, called many of them by their names, with the careful learning of the schoolgirl.

"You see, I press," she said. "Do you enjoy pressing, Catherine ? "

"Flowers, she means," Benet explained. "Isie likes to keep her verbs intransitive."

"Well, you dumb-bell, we were talking of flowers, weren't we ? Catherine knows I didn't mean boy friends."

Isie, it was apparent, took teasing with good temper. A cheerful, tranquil young woman. Possibly, were she to talk for long together in that clear bell-like voice of hers, the voice of young débutante America, confident and assertive, retailing the names of pressed flowers and boy friends, telling anecdotes of the adventures which had occupied her brief career, she might become

wearisome in her loud and girlish naïveté, so different
from the sophistication of her step-father's children.
That brown and supple beauty which delighted the
eye—had it been allied to subtlety of wit, or fire of imagination, what a creature would nature, for once in
generous mood, have made! But nature, thought
Catherine, did not, parsimonious old lady, make such
creatures as that more than once in a long age. Nature
gave the world its young Isies in their clean and buoyant
beauty, and the young Isies lit the fires of imagination
or the candles of wit in the souls of those who looked
on them, even as the kingfisher which darted, swift and
radiant, from bank to bank, inflamed the poet.

2

It was now late afternoon. The river had narrowed,
running beneath a tangled roof of boughs, from which
long scarlet creepers trailed in green water. Log canoes
still paddled up the stream, but the launch could go
no further. It came to shore at a little clearing, announced by a sign-board on the bank to be San Pedro.
Here, beneath a gold and rose-flushed sky, the travellers
landed in the forest. Mules and mozos met them, and
a little cart, on which Catherine's luggage was piled,
behind a very small mule. Mounting taller mules, they
rode through the little clearing, in which the tiny
village clustered. Out of the clearing a rough track ran.

"The path to Perdido and the Villa Sans Souci,"
said Benet, as the cavalcade took it.

"You mutt," said young Mrs. Rickaby. "Don't

give the Hacienda that name. Catherine will think
we're all morons."

"Sans Souci," Benet repeated. "That's what
Claudia and I think we shall call it, because it's
becoming rather like the Sans Souci palace at Potsdam.
But sometimes we think it should be Hadrian's Folly,
because of Adrian, and because it's rather like Hadrian's
Villa in some ways—I mean in the way it has collected
styles from all over the world, and looks so silly.
Adrian wants to call it the Follies, and Med the
Bananas, but Belle prefers Villa Maya, and after all it
belongs to her. However, as it's always known in the
neighbourhood as the Hacienda del Capitan, it doesn't
make much difference what we call it. . . . Look, those
Indians have grouped themselves like a Vanessa Bell
fresco. Rather ravishing."

"A what al fresco?" Isie enquired, but without
desire for information.

One of the fresco detached himself from the rest and
began, forcibly but without animation, to beat his wife,
who, also without animation, howled.

"I've seen things like that in Bloomsbury," said
Benet, "only a larger scale."

"Larger scale? What d'you mean, a larger scale,
you dumb-bell?" Isie asked.

A thing about her is, Catherine reflected, she doesn't
want to know the answers to any of her questions;
she's thinking of something else. Absent-minded and
self-absorbed.

The track wound round a deep barranca, following
the river. The dense wood shut the travellers into a
warm green twilight; the moist air steamed with a

thousand sweetnesses of evening, as if all the bottles
in a perfumery had been broken into clear green soup.
All the agreeable scents and spices in the world seemed
to blow towards them and kiss them on the lips—vanilla
and frangipani and orange blossom, and honey and
incense and wine. Great moths, swaying long tails and
beaming shyly out of wild, bright eyes, sipped themselves drunk among starry flowers; owls flitted, soft
and solemn bundles, from tree to tree, doubless
believing that night had already arrived, in this
deep covert shut from the golden flame of evening.

The forest was alive with plungings, scufflings, and
excitements; monkeys cried, and frogs, jaguars, and
whip-poor-wills; crickets chirped, armadillos rattled,
peccarys crashed, while from the river came sounds of
tapirs snouting among the rushes, and alligators that
gnashed their teeth.

Presently the path began to climb; it wound up the
barranca's steep, forested flank, and the air cooled
and lightened, as if into the green soup someone was
gently trickling ice water. Sometimes the forest opened
a little, revealing what was to Benet a shocking
panorama of mountains and gorges, and sometimes
they passed a clearing, patches of corn or coffee, and
a few huts. Still they mounted, and the evening was
sharp with the smell of pines; and suddenly they
rounded a bend, and the forest ran back to right and
left like drawn curtains, discovering them on a rocky
mountain side, with a range of violet peaks in front
against the clear green sky, and at their feet the rose-
flushed lake. By the lake side a wooden shack stood
among pines.

" The Cradock rest-house," said Bonet ; and it appeared that they would lie there that night, and ride on their way next morning.

They dismounted by the lake, and, leaving the mozos to prepare supper, launched forth upon the still cup of flame and violet in a boat, since Isie desired to fish for mojarra.

3

From her camp bed in the shack Catherine could see all night the dark shining of the lake, flecked, like a Christmas goblet of wine, with gold candles that were fireflies and stars, and the forest shouldering back from it, grey beneath the moon, black beneath the stars, at last burgeoning into blue and green with the dawn. She could see, against the faint sky, ghosts of shadows of peaks far off ; they must have been volcanic, for one threw up a jet of flame at dawn, as if a housemaid had risen and lit the stove. All night, waking and sleeping, Catherine heard those sounds which, when one is passing the night in Central American forests, or near Regent's Park, link one so happily with night in city streets, for jaguars and pumas howled like motor horns, wild pigs and other creatures crashed through thickets with the noise of motor bicycles, monkeys, waking or disturbed by dreams, emitted sharp cries like milkmen, alligators in the lake clashed their teeth as milkmen clash bottles, and birds whistled like boys bringing newspapers at dawn. Thus home thoughts crashed and sang through Catherine's dreams, so that she was greatly amazed to open her eyes on a pine-wood shack, on her cousin Isie sleeping at her side, and all the Guatemalan morning shining on mountain, forest and lake.

They rode off early, in the cold sweetness of the mountain morning, which warmed to a blazing noon. On the hills it was dry and clear, but down in the ravines hot and moist. All day they rode along the climbing and falling track, by hill and gorge, through deep forests and along dark warm streams, passing little lakes, and sometimes little villages surrounded by orchards full of fruit—red and yellow jocotes, oranges in blossom and fruit, coffee in berry, plantains, peaches, bananas, alligator pears, and those little sapotes whose juice drips as sweet as honey from the teeth. But most of the way ran through thick hot forest, uncultivated, uninhabited and uncleared.

" Very noble and picturesque, isn't it," said Benet, using distastefully such epithets as one applies to the valley of the Rhine. He looked tired, and it tickled Catherine's sense of queer juxtapositions to see this youth, so frail and urban, thus mincing his way through primeval forests, which he dismissed as irrevelant, if he did not condemn them as horrid. Very noble and picturesque, of course. But not civilised, not intellectually intriguing. To be these, there is required the stamp of an ancient civilisation. There was, to be sure, a civilisation ancient enough buried in the depths of these surprising Guatemalan forests ; but it made little show, it was obscured by woods, mountains and ravines. As to the scattered natives of these barbarous woods, they were, naturally, barbarians, and knew nothing of their more cultivated ancestors. Further, their command of any European language was so poor, and they seemed so reserved and abstracted, that communication was quite difficult.

So, thought Catherine, it was an odd setting for Benet, Claudia and Julia Cradock, those children of the world.

4

They rested for a time in the early afternoon, by the side of a hill stream, and under the dark green shadow of mahogany and sapsodilla trees. Parrots, lories and humming-birds made the deep covert gaudy and surprising, like a Christmas tree decked with bright glass birds. Catherine remembered that it was indeed the Christmas season, and felt it only right when the God of Christmas, at work also, it seemed, in Maya forests, discovered in an orange-coloured mistletoe above their heads a quetzal, bright emblem of his country, his lovely tail caught in a liquorice vine.

" I will admit," said Isie, " that they have the swellest birds in America in these parts."

Benet too admitted this. " Not but what we haven't got them all in the South Kensington Museum," he added, " and better arranged."

As they ate their sandwiches, anointed though they were with unguents, mosquitoes ate them. And the humming-birds and parrots ate the mosquitoes, and squirrels stalked the humming-birds and parrots, and wild cats stalked the squirrels, and snakes swallowed the wild cats, and all creatures ate, or endeavoured to

eat, those fellow creatures appointed for them as food.
Nature is very just, thought Catherine, for she has
made us all food. Not a creature but is to the palate of
some other creature. Even the skunk has his devotees.
A world of eatables, a great round spinning table, at
which we all are the diners and the victuals. Yes ;
nature, repulsive though she is in most of her ways, is
on the whole just.

"Now," said Benet, "we had better show you a
Maya town. I feel sure you will like to see a specimen
of our local industry, and there is one quite close
here."

"But it's a pretty dead one," Isie put in ; "it's
never been dug."

However, they went to see it. It lay on the hill-side
above them, overgrown and hidden by forest, a circle
of mossy ruins, broken columns through which the
trunks of trees had grown, and what had perhaps been a
rectangular temple, roofless now, and full of the trees
and shrubs of centuries' growth. At the sight of that
buried city, its streets and squares so silent and unseen,
so dead and so undug, lying in the hot heart of the
jungle, Catherine's soul experienced that leap of
recognition and surprise with which we accost the
world's masterpieces, always heard of and now for the
first time seen. Vines and tree-ferns, sarsaparilla and
great creepers with coloured flowers, made a tangled
undergrowth, rioting over the grey moss and broken
stone, and in the thicket of boughs overhead monkeys
scrambled and screamed.

"Why isn't it excavated ? " Catherine asked
Benet shrugged his shoulders.

" There are hundreds of them untouched—hundreds more, no doubt, in the unexplored parts of the forest, that no one has even seen for five hundred years and more. I believe Mr. Phipps is getting a permit to dig up this one ; it's on his land."

" Who is Mr. Phipps ? "

" My dear, the most charming little man. Our only white neighbour ; his land joins ours. He bought his hacienda six months ago from a Spanish rancher who went bankrupt because he wouldn't move with the times but persisted in going on with cochineal. Mr. Phipps made his money in straw hats in the Middle West, where they still seem to wear them, or perhaps only the horses wear them ; anyhow, they made Mr. Phipps rich. He lives about ten miles from us, and is *most* neighbourly and sociable. We adore him."

" Mother's not so tickled with him," Isie said. " He was crazy to buy our hacienda when Dad died, and when Mother wouldn't sell he bought the Hacienda del Rio and settled on it. He's crazy about our villa ; Adrian gets quite worried, always having him hanging around having brain-waves about the decoration. However, he's amiable, and brings candy over. Why, there *is* Mr. Phipps and his mule. Hallo, Mr. Phipps. Good-day."

Mr. Phipps and his mule, a plump, small, good-humoured looking pair, were approaching them, one bestriding the other, along a path that wound north-west into the forest. Mr. Phipps lifted his palm-leaf hat at arm's length above his head and benignantly smiled, beaming through horn-rimmed glasses.

" Good-day, Mrs. Adrian. Good-day, Mr. Benet.

Showing your cousin the sights, I see." They introduced
Mr. Phipps to Catherine.

"Well, Miss Grey, you've come to a mighty fine
country, at a mighty fine salubrious time of year, and
I hope you'll enjoy your little visit. I anticipate
you'll get quite a kick out of these old woods,
and these old buried cities; they're quite full of
drama and romance, and you don't need to look for it,
either. I'm informed you write fiction in England, Miss
Grey. Well, I will admit I don't read much English
fiction, but I'm told it's a flourishing industry, and I
hope you'll pursue it to great advantage in Guatemala.
Now I mustn't keep you, if you're riding on to the
Cradock hacienda. Perhaps you'll bring Miss Grey over
to luncheon at my ranch one day soon. Why, I certainly
envy you, Miss Grey, seeing this land and all its
marvels for the first time. I'll say you'll enjoy your
trip."

Catherine agreed with Benet, as they rode off, that
Mr. Phipps was a most charming little man.

"He's crazy about us," Isie said, without surprise
that this should be so. "I suppose he's quite lonely,
stuck in that out-of-the-way old ranch by himself.
He's left his wife back in their native town ; her name's
Almey, and they've four children."

"Isie knows all their names," Benet interrupted,
" and their ages, so let's change the subject. We ought
to push on now, to be back by dark. He, Luis, vamonos
ahora," he called to the mozos.

5

Throughout the languorous hours they rode along the path through the hot and sleepy forest, where wild things lightly slumbered and moaned in their lairs, and unnatural-looking birds and butterflies, hovering dreamily over bright and scented blossoms, decorated the afternoon, making it like the richly illuminated page of a missal, whereon scarlet and blue birds are poised by monks on gold flowers and green scrolled trees.

The smell of coffee flowers drifted on the air, crops began, and Indians disclosed themselves on the landscape, tilling the earth, gathering coffee berries, dealing with cattle, and otherwise pastorally engaged.

" This is where the hacienda begins," her companions told Catherine. " This is our land."

It was now dusk. Herds of milk-white cattle flowed after the travellers like a river as they passed, as do cattle in English fields. Who am I among so many, Catherine thought, as she thought in English fields, and what am I, among so much milk and beef, who am neither ? She suffered that eerie loneliness, not fear but on fear's border, which submerges the human animal when surrounded by the other animals and their strange, bright, shy eyes. What have we done to deserve the place we have gained in the animal kingdom ? How have we won it ; how long can it last ? Even now has our hour struck, and will horses, cattle, sheep, pigs and dogs, their strange and saturnine patience at an end, turn on us and stamp us out of existence ?

They emerged suddenly out of the sweet-smelling forest path, and the evening sky was green above them, and they rode between richly carved Maya gate-posts into a courtyard full of strange buildings and statues, and flanked on three sides by a most surprising edifice.

" Sans Souci," said Benet, " Villa Maya, the Hacienda del Capitan, or the Cradock house."

The mules' feet pattered on a paved court. A quick little woman like a bird ran out to meet them, uttering shrill cries of affection and delight.

" Why, Catherine, it's just fine to see you. Dickie, Adrian, girls, here they are arrived. Well, honey, did you have a good journey ? Now you come right in and rest, and remember Maya Villa is like your own home till you leave it."

But anything less like her own home, or, indeed, than anyone else's home, Catherine thought she need never hope to see, as she gazed at that superb erection, baroque on Maya, and entered through the magnificently carved lintels of the amazing front door.

CHAPTER III

ARRIVING

I

" How do you do," said a cool, clear, dragging voice, at once sweet and dry, that reminded Catherine of iced champagne, and seemed to hold, in its delicate modulations, the faint tremolo of a lurking laugh. Before her, in the long, richly sculptured stone hall, stood Claudia Cradock, pale and fragile, with narrow light grey eyes, ironic mouth and dark hair close-cut and brushed straight back from a white forehead. Over her shoulder peeped Julia's head, sleek and ash-blonde, demurely parted and coiled, above a small colourless face that smiled at Catherine with tilted lips. Catherine thought again, as she had thought before, that, in their somewhat mannered elegance, these two young ladies had the air of having strayed out of an earlier and more formal period, or out of a Bach fugue.

" I hope," said Claudia, " that you had a tolerable journey."

Catherine said that she had.

" Do you admire our villa ? " Miss Cradock continued. " We think baroque on Maya decidedly chic. Perhaps you find it surprising ? "

" A little surprising—yes. Unexpected, you know, in these forests."

Miss Cradock looked pleased.

32

" Ah, yes. The woodland surroundings. The park, we like to call them . . . Adrian has taken great pains with the villa. The triumph of civilisation over barbarous rusticity, we like to think it is. It doesn't strike you, I hope, as a trifle bogus ? "

" Well, I've not really seen it yet, you know. It's very . . . palatial."

" That it ought to be," Aunt Belle broke in, " for it's built on to an ancient palace and the new part claims to imitate half the palaces in Europe, you'd think, to hear Adrian and these children talk. Adrian, if you've done petting Isie, come and meet Catherine. You remember Adrian, don't you, Catherine ? "

Catherine did remember Adrian. A fair, thin, pale young man of middle height, an architect, wearing pince-nez over near-sighted eyes. Thirty-five. He belonged to the half-generation above Benet's, and he had its rather different set of mannerisms. He was old enough to have lost his health in the European War of 1914-18, which now seems to his generation such a fantastic myth and to the young not even this. Isie clung to his arm, full of love and chaff. Civilisation and barbarous rusticity ; Claudia's phrase floated into Catherine's mind. How queer marriage is, she thought ; and how different and how happy those two.

Her aunt was calling shrilly, " Dickie, Dickie," in the ardent yet indulgent voice with which one entreats a canary to sing. In response, Sir Richmond Cradock, Catherine's new uncle, materialised ; a good-looking judge of sixty, his mind doubtless preoccupied with Mayan problems, but still not closed to the fact that his wife's niece was apparently arrived on a visit.

S.W.R.   C

So now they were all assembled, even little Meg, a sturdy, square-headed, imperturbable-looking child of twelve years, who wore a firm and cheerful expression and a bow and arrow slung across her chest, and munched an alligator pear.

" Well now," said Belle, " you must see your room, Catherine. Catherine certainly must see her room. Why, Catherine dear, you must be quite tired out with all that travelling. You come right up and have a rest and a bath before dinner."

She led Catherine through the stone hall, so strangely carved with Mayan men, beasts and birds, and up the winding stone stairway, which led to the upper gallery of the palace. Here rococo had been laid on Maya like a palimpsest. The walls and ceiling were frescoed with paintings of gentlemen in periwigs, in armour, in little but wreaths, of full-bellied nymphs reclining on tasselled cushions, of chubby cherubs on plump clouds, of battles, of ships, of Turks, of love, of the thousand florid and whirling activities of men, women, beasts and Gods.

" Do you like the designs on the walls ? " Catherine's aunt enquired of her. " We had a Spanish painter do them, from photographs the children had of some palace somewhere. They brighten the landing, I will admit. In your Uncle Heck's time it was plain pink plaster. This way. Isn't it quaint, the way they built these old Indian galleries. And haven't we smartened it up and made it look cheerful ? "

" Too marvellous, Aunt Belle."

" Your Uncle Heck made the bedrooms. It was all little cells when he bought the house, that those old

monks built to sleep in. Your Uncle Heck threw each
four cells together to make a room. That's yours at
the end, between the painted curtains."

They went through the painted curtains, into a
circular room with a bed in an alcove. The decoration
was pink and silver ; silver trees and waterfalls flowed
up and down between pink stucco panels, in the most
elegant manner imaginable, while on the ceiling Jove
sported with nymphs.

" *Aunt Belle !* What a lovely room," Catherine
gasped.

" It's bright," said Aunt Belle. " And I thought
you'd feel homey in it."

" Oh no," said Catherine, thinking of the vicarage
at Much Potton and of her flat near Regent's Park.
" Not that. It's pleasures and palaces, no place like
home. It's too exquisite and strange for words. How
in the world did you get it done ? "

" We had Indian workmen do the stucco work,
from Adrian's designs. These poor Indians, they're
quite quick with their hands, but they had to be told
everything, they're so dumb. Here's Luis with your
grips. Well now, I'll send up Amy to unpack for you,
and if you'd like a bath before dinner, it's through the
door in the alcove. We've had some trouble with the
plumbing, but we've got it right now and you'll find
the water good and hot. Well now, dear, I'll leave you,
and you'll come down when you're ready."

Left alone with her grips in the pink and silver room,
Catherine opened a box of sweets that lay on the bedside table and ate a large chocolate. Everything had
been thought of. She would be comfortable here.

2

Amy, a negress, came and unpacked her things. She bathed and put on a rose coloured frock, in which she appeared charming and serene, almost matching all this grace around her.

Claudia knocked and entered. " How nice you look," she said, in her sweet, indifferent drawl. " You match your bedroom décor very well. And you won't be amiss in the dining-room. The dining-room is sea-green and silver. After Cuvilles' octagon room in the Amalienburg pavilion at Nymphenburg. This one is after one of the New Palace rooms at Potsdam. I assure you we had the most amusing time thinking it all out, Adrian and Benet and I. We considered it our duty to save it from Belle's timbered-hall and rude-oak-settle ideas. Americans are so fond of timbered Tudor rudeness, but we can't abide it. Baroque is so much more civilised, don't you think ? Are you ready ? Shall we come down ? "

The young ladies descended to the hall, where the family awaited them, and they went into the dining-room, which was, as Claudia had said, an octagon saloon in green and silver, decorated with clusters of silver stucco flowers and fruits, serpents, birds, fishes, mermaids, tritons and wreathèd horns, and presented the most ornate and agreeable appearance in the world, having a large mirror set in each panel, so that the silver brightness of the room and the brilliant lights gleamed round the diners as from eight artificial lakes, and might well persuade them that they dined in fairyland.

" So long," Sir Richmond said, " as they don't stick

their trumpery rococo on the Maya ruins, I make no objection, though I must say that to my mind this mixture of styles looks very ridiculous. We now, Catherine, have in this unfortunate house a Maya palace of approximately the tenth century, the Dominican priory into which it was converted by the Spanish in 1560, the ranch-house a Spanish planter turned it into in 1830, the Americanised villa built onto it in 1912 " (by his wife's former husband, he meant, but did not care to mention him), " and the baroque mansion you see now. But the Maya core remains, through all these follies. There is a lot underground, you know. Great subterranean chambers, magnificently carved, which the Dominicans and subsequent owners used for wine cellars. It must have been a magnificent manor house originally ; the centre of a whole town. In fact, it is still, only the town is ruined and largely buried."

Catherine found all this extremely interesting, and her new uncle took quite a liking for her, as indeed people usually did, for they found her an intelligent listener, with a very sympathetic, interested nature. A sweet apple, sound to the core, someone had once called her. Though a writer, she seemed little touched by the morbid introspectiveness and egotism to which so many who ply this disagreeable trade are a prey, and her interests seemed to be largely concentrated on the world of persons and objects outside herself. She was interested now not only in what her uncle was saying about the house, but in her uncle himself ; not only in the lovely octagon room after the Amalienburg pavilion, but in all those who sat in it talking and eating. As usual, the interesting differences between one kind of person and another kind of person fermented in her mind, providing the heady wine of imaginative insight which stimulates novelists. Most of all, perhaps, she was interested in Claudia, who sat opposite her, pale, ironic, and delicately spinsterish. Claudia, Catherine thought, was not robust in health ; she had never done any regular work since she left school, but had lived in her father's house, travelled, and idled, in the leisured fashion of an earlier generation. Reputed clever, she had refused a university education ; bookish, she yet wrote no books, possibly sharing with Lady Louisa Stuart a horror of losing caste by appearing in print. It was obviously more chic, more elegant, in these days of general (and so often regrettable) writing of books, not to write books, and Claudia usually chose the more chic and the more elegant path, mincing along, a delicately civilised loafer, through a rough and coarse world. Benet, so like her, had, among other differences, the differences of sex. He, for instance, had not refused a university education, and had appeared quite frequently in print, in what he, probably erroneously, held to be the more educated journals. He, being masculine, could assert himself more firmly on the world, approaching it with more of familiarity and of confidence, seating himself in its saddle and seizing its reins with the triumphant control of the male rider whose steed it has always (if one comes to think of it) been. Feminine creatures too often appear and feel unseated, alien, and a little lost, as if they knew no way of coming to terms with a world too strong, swift, and overpowering for them. Catherine had seen that lost look in the eyes of many little girls, while their brothers seemed to be immediately at home in the odd world into which they had strayed, recognising it as something which their papas and grandpapas had made and bequeathed to them. Even Isie, that jolly, handsome, firmly seated young sportswoman, had now and then this lost alien look in her clear hazel eyes ; even little Meg (who had gone to bed) had it, in spite of her stamp collection, her bow and arrows, and the hundred other sturdy links between herself and life ; even Belle, so briskly and capably the matron, mother, aunt, hostess, and estate owner, had it sometimes, this fleeting testimony to woman's incompetence and bewilderment in the face of the world's strangeness. Baffled and afraid ; that, thought Catherine, was what women were when they stopped to think. Men, on the other hand, seemed competent, assured, at home, full of energy and physical and mental robustness.

So Catherine meditated, succumbing to the facile temptation to classify humanity according to sex, to age, to type, to anything but temperament, which so readily besets the writer.

Benet and Isie were recounting the little episodes of their journey, how they had encountered Mr. Phipps in the forest, and how they had left their parish priest the better for liquor at Lake Salvador.

" They certainly do drink, these ladino clergymen," Belle said. " I've sometimes thought we ought to have an English or American preacher here instead. Such an example the Reverend Jacinto sets in Perdido. For it's not only drink, I'm afraid. No, drink's not the worst."

" He ought to be ashamed of himself," said Sir

Richmond, mechanically making one of the impertinent remarks that judges make concerning the victims before them, thus unchivalrously and impudently abusing their position of impunity.

" I think," said Benet, " it would be very charming to have an English clergyman in the forest, complete with wife, parish teas, Bands of Hope, mothers' meetings, and services for men only. It would strike another note of bizarrerie."

" Can't you just see the wife," Isie continued the fantasy, " coming up here to call, with the parish magazine under her arm, and a revolting piece of hare or rabbit fur round her neck, like the one Mrs. Macbayne used to wear."

" I always wonder," Claudia speculated, " whether hare and rabbit fur is revolting because it's cheap, or cheap because it's revolting. And whether it's revolting while still on the hare or rabbit, or only begins to be revolting when on a human creature."

" Why, Claudia," said Isie, " how do you mean ? Why, hell, you know as well as I do that hare and rabbit fur are just utterly revolting and cheesey. What more do you want to know ? "

" I agree with Isie," said Benet.

" He's a terribly inconsequent man," said Belle, still deploring her parish priest. " Sly, too. Mr. Phipps thinks he's just terribly sly. Mr. Phipps doesn't like him. But then Mr. Phipps doesn't care for Catholics he's such a Protestant. Quite a fundamentalist, he tells me."

" He ought to get on with Father Jacinto then," said Claudia. " He's a fundamentalist too. Protestants

and Catholics always seem so like one another, I don't
know what they find to dispute about. It's like right
and wrong ; there's some difference, but one always
forgets what it is. The same beliefs, the same firm
attitude of mind towards damnation and the Bible
stories, the same Garden of Eden, the same Fall, the
same Hell, only with a different set roasting in it.
They'd much better bury the hatchet and unite against
modernists, Jews and unbelievers."

" Why, Claudia, you don't need to talk religion at
dinner," her step-mother protested. " Anyone would
think we were in church. Catherine doesn't want to
hear religion spoken of on her holiday. Listen,
Catherine, would you like a quiet day to-morrow, or to
ride around and see some of our beauty spots ? I
assure you, we have more beauty spots in this old
forest than you'd dream, just looking at it passing
through. And all the interesting things your uncle
could show you, you'd never guess. But as you've been
riding mule-back these two days, I think you'd best do
nothing much to-morrow, but just stop around the
house and grounds."

When to-morrow comes, Benet thought, one behaves
in some manner about it, but why think of it before-
hand ? Plans, plans, plans.

A sweet girl, thought Claudia of Catherine. Sympathetic, polite and rather smug. The perfect guest, I
believe. Perhaps she will go up presently and write some
letters. . . .

Julia yawned when her step-mother said " beauty
spots," and " interesting things," for this was her
involuntary reaction to these, and also she had been

up too late last night. The Cradocks were not hearty,
like Isie.

"I don't care what I do," said Catherine. "Anything
I do here will be lovely." And Claudia ever so slightly
nodded, as if agreeing with herself that Catherine was
the perfect guest. So quite unlike the lazy imp, Julia,
who was lolling over the table, sleepy, languid and
pale, and munching fruit, Catherine actually sat
upright. Her beautifully rounded neck and bosom
emerged from her rose-coloured frock, charmingly full
and creamily brown, and her eyes were intelligent
and kind.

3

They went after dinner into the drawing-room, which
was orange-gold, lemon-gold, and dull blue, with ceiling
painted after Gregorio Guglielmi. These two great rooms,
all redecorated now by Adrian Rickaby, had been built
by Mr. Heck Higgins on to the original structure like
pavilions, so that the façade of the house presented a
curious heterogeneous appearance which Sir Richmond
Cradock deplored. But the rooms themselves were
magnificent. "After Cuvilles again," said Catherine,
lost in admiration of rich orange and lemon-gold
boiseries. Her reactions were ever correct, and it *was*
after Cuvilles. "Very ravishing. Very superb."

"Ah," Benet told her; "wait till you see the
chapel."

"Chapel ? "

"Why, yes, dear," Belle assured her. "We have a

chapel in the grounds. The monks built it. And the children would have it filled up with figures. Stucco groups sitting in opera boxes and painted like real people. Well, you know, I call it quite worldly, but they said the chapel must be rococo."

Sir Richmond shuddered. " Excessively bad taste. Really vulgar," he condemned, and sank into his thoughts again, for he was calculating measurements on paper.

" Lord," said Julia, stretching like a kitten. " I'm tired. Let's dance."

They turned on a gramophone and danced. Indeed, the floor seemed to exist for that purpose only, so smooth and resilent it was beneath their feet. As she trotted round the room in the arms of Adrian, Catherine felt again the comic strangeness of this handful of modern western persons tripping with their ordered steps to mechanical music round a rococo ballroom erected on a Spanish monastery, on an Indian palace, in the heart of primeval forests. Round the villa jungle creatures prowled and roared, Indians and Spaniards and half-breeds slept and waked, and a strange stone army crowded up about the house, Maya gods, sixteenth century Spanish missionaries and saints, and eighteenth century beings in togas or cocked hats.

But it was not really stranger than anything else, thought Catherine. All the world is strange. Strange looks passed from eye to eye, strange touches, strange half-phrases. There was beauty ; Isie's beauty, for example. What was it ? How did the human eye so arrange for itself the lines and colours of the human creature (surely a comparatively ugly animal ?) that they wavered and re-formed into this shape we have conceived to be beauty ? Strange illusion ! But how necessary for the continuance of the race ! And how successful in this purpose ! What a sublime creation of the animal eye and brain !

Catherine knew that Adrian's eyes, as he shuffled competently round the room with her, roved after his magnificent Isie where she danced with the lounging child, Julia. The splendid young American, perfect in health, in poise, in that vigorous, clear-cut handsomeness of colour and line which distinguishes splendid young Americans, and the lazy, derisive, slouching, colourless English girl. Primitive and decadent ; the words came to Catherine's mind as she glanced at these two. Open air creature of the wilds, and pale hothouse flower. The elegant spinsterishness of Claudia and Benet had turned, in Julia, thought Catherine, to something more sensuous. One could not well imagine Julia, any more than they, married or a parent, but one saw her as a light lady, a mistress to a succession of lovers. She was in an old tradition, and belonged more to nature than did her brother and sister.

Adrian had charm. He danced neatly, and sang adequately, if absently, at those moments of the dance when one sings.

Then, in modern fashion, some one put on " The Blue Danube," and those who knew how to do so abandoned themselves to the voluptuous rhythms of the waltz. Catherine, tired and stiff after her riding, fell out, while Adrian and Julia, Isie and Benet took the floor. Isie and Benet were still learning this dance ; but Adrian had known it before the war, and to Julia it seemed to be natural, this slinking and gliding round to a sensuous melody.

" More suitable to our period décor," Claudia commented to Catherine, indicating the room. " We should really always waltz."

Catherine said that, for her part, she would now go to bed. Her aunt came up with her to her room, to perform that hostess's duty called seeing that she had everything she wanted, as if anyone ever had this, particularly on visits. But Catherine nodded and smiled and said, " Everything indeed, Aunt Belle. Just look——" indicating her luxurious room, where Amy, the negress, had been busy with those little industries practised by domestics in bedrooms between dinner and bedtime.

" Well, dear, it certainly is nice that you've come," said Aunt Belle, and Catherine said it certainly was.

" And now you must get a lovely long sleep, and be just ever so rested in the morning. Don't mind the wild cats howling."

" Oh, no," said Catherine ; " I'm used to that in London."

" To be sure ; they spend the nights on the roofs, there, don't they. Well, the pumas and jaguars and peccaries may be a bit noisy too, but they're quite a way off."

" I'm used to that too. You see my flat is near the Zoo."

" Why then, you'll feel quite at home ; isn't that nice. And anything you want, just ring, and Amy'll come. I hope you're going to enjoy your little visit here, dear."

" I'm going to simply love it, Aunt Belle."

4

" She's a sweet girl, Catherine, isn't she ? " Belle
said to her family downstairs. They had stopped
dancing, and sat talking round the open window,
through which the dark warm forest night flowed in
on them, smelling of various kinds of animals and trees.

" She's delightful," said Benet. " So charmingly old
world and *vieux jeu*. My dears, she still reads Proust.
Yes, we spoke of books a little as we rode. Why not ?
There was so much time. And she adores Proust."

" What d'you mean, proust, you owl ? " Isie
mechanically enquired.

Her mother answered her.

" Why, Isie, you don't *know* anything. That's the
trouble with you, honey, after all these years at school.
What will Adrian think he's married ? Proust wrote
stories, of course. I'm just crazy about him. Give me
a nice long Proust, and I'm all right for weeks. That's
what it is about Proust, you don't need to be changing
him all the time. Why, he's so comfortable. I don't
care if I am *vieux jeu*, as you call it. What I say is, why
leave all the old favourites behind just because there's
something new out ? I call it silly."

" I think you're so right," said Benet.

" I mean, a book's a book," said Isie, perceiving now
that they spoke of books, " if it's a hundred years old.
Isn't it, Judge ? " She addressed her stepfather, who
was sitting in the background calculating, and knew
something about books, but said nothing to the point,
only " A hundred ? More like six thousand."

" It isn't safe, all this night air and gnats coming in,"
said Belle, rising. " That's the way to get fever."

" Well, anyhow, we are agreed that Catherine is
delightful," Claudia said. " Handsome, agreeable, intelligent and virtuous. Don't you think, Adrian that
Catherine's handsome ? "

" Very nice looking. Something of a Murillo Madonna
in her flesh-tones and colour. I like her calm too. A
very gentle, benignant calm."

" That's her father," said Belle. " The quietest,
kindest clergyman ! Never gets flurried ; never makes
a fuss. There was Hetty, hopping around like a flea,
getting all excited with everything, and Henry—' All
right, dear.—As you please, dear.—It's of no consequence, dear.—Do just as you like, dear.' I certainly
think that, if Catherine's like the Madonna, Henry's
like Joseph. Isie, love, hadn't you better go to bed,
like Catherine ? You've had the long forest ride too,
you know."

But Isie was putting on a new record.

" No more waltzes. They're so fierce, they make
me tired. Let's simmer down over some dear old jazz."

It was Benet, who had also had the long forest ride,
and was less able to support it, who went to bed.

5

All night the night air flowed into Catherine's pink
and silver bedroom, and perhaps Belle was right and
that was the way to get fever, for she lay behind her
mosquito curtains and tossed and twisted, and listened

to the lisping chatter of leaves like falling water, and the sharp crying of creatures out in the moony forest, and breathed keen disturbing scents, and faint far ghosts of dreams of scents, and thought of the pale stone army that stood on guard between forest and house, watching the Villa Maya with cold, proud, curious stares. Then she thought of the living persons within the villa, and the thought of living persons is too disturbing a fever in the night ; it set seven candles flickering and flaring in Catherine's brain, flickering and flaring and leaping among quivering shadows, like seven bonfires lit on a dark heath. Then little Meg pushed in, and an eighth candle flared and became a little bonfire on the heath. What, who, were all these people ? Who, what, were any people ? Strangers, strangers, and here was she among them on a visit, a long, long visit. Human creatures should not be on visits, but in their own homes. One was lost, abandoned, utterly at sea, if one was on a visit. One resembled a new-born infant, just arrived on this planet, flung grotesquely into a strange family, to be stared at and inspected and given, of their kindness, a place upon the earth. How it cried, the poor little devil ! I could cry too, thought Catherine, in this lovely room, this pink and silver room, among such ancient ruins, such rich sculptures, such tropical forests, such live persons, all living their separate, curious, secret, burning lives. Let me see, thought Catherine to calm herself, there are eight persons, and each quite different from the rest. She began to tell herself one of those domestic stories about large families and their different characters with which she had sent herself to sleep as a child. There is

Aunt Belle, she thought ; she is quick and kind and practical. There is Uncle Dickie—do I call him that ? —he lives (just now) for Maya buildings only, but all the time he is a judge. There is Claudia ; she is elegant and fastidious and aloof, and excites me. Benet is less aloof, but as clever and fastidious and civilised and highly strung. Julia ; she is spoilt and lazy, but gentle and amusing and has charm ; probably no scruples ; probably a rake. Isie, she is simple and open-air and barbarous and jolly, and loves Adrian. Adrian is civilised and reserved ; but no, I don't know Adrian yet. And Meg—she's just a jolly little tom-boy. How interesting people are, all so like themselves, and all different from one another. I could put them all on paper, right away. . . .

A ninth candle lit and flared, the hot, devouring candle of the writer, and extinguished the others. Then that too flared down, and Catherine thought of other living people, not in Guatemala but in London, England, and these were now strange and far and reproachful, like ghosts, now brightly intent on their own business, moving about in their lit circle, happy and self-absorbed, a solid gay phalanx of society, seeing one another day in, night out, with that superhuman gregariousness practised by others, never by oneself. Forgotten and far, Catherine lay in a forest, lost in the dark heart of the Central American night.

CHAPTER IV

SEEING THE VILLA

I

Cool and wan and empty, like grey water, dawn flowed into the pink room on a faint east wind. It lightly washed the silver trees and flowers, fruits and flames, that flared from floor to ceiling, till they gleamed, iridescent stalactites in a shell-pink cave. It spread, a pale pool, over Catherine asleep in the alcove, and woke her with the bland firmness of a hospital nurse who rouses her patients at dawn. As one turns from the nurse, seeking to elude the waking hour, Catherine turned to the wall, but, not finding night even there, she woke, and lay open-eyed beneath the faint grey wash of day.

Presently she accepted the state of affairs ; that a new day had arrived to her ; that she was on a visit ; that she lay in a rococo bedroom in an ancient palace ; that outside the palace was Guatemala, and a great forest, and mountain ranges beyond, and a landscape decorated with the figures of Indians, Spaniards, and ladinos, and many other kinds of peculiar creatures ; that immediately outside her windows was an enclosed plaza, the site of an ancient city, girdled with monastic cloisters and adorned with buildings only half-discerned in last night's dark.

Remembering these things, she threw back the bed clothes and staggered to the window, to inform herself further concerning her environment.

Yes, to be sure there was a plaza, turned into a patio, fifty yards across, half-circled with cloisters, and set about with buildings, with mounds, with sculptured figures of men and beasts. There were high mounds on some of which temples and columns still stood, in varying stages of preservation, some with trees thrusting up through them ; on others Mayans, Spanish monks, Americans and British in succession had made to themselves graven images, and there they stood, pale citizens of a dead city ; rearing serpents holding gentlemen or frogs between their jaws ; apostles, Dominicans, and a Madonna ; a large lady reminiscent of New York Harbour and doubtless symbolising some as yet unachieved North American ideal, such as liberty, democracy or justice ; and a few recently-erected wigged gentlemen with proud, pursy expressions and rolled up papers in their outstretched right hands, who doubtless represented the Cradocks' conceptions of what statues should be.

Surprisingly out of place stood this miscellaneous populace, among ancient altars, temples and broken columns richly carved with grotesque ornament. Imps, serpents, warriors, nobly-tailed birds, hybrid men and beasts, scrolls, flowers, fishes, fruits, feathers and inscriptions, were cut in rich and deep intricacy on pillar, wall and gate-post. In the middle of the paved court was a carved well, and by it a fountain played in a small stone basin. Over this strange assembly and scene a cold, pebble-coloured dawn spread, giving it an eerie stillness, as of life frozen or drowned, as of a world forgotten, entranced, or dead. Beyond, to the east, a great country rolled, forest and mountain and scarred desert, and Catherine recognised the landscape immediately for those wildernesses, dark, strange and ominous, that one traverses in dreams. But from the west came a soft and sighing sweetness, as if an orange garden blossomed.

As Catherine stared on the still scene, soft footfalls impressed themselves gently on it, lightly beating on silence, and retreating into silence again ; or rather, retreating into the forest, where no silence ever is, and mingling with the other footfalls there. Some being had been quite close to the house, perhaps in the patio itself, creeping softly about the dead city and among the silent citizens. A wild cat from the forest, an Indian, or some other prowling creature. Catherine stood listening, while the morning stealthily brightened and took colour. Into it there came new footsteps, firm and light and quick, and out of the house came Isie, bare-headed, dressed for walking, beautiful and alone. She stood for a minute, and stared about her, at the pale, strange morning, yet as one who did not see it (did Isie, indeed, ever see such things ?), then crossed the patio and turned along a path which ran westward and led to the grounds behind the house.

Isie on a dawn adventure by herself, like a poet or a child. Rather, thought her cousin, like a young Diana going hunting. Isie, abroad in this strange forest dawn, seeing nothing of its mysterious beauty and fear. Probably she was going to see after some domestic animal, such as a horse, or to chase after some wild

animal, such as a pig. Isie, young Amazon, would not
be frightened of the forest at dawn.

Catherine went back to bed, and, after one hour of
waking, slept for three.

2

One after the other, the household strayed out on to
the loggia where breakfast was laid, and consumed
coffee, bread, and fruit. The cool and bright morning
air flowed in on them ; to Catherine, climbed up by
now from the steep abysses of the night, all was happiness and beauty. She breakfasted rather early, her
natural habits unconquered by her also natural gift of
being a good guest. She found in the loggia Benet,
nursing a grey cat, and looking pale and heavy-eyed,
for he seldom slept, and the mornings were not his good
time. But he smiled charmingly at Catherine, said it
was going to be hot, surrounded her with food and
drink, and hoped that she had passed a tolerable
night.

" I should say you usually did that, don't you," he
added, guessing quite wrong. Remarkable how people
nearly always guess wrong about other people's habits.
Little did any one know or care how far from well
Catherine usually slept.

Julia lounged in, followed by Isie and Adrian. They
all said it would be hot. Julia looked jaded, but Isie
bloomed like a mountain morning.

" You were early out," said Catherine to her.

Isie, eating an alligator pear, seemed momentarily

checked. Her smooth brown cheeks assumed the blush of a peach.

" Why, yes, I just strolled out. Why, it's fine out in the forest early mornings. I don't know why we don't all get up at dawn every day."

" And I," said Julia, lying limply in a long chair, " don't know why we ever get up at all. Everything worth doing, except dancing, can be done better in bed. Pray, Catherine, couldn't you write your novels better in bed ? I'm sure I could mine."

Catherine smiled indulgently at the absurd child. She did not believe that Julia had ever written a line of a novel, in bed or out.

Amy the negress beamed out on the loggia like a black sun and said, " Mass' Phipps," and stood aside to give place to this gentleman, at whom the family glanced languidly and without surprise.

" An early call," said Mr. Phipps, smiling benignantly on them.

" Yes," said Adrian.

" Good-morning," said Benet.

" Why, Mr. Phipps, I certainly will admit you rise early," said Isie.

" Good-day, all," said Mr. Phipps, and seated himself. " I was riding around, and thought I'd look in. It's going to be hot. Thank you, I *will* have just a little coffee. . . . Well, Miss Grey, and how does the little old villa please you ? Very tasteful, the decoration scheme, don't you think ? I'll say that Mr. Rickaby's shown himself a very fine designer. He's gotten the old hacienda up real smart."

" Very smart," Catherine agreed.

" And where are Sir and Lady Cradock this morning ? " Mr. Phipps enquired.

" Sir Richmond," Adrian said, " is probably either in the cellar or somewhere out in the grounds."

" And mother's talking to the cook," Isie added.

" Is she so ? Well, I'll just stroll around and look for the Judge. In the cellar, you say ? "

" Very odd, how early people call here," said Adrian, when he had gone. " I mean, you'd think later—the cool of the evening. He can have nothing to do, Phipps. The fact is," he added, brooding over it, " Phipps is a nuisance. People who call at breakfast time."

Adrian was rather a fussy man.

" I think Phipps is adorable," Benet murmured.

Claudia came out, cool and bland in tussore.

" I was waiting for Mr. Phipps to go," she explained. " It's going to be hot."

" Say, listen, Catherine," said Isie, " what would you like to do to-day ? What I mean is, are you rested, and would you like a picnic, or would you rather just fool around the hacienda ? "

" Of course she must fool around the hacienda," said Benet. " She's not seen it yet. She's seen nothing— not the chapel, or the grounds, or the ruins, or the house properly. I hope, Catherine, that you aren't a picnic addict."

" We think picnics deplorable," said Claudia, in her faint voice.

" So hearty and jolly," added Benet. " We are trying to cure Isie of heartiness and jollity, and we hope you aren't going to encourage her, Catherine."

" But I expect I am hearty and jolly too," said

Catherine. " I'm a country clergyman's daughter, you know. I used to be mixed up with Girl Guides when I was younger. I expect one never quite recovers from that."

"Were you a Brownie ? " Benet asked, morbidly interested. " Meg's a Brownie ; they have it at her school, as well as chicken-pox, infant paralysis, hockey, and esprit de corps. Meg's had them all, except infant paralysis."

" I had them all," said Julia. " But I won through. The fact is, practically everyone has them at school. That's where grown-up novels are wrong about girls at school ; they always make the heroine contemptuous of and superior to her surroundings, and she never is ; it's a myth. The truth about girls and boys at school is too contemptible to put into real novels ; it only gets into depraved books called *The Fourth Form at St. Ursula's* or *Maitland of the Fifth*. I mean, you might as well try to write a novel about a flock of sheep." Fatigued by the idea of so doing, she lay back with closed eyes.

" What one has been through," she murmured.

Isie looked for sympathy at Catherine. " Good-night, what a family ! " she commented. " What it is, they don't have any *pep*. Only little Meg has pep, and *she* won't be let grow up with it. I never knew such girls and boys. It seems like they're all bled white."

"We definitely are," said Benet, not displeased. " We put it down to the great war."

" And what did *you* do in the great war, I'd like to know ? What part of the front were you on, for heaven's sakes ? "

" The great war was won on the playing-fields of
Winchester and of my prep. school," Benet explained.

" And for my part," added Claudia, " I was nineteen
when the affair ended, and I attended an armistice ball.
I belong practically to the Lost Generation, like
Adrian."

" And I remember an air raid," said Julia. " They
woke me up and carried me down to the basement. I
am the air raid generation."

" They're terribly generation-conscious," Adrian
explained kindly. " I believe they can't help it. It
seems a post-war disease. As a matter of fact, I believe
none of them noticed the war particularly while it was
occurring."

" Well, Catherine," said Claudia, " would you like
to come and see the place before it gets hotter ? The
day, I mean. I assure you, it's full of curious and
amusing buildings, and not in the least like any country
house you've ever seen before."

3

Catherine, animated and admiring, the perfect guest,
was conducted round the grounds by Claudia, Benet,
Isie and Adrian.

They showed her the plaza, with its ruins, its temples,
its statues, its sculptures, and its columns with ancient
trees thrusting up through them and bees hiving in the
cracks.

" But papa shall show you the details and interpret
the inscriptions to you later. We should get them

wrong. It's not really one of the best Maya ruins, of course ; not to compare with any of the well-known ones. That's why it's been let alone and we've got it to ourselves. There are probably hundreds as good strewn about the unexplored forests. But it's charming, rather, with the Dominican additions, and the nineteenth century hacienda. Now look, that's the chapel. The monks built it, and we added the gallery and the figures inside. They make it gayer, don't they ? It was very depressing before. Spanish church decoration is so melancholy ; they seem to love to look on the sad side of religion."

Claudia indicated with distaste a huge rood-screen which treated a painful theme with distressing realism.

" Latins like that sort of thing," Benet explained. " They're so strong-minded. The English are too squeamish for it. That probably partly accounted for the Reformation in England. Anyhow, we thought we'd brighten the scene."

They had brightened it by adding two galleries like opera boxes on either side of the church, and filling them with male and female plaster saints of the most gentlemanly and lady-like appearance imaginable, apparently engaged in animated conversation, elegant adoration, or amiable interest in their surroundings. None of them either wore the smug appearance of many saints in churches, or clung morbidly to the instruments of their future decease like others. They behaved, in fact, like ladies and gentlemen, and their presence in the galleries, beneath gold-tasselled stucco curtains, gave to the little church the incongruous yet delightful quality of a Bibbiena opera house.

" They're rather well modelled," said Adrian. " We had a Neapolitan sculptor here, a very clever fellow."

" Well, I think they look just terribly silly," said his wife. " Don't you, Catherine ? "

" Silly, but rather charming, I think."

" Goodness, Catherine, you don't *like* these people stuck up there ? Why, I think they look so foolish, I could die laughing ! Why, they're not like church figures at all. They're just bogus and worldly."

" Rococo *is* bogus and worldly," Adrian agreed. " That's precisely the idea, my child."

Catherine thought, he is a nice prig. But it seems rather vulgar of them to have put these figures in the old church. . . . For she had been brought up to believe that old churches should not be touched or added to, only restored when they required it, with the most careful sense of period.

Leaving the church, they continued their tour of the grounds, passing a ruined temple reminiscent of Tivoli (for they had felt they must have an artificial ruin, presumably to encourage the real, as one lays a stone egg among the eggs laid by a hen) and arrived at a pavilion they called the orangery, charmingly decorated inside with orange, lemon and peach trees of painted stucco, on which perched gay butterflies and birds more bright than life.

" After the orangery at the Bayreuth Hermitage," the Cradocks pointed out. " You know it ? "

Catherine did, and was enchanted afresh with this gay and absurd pavilion, and also with the shelly and fishy grotto near it, wherein water trickled down gleaming shell-plastered and pebble walls, and the rocks arching overhead made a cool green gloom.

In these charming pleasure grounds it seemed that everything had been thought of ; there was even an artificial lake, made by the Dominicans for a fish pond and decorated by the Cradocks with fountains and stone dolphins, mermaids and tritons, and live swans.

As they stood by this, Mr. Piper, the estate manager, strolled up to them, chewing a piece of sugar cane. He was a tall, lean man, elegantly built, with a cynical expression and a soft Devonian voice, using inflexions gathered during twenty years' residence in Texas. He had not the air of thinking much either of Maya architecture or rococo pleasure grounds ; it was his sole business to see that the coffee, sugar and coconut plantations flourished and were profitable, and that the Indian workers behaved themselves, and he was not concerned with other aspects of the estate than these. He lived in a small house on the edge of the forest, about two hundred yards from the villa, and trusted neither human beings nor animals.

" Good-day," he said, with a not unkindly contempt. " Going to be hawt." For that, thought he, even these trifling persons on pleasure bent could comprehend.

" Hawt already," Benet replied.

" Not," said Mr. Piper, spitting out fragments of sugar cane, " to what it's going to be . . . Judge about ? "

" In the cellar, probably."

" I'd be glad of a word with him, later."

He lounged off, a scornful, cynical, melancholy man,

half-turning his head to throw over his shoulder, " The minister's back, darned drunk."

Benet mopped his face, pale and glistening from the heat, with a green silk handkerchief.

" It certainly is hawt. Shall we join papa in the cellar ? We can get there by a subterranean passage from the temple."

" What does one do in the cellar ? " Catherine enquired.

" Get darned drunk, if one likes to. The Dominicans turned it into a wine cellar, and it's been used as such ever since. But that isn't what papa is doing ; he's making out inscriptions. There are the *most* marvellous sculptures there. They're not half-uncovered yet."

They trailed languidly back to the patio and entered the temple.

" Not me," said Isie. " I'm not going to waste the morning in that mouldy cellar. I'm going fishing. Come too, Adrian ? "

" I can't. I told Dickie I'd help him this morning. Don't go far, will you."

" Oh, no, nursie. I shall fish for minnows in the garden pool, of course."

She left them. They then removed a stone slab from a hole in the corner of the temple floor, discovering steps which led them along a narrow stone-paved passage under the courtyard and came out in a low, rectangular chamber stacked with wine barrels and enclosed by richly sculptured walls. The carvings were still partly concealed by the plaster of four centuries, and Sir Richmond was chipping carefully and craftily at the corner of a doorway, disclosing little by little a lizard's head. Behind him Mr. Phipps squatted in the corner behind the barrels and peered at the floor.

" Well, papa," Claudia said, " we have all come down to help you, and to show Catherine the cellar. Well, Mr. Phipps, I hope you keep cool." Mr. Phipps crawled out from behind the wine casks.

" I've had a right nice time here, Miss Cradock. I find it highly interesting watching the judge at his excavating. But now, if you'll excuse me, I must be getting back. I'll go up through the villa, if I may."

He disappeared through the doorway at which Sir Richmond was chipping.

" Dear me," said Sir Richmond, mildly surprised. " Has Phipps gone ? Very unusual. . . . Yes, this is the cellar, Catherine. An extraordinary wealth of detailed decoration in the carving, you'll notice, and only half uncovered still. Remarkable inscriptions. I am having moulds taken of them. You see the way in which the monks plastered the carving over. The usual passion for concealment ; a strange impulse to cover a beautiful thing with a less beautiful. You know the way in which they used to erase classical literature and use the parchment for writing lives of the saints. There's a chest of such manuscripts here, that they must have brought with them at some time. One supposes that the same impulse made them cover up these heathen sculptures with plaster, and paint religious frescoes on it. And so it's remained from the sixteenth century till now. . . . A lovely doorway, this. One of the best. You see the delicacy of the feather work ? And this charming imp—rather like

Humpty Dumpty ; and the other one is like the Lord
Chief Justice, isn't he ? Almost incredible that they
did it all with stone tools. How many years must it
have taken, this one piece of carving. . . . And then
to have it daubed over with plaster by a set of ignorant
missionaries. . . ."

Chipping gently and cautiously away, he rambled on,
swelling the chorus of the age-old, so frequently
unfair, complaint of art against the churches.

Catherine, just-minded daughter of a vicar, feeling
them all to be prejudiced anti-clericals, would have
liked to remind them of the beauty of the Dominican
monastic buildings above them, of the preservation by
monks of art and letters through ages of savagery, and
of the loveliness of ecclesiastical architecture over
Europe, but refrained from such a discussion, in the face
of the plastered Maya carvings. Adrian and Benet had
taken chisels and had begun to chip at the other corner
of the lintel. Claudia, no doubt not wishing to be
burdened all the morning with the entertainment of the
guest, quietly disappeared up the stairs that led into the
hall.

In the upstairs loggia she found Julia, lolling
negligently with pen and paper on a cane couch.

" I think my novel is becoming very diverting,"
said Julia, not looking up, as her sister came out.

" I am glad," replied Claudia, " that you are diverted.
But you are also selfish, as usual. This afternoon it will
be for you to take Catherine about and show her the
sights."

" No," said Julia. " She will go for a ramble, with
Isie and Meg. Catherine is a devotee of Nature. She

adores scenery. She must be taken up a mountain in the cool of the evening and shown a view. You know quite well how I find mountains shocking and can't climb them."

" I know quite well that you will do as you please," Claudia amicably replied. " And so shall I." She yawned, and lay back in a lounge chair with a book.

4

Lady Cradock, trim, energetic and heated, bustled out on to the loggia. " I will say you two girls look quiet. As if nothing upsetting could happen. Just the same, it does. Where's your father ? "

" In the cellar."

" He surely would be in the cellar, chipping away at those old carvings, and not noticing a thing. Here's Piper says the coffee pickers want to get more wages. I'm sure I don't mind them getting them, but Piper says no, it would upset the sugar-cane men. And if the sugar-cane men got more, it would make trouble in the coconut plantation. And if all the workers in the hacienda got more, it seems it would go to their heads, for Piper says they get quite as much already as peons can stand. Piper seems to think money's like drink."

" Money *is* drink," said Claudia.

" Well, maybe you're right. The men certainly do seem to get very drunk on wage days. That chicha they all take—it must be terribly strong, the way it affects those calm, reserved men. It's such a pity we don't grow hops here. Well, anyhow, Piper says they're getting quite tiresome about their wages, and he anticipates there may be trouble. Fifty years ago, you know, before our time, there was a real big trouble, a regular war between the Indians and the hacienda. The mill got burnt, and acres of canes. And all the cochineal ; but that was for the best, Piper says. That was in the days that Spanish family had the farm. It was terribly bad for the estate, of course. And the ladinos and Indians remember it still, they're such revengeful people. Piper says Jacinto eggs them on. But Piper doesn't like Jacinto, he'll say anything spiteful about him, just because he's a clergyman. What I say is, one certainly has to be just. . . . The thing is, as I said to Piper, what are we to do ? I mean, if the men want to get more, and are going to be unhappy till they do get more, what can we do about it ? Piper says, nothing ; just wait and see, and watch out. Piper really is a depressing man. Sometimes I think he downright grudges me the pleasure I take in the house and grounds. . . . Well, if your father must stay down all morning in the cellar, I shall go right down there and talk to him. But I first must eat a slice of melon. Listen, girls, where's Catherine ? "

" In the cellar too, I think. Or she was."

" How you all do love that cellar. Mr. Phipps has been down there too. He just loves to talk to your father while he chips. But Dickie doesn't listen. Your father's like all of you, he keeps calm in the middle of uproar. I guess judges have to. I shall take some melon down to him and Catherine ; they'll be needing something cool by now. It's surely going to be hot."

" Not still, Belle dear. It surely *is* hot ; the next thing it's going to be is cool."

" Why, Claudia dear, it isn't going to be cool for hours. Not till evening. . . . I suppose Meg is trapesing about in the heat somewhere. The child'll get one of those diseases she came away from school to avoid. She surely will get struck by the sun. You won't mind my saying it, girls, but I think you should worry after your little sister more than you do. I do my best, but she's all over the place and I've the house to mind."

" Oh, Meg's all right."

Belle shook her head, put some melon in a plate, and departed for the cellar.

5

Catherine, strolling alone in what her aunt liked to call the park, encountered her youngest step-cousin wading knee-deep in a stream, a minnow rod in her hands.

" Hullo, Meg."

" Hullo."

A senseless ejaculation indeed, Catherine reflected.

" Caught anything ? " she enquired.

" A few," Meg said modestly, indicating the basket by the side of the stream. It certainly was only a few.

" I don't know what they are," Meg added.

" Do you like fishing ? " Catherine asked.

Meg said politely that she did, rather, and refrained from adding that this was, in fact, why she was doing it.

" Being here is more fun than school, I expect, isn't it ? " Catherine continued sympathetically.

" Well." Meg considered this remark, as she trailed her line over a pool. " It's different," she concluded.

" I should think it was. But you like school, don't you ? "

What a lot of things she wanted to know, Meg thought : However, people so often, for reasons best known to themselves, wanted to know whether or not she liked this or that, particularly school, that she was quite used to it, and said " Yes " without any trouble.

" Well," said Catherine, " I'm going on into the forest. Where does this path lead, do you know ? "

" Into the forest," said Meg. " I think it's the one that goes on to the village."

" Is the village nice ? "

" It's all right."

Catherine went on. A sturdy, truth-telling, un-romantic, not very interesting child, little Meg ; probably unimaginative. She displayed little excite-ment or enthusiasm over her exciting surroundings. A typical British school child ; a solid, practical, Philistine Englishwoman to be. She would not grow up like her over-sophisticated sisters and brothers. More like Isie, perhaps, only with none of that beauty that turned Isie, for all her elementariness, into a poem and a flame, and had caused people all her life to spoil her. Little Meg, freckled and square-faced, would probably, therefore, grow up more unselfish than Isie. Perhaps she would be an athlete, and play hockey for counties and tennis for championships.

So Catherine reflected, as she took the shadowed

path that ran into the steaming forest, flipping at
bichos with a branch of tree-fern as she walked. These
damned insects ; they made the forest tiresome, marred
its peace. Mosquitoes and sand flies hovering in
droning clouds, ticks dropping from the trees, jiggers
burrowing beneath the skin, ants nipping the legs—
really you would think the insect world had nothing
whatever to do but eat. The other animals had
occasionally other occupations ; they sang, talked,
climbed, played, swam, slept, or merely enjoyed the
scenery. Even the vampire bats were not always
imbibing their appropriate nourishment, but often
merely sat and flapped in the trees.

Meg, left alone in the stream, jogged rhythmically
up and down from one bare leg to the other, crooning
a little poem to a vague tune of her own.

> " Oh world, oh life, oh time,
> On whose last steps I climb,
> Trembling at that where I had stood before,
> When will return the glory of your prime ?
> No more ; oh, never more ! "

From the villa a great gong boomed harshly over that
part of Guatemala. It was lunch-time at the Hacienda
del Capitan.

CHAPTER V

I

THE days passed. Each was going to be hot, was hot, expired in flame, and darkened to a purple night of stars. It became Christmas Day. The Mayas kept the fiesta with the rites with which they had kept it for three thousand years. For the last four hundred of these, since the Spanish missionaries had arrived, and had been so violently decided about the way to worship, a few new rites had been added to the old, a few minor changes had been introduced, the names of divinities had been altered, and so forth, but the spirit and ritual of these seasonal feasts remained pretty well the same. The little Perdido church and all the forest shrines were fragrant with burning pine boughs and sweet with blossoming flowers. Everyone had a holiday, and went to church, and got drunk on aguardiente and chicha. At the big house there was a Christmas-tree. All the peons on the hacienda with their families were invited to see this glittering plant, heavy with gifts, which it served out to them like some benign and shining god. They accepted the gifts with their habitual grave courtesy, and without prejudice to future financial disagreements.

To the Christmas-tree came also Mr. Piper, Mr. Phipps, and Father Jacinto, with the lady who kept house for him. Mr. Piper and Mr. Phipps stayed to dinner. " I know you English think it's only right,"

69

said Belle, " to ask your clergyman to Christmas dinner, in the country, but I know you none of you care for poor Father Jacinto, and he's stupid at talking English too, and she's a right homely woman, even for an Indian."

" Immoral too," the judge pointed out, with judical distaste for this quality. " They both are."

" Not," his wife qualified, " that one oughtn't to overlook that at Christmas time, and be hospitable and love everyone. I'm sure your father would say so, wouldn't he, Catherine ? And after all, the poor padre's only a half-breed ; it's not as if he was a white clergyman. What I mean is, you can't *blame* him."

Isie said, " Why, mother, Jacinto doesn't even wash his hands. Why, I just couldn't eat at table with him," and settled that.

2

Mr. Phipps talked at dinner about the local Indians. "Determined," he said. " They seem so quiet and patient, these Guatemalans. When they set their minds on anything, they'll wait years to get it, but they'll get it in the end. What do you say, Mr. Piper ? "

" Well, Mr. Phipps, I'd say that would depend a lot on how tenacious the fellow pulling at the other end might chance to be. Indians ain't the only tenacious men in Guat."

" They're the most patient, though, Mr. Piper. They hold on ; they don't forget. What I say is, if I was tugging against Indians I'd save my breath and drop the rope early, for I'd know I'd have to do it late."

" If the Spaniards had said that," said Sir Richmond,
" the history of Central America for the last four
centuries would have been a little different, surely."

" Ah, those old Indians were different, Judge. Kind
of degenerate and feeble, I've read ; worn out after
all that building their ancestors had done. They didn't
have such tenacity as they're gotten to-day. Just the
same, it was only some of them got subdued by the
Spaniards. Big crowds of them didn't knuckle under
then and never have since."

" Ah, yes. The unconquered tribes of the northern
and western forests, you mean ; the Sublevados and
Lacandones. A small minority of the Indian race,
however."

" Not so small, Judge. They occupy big territories,
these unconquered tribes. And no one knows how many
of them there are. Do they, Mr. Piper ? "

" Well, Mr. Phipps, I certainly did never have a
chance to count those Indians myself, and I most
likely never will."

" And," went on Mr. Phipps, his round, pink face
kindling as he lent across the table towards his
hostess, " and there's another thing about them, Lady
Cradock—they're in mighty close touch, those Lacandones of the Chiapas forests, with the Indians all about
here. These mozos on the plantations, they all got
acquaintances and relatives over the Chiapas border
among the wild men, and when they need their help,
they send for them. There were hundreds of them
helping in the big trouble here fifty years back, they say."

" Who say, Mr. Phipps ? "

" Why, the people here, Mr. Piper. His reverence

Mr. Jacinto will tell you that ; and so will every other ladino and creole for miles around. They all know it."

" Well, if that isn't quite too terrifying ! Do you want another mince pie, Meg, love ? "

" Yes, I do, please."

" To think of those wild Indians coming all around the place. I shouldn't sleep nights, worrying what they'd do in the plantations."

Mr. Piper said, " The Lacandones are mostly harmless poor Indians, Lady Cradock. Kind of mild mannered. They come around here trading copal. They mean no harm, the Lacs don't."

" Do you claim that, Mr. Piper ? "

" I certainly do, Mr. Phipps. A Lac here and there will act ugly, just the same as other Indians or niggers now and then, or whites either. But taking them all round, they're harmless poor creatures, like you and me, Mr. Phipps."

" You say so, Mr. Piper," said Mr. Phipps, eating a candied banana. " Just the same," he added, " I've heard tales of those same Indians that I surely would not care to relate before ladies. No, I certainly would not care to."

" Then pray don't, Mr. Phipps," Claudia requested him. " We know already that Indians can be shocking."

" However," said Belle kindly, " we all have our faults. There's always something, even in the best of us, Mr. Phipps."

Goggle-eyed, Meg, who knew her Fenimore Cooper, stared at Mr. Phipps. Fortunate, thought Catherine, that she was not a child of the nervous type.

" Say, listen, Mr. Phipps," Isie called to him, " I call

this cheesey kind of talk for Christmas Day. Do you want to spoil all our lovely forest picnics ? If you can't shoot a better line than that on what you've drunk already, for the Lord's sake fill your glass and get on with the good work."

" I ask your pardon, Mrs. Rickaby." Mr. Phipps beamed apology at his vivacious young compatriot. "We certainly should speak of something more Christian and seasonable than those unconverted red men."

He proceeded to do so, and became what is called the life and soul of the party, for he was a very gay, amusing man, and had seen much curious life. Mr. Piper watched him rather sourly as he entertained the table ; he was inclined to think that there was too much of Mr. Phipps and too often. He's the hell of a talker, the little fat chap, he said within himself, and left the party early, to see that no intoxicated Guatemalans were stealing his hens.

" Piper trusts *no one*," said Belle, " even on Christmas Day."

Mr. Phipps, on the other hand, stayed the night at the villa.

3

Oddly it seemed to Catherine that, after the gay evening, the night was full of tears. Did she hear or imagine them, these faint choked sounds, as of a ghost in grief ? She lay and listened, but they dwindled away and died, and the Christmas night held only the thousand animal and vegetable noises of the forest, as if no human creature waked. And yet to Catherine, lying in the faint dawn, the night seemed full of tears.

CHAPTER VI

WAITING FOR A QUAKE

I

THE year's last days slipped out, hot and sweet and golden like the fruits that dropped in the forest. The noons were steamy and languid down in the lower forest ; but, climbing the slopes, one met the crisp and lovely tang of the dry season in the templada.

Catherine was taken by her relations about the forest and the mountain slopes. They showed her Indian villages full of small, gentle, intoxicated Maya, old Spanish churches, Maya ruins, the few scattered, distant ranches owned by ladinos or (one or two of them) by Spanish creoles, and tremendous views of distant blue sierras, great brown plains and illimitable forests, at which her heart was astonished and fainted within her.

They rode over to Mr. Phipps' ranch ; a small old Spanish farmhouse with a few acres of vines and canes, close to a little settlement of Indians and blackamoors.

" I bought it from a creole," he told them. " He'd let it go to waste. They don't have any energy, these creoles. Funny how after a few generations settled in this country, a European family loses its pep. Anyhow, the Spaniards do. All they care for is to lounge in the sun and eat and drink a little, and boast what hidalgos their relations in Spain were. If they keep just enough grit to stay creole and not take up with the native

women, that about uses up all the energy they've
gotten. And no one's known that to last more than
three generations. They go mestizo sooner or later,
and are the better for it ; a little Indian blood gingers
them up, and they begin to want to be alcaldes and
run local politics. A funny lot, these Spaniards. No
pep. If the British or Americans had settled this
country instead, it would have been very different now."

Catherine saw Cortes and his handful of soldiers
landing at Vera Cruz, destroying their ships, flinging
themselves across a barbarous and astonishing con-
tinent of forest and mountain, a few hundred gallant,
ferocious and adventuring Latins among thousands of
unknown natives, taking their country from them,
claiming by fire and sword, killing by torture, dying by
torture, savagely imposing their own faith, their own
gods, building rich cities, enslaving those who were
to them a thousand to a man, dwelling arrogantly,
proud and venal sons of Europe, surrounded by impenetrable forests whence tawny enemies issued ever
and anon for assault. Pep ? Who had pep and the
Spanish settlers had it not ? Not all virtues were theirs
—as Belle had said we all have our faults—but pep,
yes. Possibly, in the steamy tropical jungle, pep
suffered and declined. Certainly the few creoles about
did not seem to have much.

2

There was a creole ranch ten miles west of Mr.
Phipps' house, almost on the edge of the Lacandon
country. They rode past it one day ; a rambling stone

house falling to pieces, with a sugar-grinding house near it, half destroyed by fire. A woman, with the pale olive skin of Castile, stout, and clad in a loose and dingy wrap, was calling to a group of dirty children in a chicken-run. The man, lean and graceful, with the same tight olive Latin skin, was lounging against a carved gate-post, smoking a cigar. He greeted the riders—Adrian, Isie, Claudia, Benet and Catherine—in the Spanish of Guatemala.

" Good-day, señores."

" Good-day, Señor Jaime," they replied, in the Spanish of Castile and Berlitz.

" Those are pretty gate-posts you have," Adrian added.

Señor Jaime deprecated the compliment with a gesture. " They are tolerable. They support the gate."

" They are Maya, surely, and very old ? "

" Doubtless they are Maya. As to their age, my grandfather found them in the forest when he came here and built the hacienda, and set them up for his gate. Many similar stones he used for the house itself. The forest is full of such." He waved a negligent hand towards the thick jungle to the north-west. " They are often in the way when we cut the wood down."

" My father," said Claudia, " is interested in Maya carvings. Perhaps you would kindly permit that he comes over one day to see your gate-posts and house."

" With all the pleasure in the world. But there is little to see—only Indian stones. The forest here abounds in them. These lazy mozos don't clear them away, though they must have lain there for years."

" For centuries, no doubt."

" Who knows ! In any case they are a nuisance to us who want to plant the land. To dig, and to come on great broken fragments of stone—that is troublesome. So my cultivated land here is small in extent ; one cannot contend against such difficulties, with these lazy and drunken mozos. There is enough to do without that. For my part, I never have a minute to rest in, and often I wish I was back in Spain, where my relations have without doubt prosperous vineyards and great dignity, and Christians to work for them instead of these miserable Indians and negroes. Goodbye, señores, go with God."

Polite he was, but languid and bored, leaning against his Maya gate-post talking of dignity,.but thinking of the miserable meal that was being prepared for him in the house.

" He is very good-looking," Claudia said, as they rode away. " And it is nice for him to come out here and believe that his Spanish relations are people of substance. His grandchildren will be ladinos or mulattos, no doubt. . . . Certainly we must take papa to see those gate-posts."

But Sir Richmond refused to stray after the gate-posts of neighbours. He was absorbed in researches about his wife's house and grounds. He had become a man of one occupation, one aim ; from morning till night he delved, chiselled, hewed, and wandered about the plaza, the buildings and the chapel with stooping mien and an iron rod wherewith he prodded the cracks between the stones of the floors and walls, for he conceived that further treasures might be lying hid behind some paving or monastic wall.

" Of course all the forest to the north-west is full of interesting ruins," he allowed. " But, with all we have here, I have no time to go looking for them."

And Belle said, " For goodness' sake don't tell Dickie of more old stones." So Señor Jaime and his señora expected in vain the second visit of the wealthy gringos, to whom they hoped to sell various Indian antiques, for, living among the descendants of the Maya, one acquires in faking antiquity the skill and enterprise of those small shops in London by-streets whose windows are so picturesquely stocked with cottage brass, china, oak settles, and samplers embroidered by " Mary Ann, A.D. 1813."

3

It had turned unusually hot and moist for the dry season. The family lay much in the bathing pool ; the river was not so restful, because of crocodiles. But life nowhere out of doors was really restful, because of mosquitoes, ticks, ants, flies, jiggers, caterpillars, bichos, snakes, scorpions, and other inhabitants of the forest. Forests are not restful, even in Europe ; those who dwell in them are intrusive and interfering ; they will not let one another alone. Civilisation, as the Cradocks complained, does not prevail there.

" Prevail," Adrian repeated. They were lying, through the hot afternoon, in the shade of the grotto. " I am sure I don't know where civilisation does prevail. Certainly nowhere where human beings are gathered together." However, as Benet pointed out, that entirely depended on how you defined civilisation. If you meant by it a certain proficiency in the arts and

sciences, and an elaborate meshwork of laws for
regulating behaviour, a certain amount of tolerance and
indifference to one another's habits. . . .

" That," said Claudia, " is not compatible with your
laws for regulating behaviour. You can't have it both
ways. Civilisation may mean laws, or tolerance, but
it can't mean both."

" You must surely include in civilisation," said
Catherine, " a more or less prevalent and not too low
ethical standard."

" Too low ! That means nothing. What is high and
what is low ? Each community and each age decides
arbitrarily for itself. There's no absolute high or low
in ethics."

" I think there is. There's cruelty——"

" What's cruelty, once you get beyond the purely
physical ? Cruelty and kindness—a hopeless bog of
muddled standards."

" Well, why get beyond the physical ? Torture is
cruel. Slavery is cruel. The Spaniards were cruel to
the Indians. The Indians were cruel to the Spaniards.
Russians are cruel. So Russians haven't civilisation."

" They certainly have not. But at that rate, what
nations have, or ever had ? At that rate it doesn't
exist, except in individuals."

" My dear Adrian," Benet languidly protested,
" everyone knows it doesn't. What a suggestion ! But
I agree with you that civilisation hasn't much to do
with ethics."

" It's no use talking about it," said Claudia, " since
everyone means a different thing by it—learning, or
culture, or applied knowledge, or virtue, or good taste,

or good manners, or good laws, or good housing and drainage. So one may just as well not use the word at all. Conversation about anything is useless. There are simply not enough words that mean the same thing to everyone. We talk entirely too much. St. Thomas Aquinas was so right to smash the talking machine that Albert de Groot invented. Those who act from religious motives are so often right. What are words? We could get on quite as well with a few gestures, howls, and what not."

She indicated a group of monkeys in a sapsodilla tree, who were making themselves, by their noises, intelligible one to the other.

" But that," said Benet, " would make us even hotter than conversation does. They must get as hot as Italians do when they talk."

" What is heating," said Julia, " I mean, what are heating, are the passions. We must not yield to them in hot weather."

" In no weather, in Guatemala," said Claudia. " It's not the climate for them. They do very well for Europe, like hot bottles and fires. I am keeping all mine well under until we get back."

" You have such self-control," Julia sighed. " You all have, except me. Now I am devastated continually. It is, perhaps, all this fiction that I can't help emitting. You can imagine how it rouses and heats the imagination. Don't you find it so, Catherine ? But still, I must say that you always appear cool and collected."

" Oh, indeed, I'm not," Catherine replied. " That is merely my placid manner and my uninteresting complexion."

"Really? If you don't mind telling me, Catherine, are you devastated by the passions, like me? But there, of course, you would mind telling me, with all these people gaping round us. I will ask you again, when we are alone. But I'm nearly sure you are not. Of course I don't mean never, but just now, in this heat. No; you are sensible, and calm, and wise, and know how to keep cool. Not like these poor Indians, with their unfortunate complexions. However cool an Indian might feel, no one would guess it."

"One understands," said Benet, "that they don't even feel it. Their minds are on more money, in order to afford more alcohol, and those are not cooling thoughts. Here come the children."

Isie strolled into the shadow of the grotto, and beside her walked Meg with her bow and arrows, her white sun-hat pushed back from her hot, round, freckled face.

"Hullo, everybody. Having a siesta?"

In the grotto, thought Catherine, half asleep, voices sound hollow and strange and not real. Isie looked cool and far off, like a stalactite, like a chill and beautiful nymph of the rocks. Looking up at her, Catherine saw Julia looking too; then Julia's eyes rolled for a moment to Adrian lying quiet in his long chair. A little door was pushed ajar in Catherine's mind: a little cranny of light stole through. . . . Julia, limp and languid and devastated, so she admitted, by the passions. . . . What passions devastated young Julia, in this family circle? Were they the purely fictional passions to which she had owned? Julia was surely a light-of-love, and without scruples; an honourless imp.

But Adrian and his beautiful Isie? Yes, surely Adrian loved his Isie. . . . Well, then, poor little Julia. Only could Julia take anything seriously, with her rolling comic eye and drooping indiarubber mouth?

Absurd, thought Catherine. I have imagined it all. But it had not taken her longer to imagine it than it took Adrian to say, in his tired, gentle voice, " Come and sit down, my dear. There's no such hurry as you think."

Isie came farther into the cool shadow of the grotto. Julia pulled herself limply up from her chair by Adrian's side, yawned, stretched, and said, " I shall go and sleep alone in the loggia. One gets no peace with all this chatter about civilisation, monkeys, and the passions. It is odd that everyone talks so much, when really there's so little to be said about anything." She lounged off.

" Meg, you're too hot," said Claudia, being suddenly an elder sister, but without zeal, and rather commenting than admonishing.

" Yes," Meg agreed, " I'm going to bathe in the lake now."

" You had better cool off first," Claudia suggested.

" No. That would be silly," replied her sister, and began to remove her clothes.

" She is quite right," said Benet. " It would be silly. Meg is a hedonist."

" She will come out in a rash," Claudia predicted. " But there, she is used to that, with all these diseases that are part of her school curriculum. We perhaps make too much fuss about coming out in rashes. Some people, such as Cleopatra, have refrained even from strawberries and shellfish on that account. And all this vaccination. . . . It seems certain that we make too much ado about our skins and our insides."

" Well, hell, Claudia," said Isie, " they're all we've got. Why, if you take away our skins and our insides, I'd like to know what's left ? "

" Only the soul, I fear. An inconsiderable wraith."

" Oh, if you're going to pull that raw pre-war stuff on me. . . ."

Benet looked pleased. " Raw pre-war stuff. That's an entrancing description of the soul. Go on, Isie."

" No. I'm not going to talk for you all to laugh at. I'm not standing for it."

Catherine glanced at her cousin, in surprise. The heat would seem to have made her quite disagreeable. Red stained the ivory brown of her cheeks ; her thin black brows were drawn sullenly together.

" The way you all sit here talking about nothing," she added. " The kid's the only one who's gotten sense."

A splash announced the kid's entry into the lake.

" Oh, I shall go and bathe, too." Isie jumped up. "It's the only thing worth doing, in this damned place."

" For my part," said Claudia, " I shall go and look for papa, and help him in his researches."

She got up, and strolled out into the glaring garden. She walked calmly, casually, and negligently, thought Catherine, as idle spinsters walk. Isie was already acquiring the tense, hustling, busy air of the young matron, who must be up and doing, lest something should go undone. By all means, Claudia had the air of saying, let, so far as I am concerned, everything go undone.

" Unmarried people get quite selfish," as Belle complained.

4

Claudia found her papa in the temple, digging behind the altar.

" Any luck, papa ? "

" No," said papa, wiping his face. " The heat is scandalous," he added severely, as if he would like to give it at least two years. " Really outrageous in the dry season. Piper says it's working up to a storm."

" Well, that will make a change."

" And Piper dislikes the attitude of the peons. He thinks Jacinto is working them up."

" Well, perhaps when Jacinto and the peons have all had a good wetting, they may feel cooler."

" Piper thinks Jacinto has some idea in his head."

" Oh ! That wouldn't do at all, in one's parish priest. I must say, he doesn't show it."

" They're dark horses, these ladinos. Very dark horses. And traditions linger on, in these country places. They linger on ; they never die out, though they get distorted."

" Whereas in towns, there's always so much new gossip that the old dies in a week. That is certainly healthier. Less stagnant."

" I must say, I don't trust Jacinto."

" No. That would be a mistake, and quite unnecessary. . . . But then I wonder what one means by trusting people ? People who are inquisitive about servants ask, Can one trust her ? The truthful answer usually is, unfortunately one can and did. However,

certainly it's difficult to imagine any one going so far
as to trust Jacinto. Unless one might, perhaps, trust
him to get drunk on fiestas, and not to neglect to ask
for money for church expenses. In a few little ways
like that, we're all trusted by our friends, I think."

" An untrustworthy parish priest in a place like this,
a country place, with no other priest for miles, is an
outrage. Misleading the simple people."

" It would really be worse if there was another priest
for miles, as he might so easily be untrustworthy too,
and then the simple people would be doubly misled.
For my part I feel that one Father Jacinto is all that
is required."

" Well, I must get on. I confess one grows a little
discouraged as the days go by."

" I think you're wonderful, papa dear. You have
so much faith and hope and industry. I have none of
the three. There is one thing I really can't believe,
and that is that, after all these centuries, with all these
Indians and ladinos about, and always a parish
priest——"

" Hush, my child. That's enough."

" Yes, papa. But still you know, I can't bring myself
to believe it."

" If you had been a judge for years, my dear, you
would be able to believe practically anything."

" Yes, I've noticed that they do. I always feel it a
weakness in them. It is partly what makes them so
childish and unfair. Not you, of course, papa, but
some of the others. However, in this case it's a
strength, and I admire it in you. So go on, papa dear.
It will be cooler when the storm breaks, they all say."

Lady Cradock appeared, via the passage from the cellar, looking hot.

" Why, Dickie, if you aren't at it again, when you know you should be resting in the heat of the afternoon. Why, you'll only knock yourself up. The carvings aren't worth it. Claudia, tell your father the carvings aren't worth it."

" Certainly, Belle. The carvings, papa, aren't worth getting so hot about. But we waste our breath, Belle ; you see how he doesn't heed our words. Judges, you know, acquire and retain their own ideas, quite impregnably, and are not to be assailed by argument or reason. You must have noticed that, even in your short experience of a judge."

" My poor Dickie, it simply never is done, in Guat, to work in the heat of the afternoon. Why, if Heck ever did a thing between noon and five ! "

" Mr. Higgins doubtless understood his own constitution and had his own habits, as I have mine."

" It's not as if you were a young man, either. Why, for any one past fifty to do a thing between noon and five during a hot spell in Guat ! Amy says we surely are working up for a big storm. She's gone to bed ; she's terrified of the storm breaking while she's up. But Piper says it won't come yet. He says it will lay the canes and dash the coffee berries and soak the cotton and spoil the fruit. Still, it always is the way on this hacienda ; as soon as the crops look good, something comes along to spoil them."

" That," said Claudia, strolling out of the temple, " always is the way on every hacienda. It's nature's way."

5

Mr. Piper was crossing the patio, his thin shirt clinging darkly to his lean chest and back. He said gently to Claudia, " Good-day. It's hawt. Storm coming up sometime this week. Shouldn't wonder if we got a quake as well."

" A quake ? "

" Yeah. A small quake. Sometimes get them here after a hawt spell in verano. Not often, but sometimes."

" A *small* quake, you think ? I trust you are right."

" Yeah. A little one. Quakes don't run big hereabouts. 'Twon't do much harm, the quake won't. Not like the storm. It may strike some sense into the Indios. They're right scared of quakes, poor creeters."

" On the whole, I agree with them. Still, if quakes give them more sense, they ought to be glad of them. Will it give us more sense, too ? "

" There's some jobs," said Mr. Piper sardonically, " take more'n a small quake, Miss Claudia. Judge still busy in there ? " He jerked his chin at the temple.

" Very busy."

" Ah."

Mr. Piper lounged off towards the plantations.

" More sense," thought Claudia. " That would hurt none of us, I suppose."

6

Catherine appeared in the patio, looking cool in her broad-brimmed sun-hat and thin white dress, swinging a light cane, and smelling of such unguents as she believed to be repellent to the insect world.

" Have you seen Isie ? " she asked Claudia.

" Not since we were all in the grotto."

" I thought she might like to come for a little stroll in the forest."

" You were probably right. That is the kind of thing Isie likes."

" But now she seems to be nowhere about. She didn't bathe after all, but just went off somewhere alone."

" You may well meet her in the forest," said Claudia, not wishing to hinder or retard the guest's departure for her stroll.

" How nice you look," she added. " How cool."

" It's very deceptive," said Catherine.

" Of course," said Claudia. " Well, I hope you'll have an agreeable ramble."

Catherine, who was a little in love with Claudia, perceived that she was by no means, as she had half hoped, to have Claudia's company on her ramble, hovered vaguely for another moment, said, " Well, I shall start. I shan't go far, I think." And walked away.

She is really a very pleasant visitor, thought Claudia, and went into the house to be idle and alone.

In the great saloon, which faced south, the green shutters were closed against the moist heat, and it was dim and gold and languid and sad, and seemed to smell, faintly and remotely, of the ghost of a mouse. Seeing the room, with its rococo décor, one would have said, here move the ghosts of silken courtiers and ladies, here has been life of the most artificial, polite society of the most elegant.

" Whereas actually," Claudia reflected, " if ghosts stir here, they are the ghosts of ancient Maya princes,

of Spanish monks with their rude ways, of Spanish
planters with theirs, and of Mr. Heck Higgins with his.
And all that seems to linger on the air, out of that bluff
crowd of spirits, is the tiny ghost of a mouse. Ah, well."
She strayed about the room, admiring its light
elegancies, taking pleasure in the florid grace of
each fantastic, flower-like curve. " A sweet room,"
she murmured, " an admirable room. How remarkably
well we have done it."

She sat on the brocade sofa, and sighed. She thought
of Yucatan, its wild landscape, its palaces, its cities and
temples of the New Empire.

" I will go to Yucatan. I will take Benet. It gets too
hot here. What waste ! All this lovely civilisation one
makes, and then to have it get so hot and spoilt. Oh,
I must go to Yucatan."

She lay still and pale, and felt herself swimming at
the bottom of a dim warm tank, remote and panting,
like a goldfish on a carpet, while, in the passionate
tropic afternoon without, storms brewed, worked up,
lurked at the heart of stillness, like time-bombs waiting
to burst.

Something in the room faintly went tick-tack, and
one perceived that the little ghost on the air was not
that of a mouse, but of a land crab, for one of these
was sidling and clicking, a grey-green phantom, across
the polished floor, smelling quietly of earth and of
death.

CHAPTER VII

LOSING ISIE

I

THEY met at dinner, after night had come down on them, and a little coolness.

" Nearly as hot as ever," said Sir Richmond.

" I suppose you've tired yourself to death digging, you silly old man," said his wife. " Now, where are Isie and Adrian ? Who's seen Adrian and Isie ? I've not seen a speck of either of them since lunch."

" Adrian went up to change when I did," Benet said.

Adrian came in. He had not changed, and looked distressed and odd. He stood by the door, looking at them, hesitating.

" Isie seems to be out still," he said. " I've been looking about the grounds, but she's not there."

" Why, for heaven's sake ! " Belle started up. " She can't have stopped out so late by herself. Why, she couldn't——"

" Who saw her last ? " said Sir Richmond.

" Well," said Benet, " she left us in the grotto about four. Then Catherine went to look for her, to go a walk, didn't you, Catherine ? "

" Yes, but I didn't find her. She must have gone out before me."

" She went riding," Meg intervened, with the matter-of-fact informativeness of a child. "She went on Pocohontas. I ran after her, to go too, but she said she was going alone. She started along the path by the creek."

"She went riding out alone in the forest and has never come back!" Belle cried it to them shrilly. "And it's been dark for hours now. . . . *Why, Dickie* . . ."

Adrian stepped forward, and they saw that he was frowning and pale. "I had better say," he said, "that she left a note for me, saying she was going away for a time."

"Going away *for a time*? For a *time*? Have you the note there?"

"No," said Adrian.

"Where is it, then?" asked Dickie.

"I destroyed it. I'm telling you what she said in it. She said she was going away, and we weren't to expect her back at present, as she might go anywhere."

"Go anywhere?" Belle cried. "What did she mean, go anywhere? She might have gone over to see Mr. Phipps. Why, she surely has gone to the Phipps ranch, and dark came on, so she stopped. She and Mr. Phipps are the greatest friends, and she certainly is in the Phipps house this minute. You boys must ride over and see if she's there. But you first must eat something."

Belle was talking shrilly, as she stood by Dickie's chair, her hand gripping his shoulder.

"Of course, that's where she is," she said. "Isn't she, Dickie?"

" Quite probably," Dickie answered, his hand covering hers. " I think, though, you should have kept that note, Adrian. It might throw some light which you didn't notice on first reading it. You *destroyed* it, you say ? "

" Yes. I remember perfectly all it said."

" And that was all—what you told us ? "

" All that was of relevance. All that could throw light. Yes."

The judge moved impatiently. This destroying of evidence annoyed him. " Anything may be relevant. You should have kept the note. She gave no reason, then, for going in this expedition so suddenly ? "

Catherine observed that Adrian passed the tip of his tongue over his dry lips, and looked across at Julia.

" No reason," he stumbled, " that matters. Only that she wanted to be away . . . for a time. . . ."

Julia rose. " Should we sit talking here ? Shouldn't we be looking for her ? "

" Certainly we must look for her." Sir Richmond got up. " But we must remember that searching miles of forest by night for someone who rode into it four hours ago is not a light task, and will need organisation and numbers."

" Nonsense, Dickie," Belle's voice rose higher. " I keep telling you, she's at the Phipps hacienda. That's where she'd go, right away. Of course it is. Someone must ride over there this minute."

Miles of forest by night. From that awful image they all turned away. All but little Meg, who, at the shocking words began to snuffle, and now was sobbing loudly, her

face hidden in the back of her chair. Catherine tried
to console her, but only produced a louder despair.

" Oh, for the land's sake, Catherine," Belle snapped,
" take that child away. She'll be working herself into
hysterics. Have Amy take her to bed."

Catherine, her arm about Meg's solid little body, led
her from the room and up the stairs, during which
journey she ceased not to cry bitterly and make lament.
The idea of anyone being lost, particularly in a forest
by night, is horrifying even to a robust, unimaginative
child, Catherine reflected, and soothed her with
meaningless comments. " Don't cry, dear. It's all
right, Isie is quite safe. She'll turn up to-morrow.
Now, you must go quietly to bed and to sleep. Amy
shall bring you some bread and milk."

Then, having summoned this amiable negress from
the bed in which she was seeking refuge from earthquakes, Catherine rejoined the party downstairs, who
stood about the hall, an anxious, undecided group.

" How is Meg ? " Julia asked her. " That child is
such a bundle of nerves ; if she gets worked up, she
makes herself ill."

" A bundle of nerves ? Meg ? I should never have
supposed that."

" You would if you had lived with her for twelve
years. She had meningitis once, and oughtn't to get
over-excited. But she always does."

" How queer. She doesn't seem that type of child,
does she ? "

" Type ? " Absently rather than curiously Julia
seemed to look at the word, remotely, and from far off,
as if in more leisured and tranquil circumstances she

might have found it odd. But now she turned from it with indifference. " Well—I don't know. . . . Benet's riding over to Mr. Phipps. Adrian is riding over somewhere else. Papa and Belle are going across to consult Mr. Piper. I don't know what you and Claudia and I are to do. Nothing of use, I'm afraid."

" Perhaps," Catherine suggested, " she rode further than she meant and was caught by darkness and delayed, and may be in presently."

" Oh, perhaps," Julia agreed. " Even that," she added, " would be bad."

" But if she's safe and all right ? "

" Isie wouldn't be all right, alone in the forest after dark. She'd go nearly mad with fear."

" *Isie* would ? I can't, do you know, imagine Isie doing that. She's so adventurous and calm, and used to the forest."

" Calm ? Upon my word, Catherine, you have some odd notions about people."

" Well, anyhow tough, and pretty fearless. Now, Benet, who's riding off alone to Mr. Phipps, I should say had more nerves."

" Benet ? Another odd notion. Benet's tough and calm and fearless if you like. That is, as people go. No one's really tough or calm or fearless, should you say ? After all, the world is very alarming, and one would be foolish not to be alarmed."

Julia, thought Catherine, was behaving with admirable composure, giving nothing away, of all that there might be to give away.

Calmer still was Claudia, standing in the patio outside the great open door, leaning against one of the carved door pillars and smoking. Catherine, looking at the small sleek dark head with its jade earrings and the pale line of an averted cheek, wondered what were Claudia's reflections on the situation, and knew that, anyhow, not Claudia would communicate them.

Belle came hurrying across the patio among the statues, with the lack of tranquillity of a mother who has mislaid her young. Behind her came Sir Richmond, in the less violent hurry of a step-father who has mislaid his wife's.

" Listen, girls. Piper is rousing up all the peons he can get and sending them into the forest to beat it. They're all drunk, he says, this time in the evening and it's just as well, because when they're sober they're scared to go by night into the forest. Piper says he's going over himself to the Phipps hacienda, with Benet. Adrian's riding off with the peons to keep them at it, and Dickie and I are going too. I can't rest unless I'm out about the place looking for the child ; I don't care to think of her being found by a pack of Indians, perhaps lying hurt, and me not there to mind her. You girls do just what you like. Tell Pedro to have some supper ready for her ; we may bring her in quite soon, or any time to-night."

She hurried upstairs to change her dress.

Claudia came into the hall. " I shall go searching too," she said to her father.

" Very well, dear. As you like." Being a judge, he did not think that woman's place (particularly by night) was in forests, but in the home (if one could so term the Villa Maya) ; still, he perceived that his female relations intended to ride out.

" Shall we go searching too, Catherine ? " said Julia.
" No ; let us stay and receive Isie, in case she returns
before the searchers."

But Catherine thought she would not miss the dark
forest ride, the peons with flaring torches, the wild
jungle in the strange hot velvet night, and was already
half-way upstairs after Claudia.

" Then I shall stay alone to receive Isie," said Julia.
" Unless you all think that it would be precisely I that
would find her if I came with you. For I do find things,
I know ; it's my gift."

" You joke, Julia," said Dickie gravely as he went
upstairs, " but there is real cause for anxiety."

Julia answered, beneath her breath, to his back, " If
I joke, papa, it's because I know more causes for
anxiety than you do."

CHAPTER VIII

LOOKING FOR ISIE

I

MR. PIPER and Benet rode into the forest. It was pitch dark, and very hot and heavy and still ; that is to say, without motion of wind ; it was not silent, but loud with howling monkeys, the scufflings and lurchings and leapings of hunting animals, the sudden shrieks of victims, and the droning moan of a vast army of insects seeking food. These sang about the riders' ears and bit their hands and faces, in spite of the unguents with which they were anointed.

" A dreadful place," said Benet.

" Huh ? " said Mr. Piper, casting the yellow circle from his torchlight on to the black bush as he rode first along the narrow trail.

" Dreadful," Benet repeated. " The forest by night. Isn't it ? "

" Hell, yes," Mr. Piper agreed, mournfully slapping a bicho on his cheek. " It scares me stiff."

The heat increased as they got more deeply into close jungle. The brooding air was damp, and the sky hung heavy and black above the tree-tops.

" Hell," observed Mr. Piper again, for, when he was feeling worried, he was apt very frequently to refer to this future state. " It's like gravy stoo. When's that storm breaking ? "

They passed over a swampy patch set about with prickly, spiney trees and shrubs and a few mangroves. The horses sank in oozy mud to the fetlocks.

" Watch out for snakes," said Mr. Piper. " You should use your torch more, son."

They got into tall forest again. Benet started when a great ape suddenly roared at him from a sapsodilla tree just above his head.

" We've waked him up," said Mr. Piper.

Benet said presently, " Have you noticed that all the way as we go there is rustling in the trees on our left ? It seems to be following us."

" Yeh," said Mr. Piper. " A cat."

" A wild cat ? "

" They don't grow 'em tame in the forest. Yes, he surely is tracking us, that cat. You can see his eyes, times. Look now. Up in that tree."

Benet looked ; and it seemed to him that on the bough of a tree, among the hovering fireflies, two green points suddenly gleamed and went out.

" If I could get one good view of him, I'd shoot," said Mr. Piper. " He won't spring, though. He don't fancy our lights. They like tracking better'n attacking, these creeters. I've had one track me a week. You'd be surprised. They've a lot more perseverance than tigers. . . . Mind that creeper."

" How long," enquired Benet interested, " have you had a tiger track you ? "

" Oh, a tiger won't go far. He'll usually go off after other game in an hour or two. Impatient creeters. Greedy, too. Now, that little cat, he'll wait for his good meal for days, licking his whiskers thinkin' about

it, while he makes do with trifles he picks up on his
way."

" And then he doesn't always get his good meal in
the end. I am glad of that."

" Oh, he gets it darned often. . . . Hold him up
over the gully."

" ? . . . Oh, the horse, yes. . . . You know, I
think it's confusing calling wild cats he. I mean, it
confuses them with horses. When they're not wild,
they're she, aren't they ? "

" Sure," Mr. Piper agreed.

They picked their way across the wet gully, and up
again among steaming trees. The air upon their faces
and bodies was like warm soup, and made them sticky
and moist.

" It is really most peculiar weather," said Benet,
wiping his forehead.

" Hell of a night," said Mr. Piper placidly. " Proper
quake weather."

" Do you mean," said Benet, " that, in your opinion,
the earth is about to open ! "

" Cain't say when. But it's goin' to open all right
before it's done. Never have this weather but we get
a little quake."

" Dear me," Benet exclaimed. " Isie won't like that,
wherever she is. She's very nervous of things like
that."

" Dessay. I hope we may find her before it
occurs."

Mr. Piper rode for a time in thoughtful silence.
Presently, " Where's she got to, do you reckon ? " he
asked.

Benet raised his eyebrows and shoulders in despairing negation. " My dear, I don't reckon. I can't. I simply can't imagine."

" Think she did go to pay a call on Mr. Phipps and get caught by dark and stay ? "

" I don't know." Neither did Benet know whether Mr. Piper had been told about Isie's note.

" Might have done," said Mr. Piper. " Ladies—young gals in particular—are very unthinking, times. What I mean to say is, they don't think. They don't calkerlate ahead, or remember what o'clock the sun goes down. Thoughtless young creeters."

" Well," said Benet, " she will be all right if she is there. She must be there, I think." She could not be straying alone, he thought, in this starless and nightmare forest, this steaming, sighing jungle, watched by hostile eyes that pricked the hot gloom, going out and in, in and out, like lighthouse lamps.

" Tasso or someone used to write by the light of cats' eyes," Benet remembered.

" Did he so ? Why'd he do that ? "

" I forget. I think he hadn't a candle."

" Nothing'll stop some folks writing," said Mr. Piper, with pity for a disease unshared.

" There's some South American bird that gives enough light to read and write by, isn't there ? " Benet added, his mind groping in the heavy darkness after nature's various lamps.

" I guess you've been misinformed, son," Mr. Piper cautiously hazarded. " You better confide in a torch, if you feel you must study out-doors."

A chorus of tree-frogs began ; it was caught from

one tree to another, near and far, till the whole forest seemed a-croak with hoarse voices.

" Now," Mr. Piper ponderingly drawled, " how much sense has the gal ? Mind the bats."

" Yes, I am minding them. One of them has just flown into my eye. Sense ? Why, none that I know of."

" Pity. Mind that poison-creeper."

Some way off, they heard the sharp, continued thud of axes on trees, and saw a faint flare of light.

" A chicle camp," Mr. Piper said. " They're at it all night, times. Rapacious men. Guats are lazy as a rule, but it seems like the sight of chicle trees turns 'em into the world's hustlers. Gentlemen of pretty easy virtue, too, as a rule. Escaped convicts, deserting Mex soldiers from over the border, and that kind of crowd, mostly. Do any darned thing for a few pesos. You'd be surprised. Pity if a lady should come on them alone, particularly after dark. They mightn't be too respectful."

Benet felt rather sick.

" Should we go to them and ask if they've seen her pass to-day ? "

" No. Not now. Time for that later, if she's not at Phipps's."

They were now only about three miles from the hacienda, and those little signs began which indicate human intelligence and appetites—clearings for cassova, plantations among the forest trees of apples, oranges, plums and coffee, but now all running wild into the jungle, as if no one had cultivated them for long.

" Phipps don't cultivate much," said Mr. Piper. " He's a darned poor planter. Busy elsehow, I reckon."

" Why, what does he do ? "

" Talks to the Indios. Explores around, hunts in old churches. Digs up mounds, like he was a dawg scratching for bones. Pays morning calls. *You* should know that."

" In fact, a dilettante, like us."

" Dessay. He's the hell of a bad planter, anyway. Doesn't give a curse for his crops."

" I suppose he just enjoys the forest life."

" Cain't say. He's a funny little fat guy."

They came to green patches of sugar-cane, and yellow patches of maize. The savage loneliness of the forest seemed to become decorated and smoothed by man's hands, as if a lion were patted and combed and put into a little frail harness and set to drag a fruit-cart. Round the maize there were coffee bushes, heavy with red berries, and orange trees, in blossom and in fruit, smelling sweetly on the night like a wedding.

" *I* think," Benet commented, " that Mr. Phipps keeps his place very nice."

Dogs began to bark, and a turn of the trail showed a tiny settlement of palm-roofed huts. Family groups sat outside them, cooking food and drinking by the light of pine torches. All the dogs belonging to all the huts ran at the horses and barked.

" Hey," called Mr. Piper. " Ha pasado por aqui esta tarde una señorita montada de caballo ? "

The inhabitants peered at the Englishmen as they rode into the torch-light. They looked stupidly at one another, then stolidly at the white men.

" No sabemos, señor."

Mr. Piper shrugged his shoulders. " That means

nothing. Our hacienda is unpopular with the peons just now, and they won't tell us anything. They all hang together, those darned Indios."

2

A quarter of a mile ahead lit windows gleamed through the trees ; the Phipps ranch house. To them, as they rode near, sweetness drifted on the night from the blossoming fruit trees that glimmered palely about the house, and from the tangled garden of what one saw by day to be scarlet salvias, huge purple dahlias, sunflowers, heliotrope, roses, jasmine, arum lilies, and something that smelt like syringa, with great pale waxy flowers.

They rode up to the timber rail that ran round the garden, dismounted, hitched the horses to the gate, and walked up a white-paved path through the sweet dark tangle to the house door.

" Still up, anyway," said Mr. Piper, as he knocked.

Now, Benet thought, it all turns on this, whether she's here or not here. She must be here.

Gladys, an old negress, opened the door, grinning at them.

" Mr. Phipps at home ? "

" Yes, sah, Mr. Phipps at home."

" Mrs. Rickaby here ? You know the young lady ; she's often been over."

" Oh, sho, sah. The young lady been heah, and she done gone away."

" Gawn away, has she. Gawn back home, I suppose."

" Don' know, sah. She gone away. Mr. Phipps, sah."

Mr. Phipps, plump and trim in amber tussore, came into the hall. His round face was solemn and worried.

" Pleased to see you, Mr. Piper. And Mr. Benet too. I guessed some of you'd be over to-night. Come right in and have something. I'm afraid I've bad news for you."

" Mrs. Rickaby's been here and gone home again, I understand ? "

Mr. Phipps shook his head. " Unfortunately no, Mr. Piper. Unfortunately I don't think she has gone home."

" Not ? Then where the hell has she gawn ? "

Mr. Phipps flung out his hands. " I wish I knew, Mr. Piper, I surely do wish I knew. She rode in, late this afternoon, and seemed not herself—a bit peeved and upset—and asked if I could put her up for the night. Surely, I said, and had Gladys get a room ready, and we had a little dinner later, and she told me she didn't plan to go back for a bit—some little domestic trouble, I guessed, knowing what young wives are and how they fly off the deep end—and then she strolled out into the stables to see her horse was all right. I stayed behind and followed her in a few minutes, and when I got out, she was gone."

" Ridden off alone had she ? Hell."

" Well, I fear *not* alone. Both my horses too were gone."

" Hell."

" Believe me, that's precisely what I said, Mr. Piper. Of course I got the peons and started a search. They beat the forest all around the hacienda, but the tracks run all ways, and there's no clue. Do you know

what I fear ? We've had some Lacandones prowling
around here lately, and a set of them might have come
on that poor girl as she stood alone there by the stable
and carried her off with the horses. If so, they'd make
right for the Chiapas border country and hide there in
those jungles of theirs, where no whites ever go. That's
all I can think of, anyway ; unless she rode off alone
into the forest and let my horses loose. She was in a
mighty queer state ; she might have done anything.
But I don't think she did that, I certainly don't ; she
was too scared. It's my opinion she only came in here
at all because she was scared of the evening coming on
while she was alone in the forest."

"You'd have done much better," said Mr. Piper
gloomily, " to keep an eye on her, and not have let her
trapes around by herself in that state."

"I'm sorry if you look at it that way, Mr.
Piper."

"Like hell I look at it that way, Mr. Phipps. You've
let her get carried off by drunken Lac horse-thieves to
their darned swampy hell of a country where we might's
well go hunting for a dropped pin."

"No, I'm afraid hunting would be no use. We must
send messages by the peons. We must hope it is only
an affair of negotiation and ransom."

"Ransom hell. Any messages we send will be to say
that they'll be shot up unless they bring her back safe
at once."

"Unfortunately, Mr. Piper, it's not so easy to shoot
up those wild Indios in their forests."

"We'll send for the armed police."

"You wouldn't get them to go hunting Indios in

the wild Lac country. Believe me, it would be no use if they did, either. No, I fear negotiation will prove to be the only way. It's a trick they've tried before, the peons tell me. They took a creole child once ; that turned out badly, for the father wouldn't come to terms quick enough—you know how slack these creoles are—and he sure never set eyes on that child again. That is, never set eyes on all of it. He saw a finger or two. . . . You've got to act slick, dealing with Indios, you tell the Judge and Lady Cradock that, Mr. Piper. I wouldn't like to have them act too late. I surely am concerned for that poor girl, in the hands of those un- cultured Indios—she'll be scared stiff. I don't know when I've felt so upset about anything. And it having occurred at my house, I will admit that makes me feel peeved."

" What time was it ? " Mr. Piper growled.

" Ten minutes of nine."

" Christ. And now it's eleven-thirty. That's a long start. . . . You'd given it up, had you ? Were you going to go to bed, or had you thought of sending a message over to us ? "

" Well, Mr. Piper, I guessed some of you would be over. I was waiting for that. I certainly thought you would guess she might have come this way . . . I hope that little trouble of hers at home was nothing serious, by the way." He addressed Benet, who answered, " Oh no, nothing worth mentioning, I think."

" Young wives," said Mr. Phipps.

" Those darned Indios down there," said Mr. Piper, " told us they didn't know she'd been here, damn their eyes. I reckon they're up agin us on account of the wages trouble at our place."

" Those peons," said Mr. Phipps. " All the same," he added, " they'll take messages for us to the Lacs. What I would predict will occur is this. The men who've captured Mrs. Rickaby will send someone over quite soon—perhaps to-morrow—to give us their terms. They won't dare to come to any of us, of course ; they'll probably give a message to peon friends of theirs, either my peons or yours, who will pass it on to us. Then we shall have to act promptly, and in whatever way they select."

" In fact," said Mr. Piper, " we're to wag the white flag good and hard."

" I'm afraid that is so, Mr. Piper. It may be a matter of life and death, you see. When I think of that beautiful girl in the hands of those untutored men——"

" Hell," said Mr. Piper. " You don't need to keep on saying it. I reckon we can all think like that if we want. Listen ; we've got to make these darned peons get into touch with their Lac friends, and look lively about it. If they can take a message from the Lacs, they can take one to 'em. They can just go and tell 'em that, unless Mrs. Rickaby is brought back unhurt by to-morrow night, it'll be the worse for every Indio in this district."

" You said it, Mr. Piper. Only the weak point of that is that the thieves are not in this district, but in their own place, and they know right well we can't get at them. No, no ; it's a case for diplomacy, not threats. We must feel our way mighty carefully."

" Carefully hell. If we once give away a peso in

ransom not a hoss or a human will be safe from brigands for ten years to come. You darned well know that, Mr. Phipps."

Mr. Phipps shrugged his shoulders. " And yet, Mr. Piper, you would hardly suggest risking Mrs. Rickaby's life by holding out. The Judge and Lady Cradock would scarcely be with you there. Would they, Mr. Benet ? "

" I imagine not. No."

" Well," said Mr. Piper, " I'm going down to rouse those peons and talk to them. If they know anything, or think they can find out anything, I reckon they'll find they'd better put me wise."

" Third degree's no use with Indios, Mr. Piper ; and I don't think they know a thing that would help ; I put them through it myself. Just the same, we'll go and talk to them again. I'll ride down with you. They'll tell me more than you, if they do know anything."

" They left you a hoss, then."

" One, yes. Fortunately he was in the corral when they raided the stables."

But Mr. Piper did not wait. When Mr. Phipps returned with his horse he was already riding down the track to the little settlement where Indian families, shut close in huts from the night air, slumbered.

Benet waited at the garden gate for Mr. Phipps. " Piper has gone ahead," he said.

Mr. Phipps mopped his forehead. " Mr. Piper," he said, " is a somewhat impatient man. We must all keep our eye on him, or he may upset the cart. If we get the peons here peeved, they may refuse to be go-betweens. When I think of what may be at stake——"

" Well, of course. Naturally, we shall be extremely careful."

" Then we certainly had better catch up Mr. Piper quickly, before he gets going, for he is not a careful man. Mr. Piper makes a big mistake; he despises the Indios. That doesn't do; they have the whip hand of us over this, and we have to face it. We must wait to take our revenge on them till we have Mrs. Rickaby safe."

" Yes; we must wait," said Benet mechanically.

The forest had become a black pool of horror. Benet had always known that forests were like that—greedy beasts of prey, devouring lives. Guatemalan forests were the original Forest, of men's childish nightmares; the Forest of which lesser and tamer forests elsewhere were but shadows; the primeval dread, the ancient trap. Now its jaws had shut on one of the puny strangers who had ventured into it. They would not open, except to close on the others. Isie had vanished, like those nymphs whom some mischance changes into a tree; you might as well go seeking for a lost flower in the jungle wilderness.

The peons knew, or would say, nothing. Nothing to Mr. Piper, nothing to Mr. Phipps, nothing to Benet.

Why the hell, inquired Mr. Piper, had they said they had not seen the young lady passing, when the young lady must have ridden straight through the village to the hacienda? They replied that they must have been elsewhere, looking in another direction, for they had not seen the young lady pass.

If the Lacandones had kidnapped the young lady, said Mr. Piper, where would they take her? Who knew, they answered. Somewhere in their own country, but one could not guess exactly where. No use to search ; one might search for ever and not find.

Would they be likely, asked Mr. Phipps, to send a message soon asking for money ? That is surely what the Lacandones would do, quite immediately, they answered. The only thing was to wait for that.

" If any messenger should come from them to you," said Mr. Piper, " you've got to seize him and keep him till we can get our hands on him. You must send at once to the Hacienda del Capitan. He will then conduct us to where the young lady is. Is that entirely clear ? "

They said that it was, and the gringos, obliged to leave it at that, departed.

3

Mr. Piper and Benet started to ride home. They left the track half-way to go and find the chicle camp, guided to it by the sound of axes and the faint twinkling of light. They found the camp in a clearing ; a few men, less industrious than the others, had stopped work and come into the camp, and lay sleeping in hammocks ; a few women were there too, lying with the men or cooking food for those who were still at work among the trees. They looked without interest at the gringos as they rode out of the bush into the torch-lit clearing. One or two of the women grinned ; the men were apathetic and expressionless.

Mr. Piper questioned them ; they knew nothing. He offered them reward if they would all leave their

work next day and assist in the search expedition to
the Lacandon country. They shook their heads. Such
expeditions were no use, and they could not leave the
chicle. As to the Lacandon forest land, they seemed to
regard it as an undiscovered country from whose
bourne no traveller returned. They were dull, un-
interested, lethargic. To them disappearances were
common chances of the forest, and human lives trifles.
They suggested that a tiger might have carried off the
lady, or, indeed, any other accident. The forest was a
bad place by night.

A bad place always, thought Benet, as their stumb-
ling, sweating horses pushed back to the trail through
the steaming bush. A dreadful, thrice-damned, barbarous place, unfit for human habitation. Forests
should remain virgin. They always might, in future,
so far as he was concerned.

In a tree above them a party of monkeys were
chattering to each other with the fantastically ill-bred
rudeness of a French social gathering as depicted by
Proust. They flung down little yellow apples on to the
ground with the contempt of an English bus conductor
who has been given farthings by a passenger, and, seeing
no reason why he should take his share in bearing the
burden of these small coins, flings them on the floor.

" Hell of a night," said Mr. Piper, slapping mosquitoes to death on his wet forehead.

" Oh, my dear, it is," Benet heartily agreed.

" And the hell of a forest too, don't you think ? "
he added presently. " Raleigh said of Guiana, ' It is a
country that hath yet her maidenhead.' Don't you
sometimes wish Guatemala had hers ? I do."

" Yeh," said Mr. Piper non-committally. " Feels like that quake won't be long now."

It became intensely still.

" Well," Benet presently observed, " I almost think this must be it, don't you ? The quake, I mean. . . ."

" Yeh," said Mr. Piper. " Mind the hoss. Get off and hold him tight."

They slipped from their saddles and stood, gripping the bridles.

" Soothe him," said Mr. Piper. " They get kind of restless in a quake."

" Good boy. Nice fellow. Down, sir," said Benet.

" He ain't a dawg," said Mr. Piper. " But never mind ; he won't notice anything but the queer weather."

It was indeed queer weather. From the now coppery sky the moon glared down at them, a red danger signal to an earth that had already become an express train, leaping and vibrating as it rushed through space. There will be an accident, thought Benet, gripping which his left hand a mahogany tree, while his right held the horse's bridle ; there will almost certainly be an accident. Indeed, there were already, it seemed, a thousand accidents, for the trees flung to the ground their branches and fruit, together with the parrots and monkeys who clung to them chattering for fear, and who were hurled earthwards among bananas, apples, sapsodillas, and great boughs. The forest shook and roared, the earth shivered and heaved in three crescendo spasms. The great cats shrieked as if they rambled on tiles ; the two human beings were flung this way and that, clinging wildly to shuddering horses

" Dear me," said Benet uneasily, when the third vibration was over. " We are still here, then. What is to occur next ? "

" Bit of a storm," said Mr. Piper, squinting up at a sky become an inky pool. " We must get on through it. In an hour the place will be a swamp."

Thunder rolled round the sky.

" Long way off," said Mr. Piper. " But coming this way. We must get a move on. Hold him tight ; he'll be jumpy."

" You don't think the earth will quake again, I suppose ?" Benet enquired.

" No ; quake's over. We shall have a spot of rain, though."

" Yes, it's just fallen on my nose."

Other spots fell, immense, heavy, hot ; they crowded on one another's heels, becoming a running battalion, beating up the forest like drummers at the charge. Horses and men bent beneath it ; it lashed and sluiced down their heads and bodies as if they had turned on the shower in a bath. Already pools swamped the track, so that the horses splashed and slipped. Twigs and leaves and fruit spattered about them, as if flung down by monkeys, but no monkeys were throwing fruit ; they were huddled in the trees or on the ground where the earthquake had flung them, scared and complaining to one another about the strange chances of life.

From a sighing and moaning wilderness of rain, the forest became a battlefield. The sky flared as if with a thousand rockets, the great guns barked at the lightning's heels like angry dogs, till soon they caught it, and rockets and guns came together. The forest was rent and split ; all was confusion.

" I don't believe it's a bit safe, going on through the storm," Benet called out, complaining.

" Safe, hell," Mr. Piper called back. " We're searching for a shelter."

" What shelter ? "

" A nice cave. In the opposite side of the barranca. If we get as far."

They plunged down the barranca, which was now as soft and wet as a clay pit. For a few minutes they came away from the trees, and the storm broke directly on them. The lightning played about the boulders and struck a great tree in front of them ; it roared to the ground, split asunder.

" Gentle Jesus, help and hear us," chanted Mr. Piper. " Bless thy little child to-night. Through the darkness be Thou near us, Keep us safe till morning light. Amen."

Benet wondered if he were a religious man, or if it only came on in a storm, or if what he had said were merely a kind of swearing.

They were struggling up the other side of the barranca. " That's the cave," said Mr. Piper, pointing to a hole between two boulders, overhung by trees. " Can't get the hosses in. We'll have to sit inside and hang on to the reins. Get off, and keep your gun ready. Might be some creeter in there."

" We shall be rather overcrowded if there is, shan't we ? "

Mr. Piper bent to the opening, his gun levelled, and flashed his torch inside.

" Empty, for a wonder. Come on in, son. Hang on
to the reins. We'll get out of the worst of it here."

They crouched in the darkness beneath the over-
hanging rocks, their left hands wound in the slippery
reins against which the frightened horses strained.

Above them the trees raved and moaned and the
storm crashed, and the rain was as if a thousand waterfalls came down.

" Nice drop of rain," said Mr. Piper. " Plantation
needed it."

" Guatemala must be just like England," said Benet.
" That's what people say there when it rains. And
when it stops raining for a bit they say it's a drought.
I suppose it comes from the earth once having been all
under water, so that we feel that is the right and natural
state for it. Really, it's a kind of water-plant that
can't live when it's dry."

" Smells of cat in here," said Mr. Piper.

" Oh, is that what it smells of ? But you think it's
past cat, not present ? "

" Yeh. If it was present, you'd know it all right.
Just the same, a storm brings us creeters all together
wonderfully. I dessay puss would be too taken up with
the storm to hurt us, even if he was here.

" But we shouldn't be too taken up with it to hurt
him, should we ? "

" Well, I don't reckon we should just sit quiet and
read by the light of his eyes, same as the character you
mentioned. . . . That was a near one. . . . Nearer
my Gawd to Thee. I ain't pining to get any nearer
than this, just the same, thank you, Lord. Are you,
son ? "

" Tell me," said Benet, to pass the time, " do you really believe in the Lord, or were you only ejaculating ? "

" Sure I believe in the Lord. I was brought up to chapel, to Brixton-on-Sea. You don't, I presume."

" Well, no, it never occurred to me."

" You better, son. It may occur to you too late, if you ain't careful."

" Better late than never, surely."

" Well, religion won't be much pleasure to you in hell, if you're thinking of leaving it till then. . . . I hold Bible meetings for the peons, Sunday evenings."

" Do they come ? "

" Cain't say say they do. The poor ignorant creeters prefer that church of Jacinto's."

" Do you hold the Bible meetings alone, then ? "

" Well, Amy likes to come. Those blackamoors are great Bible people. Myself, I've no kind of resentment against blackamoors, coming as I do from Brixton-on-Sea. I prefer them to the Indios and ladinos. . . . To-morrow, we make every son of an Indio in these parts sorry he was born, unless we get news pretty quick."

" Do y u suppose we shall hear to-morrow ? "

Mr. Piper shrugged his shoulders, and his unusual flow of speech ceased. They both thought of Isie, somewhere lost or captive in the forest in the dreadful night.

CHAPTER IX

I

Isie lay sweating and shaking in a tent, and two Indians sat at the opening, talking. The night was hot, and full of the menace of storm. Isie did not know how far they had brought her from Mr. Phipps's ranch ; they had ridden for a long time, till they had come to a group of huts in a clearing, and stopped there for the night. Nothing said to her or about her by these barbarous men could she understand. She had hoped that she might fall dead, as she rode between them on her roped horse, crashing quickly through the darkening night, plunging deeper into the dense but unfortunately not impenetrable jungle, along wild and hidden trails. She had, however, not fallen dead, and here, in the hot, black midnight, she was huddled on the mud floor of a hut in a clearing, somewhere in the lost lands, with two wild red men keeping guard at the door.

Adrian, Adrian, she cried in her soul, not daring to cry it aloud. Come to me, Adrian, and take me away. Adrian, Adrian, do you know where I am ?

Adrian's certain ignorance of this left her sick and trembling, even while the thought that she must by now have made him really anxious, warmed her a little and filled her eyes with tears. But even if he loved her again now, because she had so abruptly and alarmingly disappeared, leaving that little pathetic note—even if his response to these activities of hers were, as she hoped, one of love, he could never find her. She was lost, lost, lost. If she could not escape, she was for ever lost and destroyed, for she had already tried to indicate to her captors the huge rewards that would be showered on them should they return her to her home, and they had rejected her plea, they had shaken their heads and said not a word. They meant, she thought, to keep her, for sacrifice, for torment, for a mistress, for a wife.

Is it me, she thought. Me, Isie, it can't be, this can't have happened to me, I can't be here, it's a dream. Oh, God the Father, Oh, God the Son, Oh, God the Holy Ghost, make it be a dream. If I get out of this, oh, God, I'll say my prayers again.

The Indians sat silent, smoking pipes. They were drunk, but calm. They felt that they had done a calm deed that night. They were too drunk and too good to feel afraid of anything ; they did not even fear the heavy brooding of the coming storm that whispered its menaces in the sullen trees, setting them stirring and shivering like a man with ague. By dawn the storm would be over, and then they would push on.

Drowsy with pulque and lulled by the warm and rustling night, the weary Indians slept.

2

They were wakened by the earth, which, bucking beneath them like a restless horse, flung the hut against which they leaned in ruins to the ground. They remarked that it was an earthquake, and ran over to the horses, who, tied to trees in the clearing, were leaping in the air with screams of annoyed surprise. Their desire to retain these animals, combined with their own amazement and fear, caused them to forget their human captive. It was not until the shocks had ceased that one reminded the other how they had captured a young lady and left her in the hut which now was a mass of wreckage on the ground. They then went to find her, but found nothing except wrecked posts and a smashed palm leaf roof sprawling on the shaken earth. The young lady was gone ; she had slipped off into the blackness of the night, into the hot, dense jungle on which the storm that follows earthquakes was already rolling up. They beat the bush round about, terrified themselves of the storm, then gave it up, and sought such shelter as they could. The young woman would perhaps perish in the storm, or be caught by wild beasts, and, for their part, unless they were careful and elusive, they would get into trouble.

3

A hundred yards away, bruised and torn and quivering Isie crawled through swampy bush, hidden by the hot darkness, by the crashing barrage of the thunder, and by the dense, twisted tangle of the jungle. This was the acaiche country, of swamps and low, spiney scrub. A little rain, and it became impenetrable bog. Rain was falling now ; enormous drops thrashing the bush, beating through on to the frightened animals

beneath it. Isie, an animal crazed with fear, blindly
pushed and broke her way through scrub and swamp,
her arms up to guard her face, her legs in their long
riding boots and cord breeches squelching in sticky
bog. She felt herself to be among snakes, among cats,
among peccaries, among tigers, among barbarous
men, with poison trees to sting her, spines to pierce
her, thunderbolts to slay her, and the earth to swallow
her up. She was all astonished and dismayed : she
was crazed with the variety of her peril ; yet the
sharpest peril, the Indians behind in the clearing, drove
her blindly on.

The storm came nearer : the night blared and
crashed on the jungle, full of those unlucky accidents
and explosions which cause so much stir in the
heavens and such collisions on the earth. A great
mangrove tree was struck and split, and crashed roaring
to the ground. The lightning was now almost continuous ; the sky was a fire which a million firemen,
deluging it with their hose, tried in vain to extinguish.
Such fire, such deluge, and such crashing blinded and
deafened and stunned ; beneath it, Isie crouched
under a prickly tangle of boughs, her face on her
drawn-up knees. She was utterly forsaken and alone ;
lost in the forest, to be soon destroyed, she would not
see anyone again ; not Adrian, not her mother, not
one among her friends. She would die in anguish and
terror, and they would not know how she had died.

The storm presently rolled back a little ; it receded
like heavy trampling feet, like an army which has
attacked and retreated. The thunder pursued the
lightning at an increasing distance ; Isie perceived

with surprise that she would not this time be struck, for the celestial explosions had retired. The rain still drove down, smashing through the forest trees, pounding the earth to primeval swamp. Isie crawled out of her bush into it, and pushed on, blindly fleeing from the clearing, plunging deeper and deeper into trackless jungle. So trackless it was, so blind, so dense, and all but impenetrable, that only the craziness of terror could have driven a human creature into it. Spiney branches tore at her ; wet ropes of lianas flung themselves about her, trapping and holding her like snakes ; prickles and stinging leaves stabbed her hands and face till she was swollen and bleeding ; solid thickets of dense scrub blocked her way like walls. Still she pushed on, clinging to the belief common to those who have not yet been lost in tropical forests that if she went far enough she must get at last to a track.

Since time was dead, she did not know what hour of the night it was when, having stumbled through a tangle of thorns, she came out of it into the mouth of what seemed a cave. No ; not a cave ; a rectangular building, supported on stone pillars. It loomed above her head, a shadowy mass in the dripping darkness of the night. A temple, she supposed, long ruined and probably never since discovered, buried in the heart of the jungle, which had, through the centuries, grown over and about it. One of those hundreds of ruins which lie hidden about the forest towards the Chiapas border, never to be seen by white archæologists seeking temples.

Isie knew suddenly that she could go no further ; she was beaten. Here was a shelter, a house made

with hands, and into it she could crawl from the savage
night and lie still. It had at least some roof, though
trees had planted themselves beneath it and thrust
their boughs up through it. It seemed to have had,
once, two stories, but the roof had long since gone from
the upper one. Isie pushed into it, between the trees
that grew there, and lay on the wet drifts of leaves
that covered what was probably, far below, a stone
floor. Snakes might be her companions, wild cats
her room-fellows, but she, numb and without hope
or thought but that she must cease to move, abandoned
herself to these. Her mind made one of those re-
leasing gestures with which London policemen, with
a wave of the hand, let loose on pedestrians a snorting
herd of vehicles. With vampire bats flittering clumsily
about the broken roof as they hunted mosquitoes,
crabs clicking like clocks as they scrambled about the
stone altar, tree-frogs hoarsely chorusing in the trees
at the temple's mouth, and the steady beating of rain
on the jungle that engulfed her, Isie curled up and
slept like a tired animal.

4

She was wakened by a most exquisite fluting close
by ; it was as if someone were playing a flute in her
bed chamber. The thin, sweet, liquid notes seemed like
golden rays of light, delicately piercing the grey dusk,
calling the sleeper from shadowy dreams.

She opened her eyes, and saw how she lay in the
twilight dawn on the mossy, leafy floor of a grey
stone temple ; a temple into which, down the centuries,

the forest had flowed, so that trees and shrubs were
rooted in its floor, and, thrusting up, had broken through
the crevices of its stuccoed roof. The nearest of these
trees stretched a bough just over Isie's head ; it was
laden with small pale-green fruit-like apples. It was
from this tree that the fluting came, for high on a branch
among the fruit a golden bird was trilling a song to the
dawn. An oriole, thought Isie, half-asleep. She sat up,
and shivered. She was wet through and stiff, swollen
with bites, torn by savage plants, lost and alone in the
jungle. The night of storm was over ; a still grey dawn
lay like evening on the soaked and littered forest. Isie
crouched against a carved and lichened wall, while
land-crabs scuttled about her with their earthly smell,
and little snakes uncurled themselves from the crevices
of the walls and wriggled about the floor. She felt that,
if the oriole in the jocote tree should stop his fluting,
she would let go of life, of the few links that still held
her to sanity, and drop down and down, drowned in the
lonely horror of the drowned forest. She was as a
wrecked sailor alone on a small and dreadful island in
a heaving ocean, wrecked utterly, irrecoverably lost.
Into the silent grey forest that enveloped her, that
drifted and lapped about her feet, slowly submerging
her lost island, she dared scarcely look. She knew that
she must cast herself into it again, struggle with its
bruising, beating waves, be devoured of it in the end ;
but now, poor castaway, she crouched safe and hidden
at its brink, its menacing whispers drowned in the
sweetness that shrilled in her ears. A bird singing in an
apple tree—that was like home ; that did not speak
of fear.

And presently her bird's song was caught up by other birds, in the forest outside, and the morning concert began in earnest. Some birds trilled, some piped, some chirped, some screamed ; a toucan yelped like a little dog ; it was like dawn in Europe, in a garden full of trees. The dark, drenched forest released its music ; from each bough a bright and bustling bird proclaimed the morning, triumphing with shrill cries over the dead and drowned.

As the light grew, the monkeys too fell to chattering their ejaculations, yapping, and gossiping cries were like those which human beings and dogs make after a great storm. The forest lost its grey ; colour and warmth struck down through it from the coming sunrise. The temple must face east, for from it Isie saw, through the close denseness of the tangled trees, the golden morning born. The terror of the night stood back, making way for the new and less dreadful terror of the day.

Stiffly Isie sat up, looking about her temple. How her step-father would rejoice if he could see it, she thought. Herself, she knew nothing of archæology ; she did not know if the temple were Old Empire, New Empire, of the Middle period, of the Great period, or when. But even she could see that it was a wonderful archæological find, or rather loss, since no archæologist would ever find it. It was in two stories, and the roof was supported by serpent pillars whose rich stucco carving was still faintly visible through the deposit of ten or fifteen centuries. The altar was a grey mass of lichened stone, a home of bats and birds, with shrubs growing out of it as out of a window-box. No doubt if one dug deep through the layers of forest on the floor, one would come to stone pavement, and find earthen pots, incense-burners, carved gods, and who knew what. A pity, thought Isie, that no one who cared for such treasures was here to dig. At that thought, at the vision of her step-father bent over his excavations, of Adrian assisting him, and of her mother chattering beside them, Isie broke at last into wild tears. Crouching on the temple floor, her head against a carved column, she wept and cried aloud :—

"*Adrian! Adrian! Oh, mother, mother, mother! Come to me! Come to me, I am lost.*"

Thus weeping, she seemed to dissolve away in a storm of sorrow, till nothing was left but tears, not her grief itself, nor fear, nor pain, but only weeping like rain, which drowned her body and soul. In its tide, nothing was left of " cette folie furieuse, cette rage revolverisque des amants," which had driven her forth ; all that had receded like a far and foolish dream.

"*If you go over desert and mountain,*" she sobbed, for she knew a great deal of verse by heart, and used it often to express her emotions,

> "*If you go over desert and mountain,*
>   *Far into the country of Sorrow,*
>   *To-day and to-night and to-morrow,*
> *And maybe for months and for years ;*
>   *You shall come with a heart that is bursting*
>   *For trouble and toiling and thirsting,*
> *You shall certainly come to the fountain*
> *At length, to the Fountain of Tears.*

" *Very peaceful the place is, and solely*
        For piteous lamenting and sighing,
        And those who come living or dying
    Alike from their hopes and their fears ;
        Full of cypress-like shadows the place is,
        And statues that cover their faces :
    But out of the gloom springs the holy
    And beautiful Fountain of Tears.

" *Then alas ! while you lie there a season*
        And sob between living and dying,
        And give up the land you were trying
    To find 'mid your hopes and your fears ;
        O the world shall come up and pass o'er you,
        Strong men shall not stay to care for you,
    Nor wonder indeed for what reason
    Your way should seem harder than theirs.

" *But perhaps, while you lie, never lifting*
        Your cheek from the wet leaves it presses,
        Nor caring to raise your wet tresses
    And look how the cold world appears—
        O perhaps the mere silences round you—
        All things in that place Grief hath found you—
    Yea, e'en to the clouds o'er you drifting,
    May soothe you somewhat through your tears.

" *You may feel, when a falling leaf brushes*
        Your face, as though someone had kiss'd you ;
        Or think at least someone who miss'd you
    Had sent you a thought—if that cheers ;

Or a bird's little song, faint and broken,
May pass for a tender word spoken :
Enough, while around you there rushes
That life-drowning torrent of tears."

It was gentle and consoling to be thus for a space
withdrawn into poetry and tears. Drained at last of
emotion, she lifted tired, swollen eyes and looked about
her, and saw how the little plants and leaves grew out
of the crevices in pillars and walls. There, near by,
was the fever grass, that one eats to cure malaria,
and beneath it the nettle that one chews when one has
inadvertently been spattered by the milky juice of
the poison-wood tree. God had placed at her side all
his remedies for the diseases she had doubtless con-
tracted in the night. And here, most useful of all, was
the leaf called corazon de Jesus, which alleviates
jealousy and love.

Strengthened by looking on these medicinal herbs,
Isie rose at last and went outside her temple. Standing
there, while the forest morning gently stroked her
aching body and face, restoring to her a little sense
of life and of love, she marvelled at the density of the
jungle that besieged her, and through which she had
somehow driven her desperate way last night. It
seemed to press about her like an unbroken army,
through whose lines she would never force. How its
greedy waves beat at the stone temple, drifting into
it, over it, all but submerging it ! Yet it still stood,
human ruin, against nature's siege, broken but
unbeaten. Outside it, what had once been a winding
stone stairway ran up to what had been a pillared

gallery on its roof. Now only bases of piers remained, standing broken on the broken roof through which the forest thrust green arms.

Isie climbed up to the roof, and sat there among its greenery, her legs dangling over the stucco edge, where had been carved a rich frieze of men, beasts and gods. From here she looked into the limitless sea of green, wet with rain, littered with the broken wreckage of forests after storm. The sweetness of pines, of eucalyptus, of a million steaming trees and a thousand blossoming shrubs, was blown to her on the wind of morning.

With the desperate hoping of a derelict sailor she scanned the undulating wild for some mark by which to steer, some break which might indicate a trail or settlement, but saw only dense jungle alternating with acaiche or low scrub, broken by barrancas and hills, but giving her no clue as to her whereabouts. Vaguely she thought they had ridden north-west, and that south-east would be her direction. At the thought of plunging again alone into that pathless waste where wild beasts and wild men prowled to devour their prey, where the very plants joined in the war, fighting and hurting her as she pushed through them, she quailed and shrank. Yet she could not stay where she was ; she felt that she could not spend an hour more without action, in that still and lonely place of terror. She plucked one of the apple-like fruits from the tree which thrust up through the temple roof, and bit into it ; it was sour, like a crab. She spat it out, and climbed down to the ground, moving stiffly and gingerly in her damp clothes and high boots. Perhaps, she thought, perhaps if she walked steadily towards the sun for an hour, by that time she would strike some path or see the smoke of some hacienda or settlement rising. She started to walk over the swampy ground, picking up a broken branch for a stick and beating a way through the tangled bush that surrounded the temple.

The day grew warmer. The dawn wind died, and the wet forest steamed in muggy heat. The air was like a warm bath into which all the contents of a perfumery have been poured. The dwellers in the forest, rejoicing after the terrifying night, ran leaping and ejaculating about the trees and earth. The swampy acaiche had been beaten by the storm into a wilderness of mud, over which clouds of insects hummed and droned. They crowded about Isie, biting her face and hands; ticks leaped on her from the bush, digging themselves in beneath her clothes and boots. Perhaps these insects had never tasted a human creature before, and she was to them as manna sent by their god. Once a little yellow-jaw snake fell out of a tree on to her arm; she flung it from her with a gasp of horror and pushed on. If a tiger should spring out of the thicket, she kept thinking . . . if a wild cat is tracking me . . . if I should suddenly come on Indians and they should catch hold of me . . . if I am lost for ever and shall die in the forest . . .

When she thought thus, her breath would come in quick pants, and her heart would leap and struggle like a bird in a cage. I mustn't think, she said, or I may go mad, and then I shall really be lost. I must believe I am getting somewhere, and shall meet nothing that will hurt me.

S.W.R.   I

Soon she saw a cloud of piebald butterflies, gaily clicking their wings in the warmth and, a little comforted, she began to say poetry and to sing hymns, forgetting how she did not believe in God and how religion was an exploded myth. She sang softly, so as not to draw attention to herself in the hostile forest, a number of hymns for those in trouble, such as " Lead, kindly light, amid the encircling gloom," and when she came to " And with the morn those angel faces smile, that I have loved long since and lost awhile," she was so transported by the thought that she almost forgot the tigers, the wild cats, the snakes, and the Indians, though she could never forget the bichos which bit her all the time, nor the spiney, prickly bushes. She went on, recalling snatches of the consoling hymns she had learnt as a child, such as

> " My God, my Father, while I stray
> Far from my home on life's rough way,
> O teach me from my heart to say
> Thy will be done."

and

> " Lead us, Heavenly Father, lead us,
> O'er the world's tempestuous seas."

Then she said poetry, some of which was her own composition, and which she knew, therefore, particularly well by heart.

" How softly did the river sigh
Upon the golden sand
That lovely day when you and I
Went walking hand in hand.

The trees were arching overhead,
And in them a blue bird,
Did sing the cutest song, we said,
That ever we had heard."

There were a good many stanzas of this, and to remember how they went was a good occupation for her mind, though they dealt with a disturbing subject.

The acaiche gave way to deeper forest, the prickly bush to giant trees. The vastness and gloom of this primeval wood was so awful that Isie's religion and poetry fell dead ; she could not remember anything but fear. It seemed to her that wild cats prowled overhead, tracking her, and she remembered how they would track a man for days and nights and then spring. She would begin to run, and then, aghast at the noise she made, would stop and creep along stealthily. She came on more ruined buildings ; mostly they were so deeply buried and smothered by the bush and grown over by the ages that one could scarcely distinguish them from the surrounding forest. Once the scent of orange flowers drifted to her among the steamy perfumes, and she seemed to be approaching the Hacienda del Capitan, with its orange gardens sending their nuptial sweetness into the brooding afternoon. Her heart lifted ; perhaps there was some plantation near, where men lived. A little later she struggled through

prickly thickets to orange trees in flower, pale among
the lush green, and with them grew plums and cacao
and coconut palms and a coffee bush red with berries.
Surely a settlement. But when she looked she saw
that it was only the ghost of a settlement ; there had
perhaps once been some huts here, in what had been a
clearing ; houses of sticks, palm leaves and lianas, long
since lost and merged in the jungle which had flowed
over and devoured them ; and now all that remained to
speak of man were a few fruit trees and some green
blades of maize still growing up among the wild grass,
and the ghostly air that broods over those deserted
places where men have once been. Long ago, perhaps,
some little colony of Indians had dwelt here and grown
their food and kept their animals ; long ago they must
have left it, perhaps after some earthquake or storm
had destroyed their habitations, perhaps merely from
Indian desire for change ; or perhaps they had been
destroyed by some enemy. Anyhow they had fled and
vanished years too soon, leaving behind them nothing
but the ghost of an orchard to companion the lost
traveller, and, of all their animals, only a little ant-bear,
who, standing in the ghostly orchard, lapped up
regiments of ants with a gentle, swishing tongue.
Isie stood in tears among wild plums and coffee berries,
with the dry rustling of palm trees whispering harshly
in her ears.

But she lingered for a little while in this place ; it
was, even after all these years of wildness, less terrifying than the never-inhabited jungle. She found water
ti-ti here, hanging in great ropes from trees, and
broke off a piece to drink from. Then she saw a milk-

tree, and sucked from its trunk a few oozing drops. She ate a quantity of small blue plums, and filled her pockets with what she could carry of them. Reluctantly she left the place; she felt as if she had lived there long ago, and been happy; as if she had found in the wilderness of death a tiny patch of life.

Not far from this little grove she got into a jungle of giant maidenhair fern, arching high above her head, and so close and dense that she could scarcely push through it. At its heart she stumbled on a little ancient Spanish church, dating, only she did not know it, from the Conquest. It was built in shape like a Maya temple; but now it was all in ruins; shrubs sprouted from the broken walls and trees grew out of it; bees had built their comb in the cracks, and wild pigs snouted about what had been the altar. Round about it the steaming maidenhair jungle towered high.

Here again Isie had a little ghost of comfort and the abatement of fear.

But soon after she had left the church she climbed up and up the hot scrub-grown side of a hill, and plunged down on its other side into a deep valley, half sand and rock, and sharp with cactus, and hot with a smothering heat, and it seemed as if no one had ever come that way before her, nor would again, and that here she must leave her bones.

There were more valleys and mountains ahead of her, towards what she believed to be the east, and deep jungle on her right, and mangrove swamp on the left, and whichever direction she turned seemed to plunge her more and more deeply into lost wilderness.

She knew then that it had been of no use her setting out to encounter with that wilderness ; it had beaten her. For she could go no more, and sank down in the shade of a cactus, laying her head on her arms, while a cloud of insects droned over her and bit her. Insects do not have meal-times ; they eat all day and all night, and even so never know satiety.

She could not lie there ; she got up and began to run beating the cloud from her with her hands. She had now no sense of direction ; she merely stumbled on, mad with terror, grief, insects, and forest loneliness.

" Oh, it's the end," she sobbed, " I shall end here all alone. . . . *Adrian. Adrian. Adrian !* " She was screaming now as she ran, caught in the surge of blind fear, that had broken over her like a wave and would drag her out into the waste seas of madness that wait to drown the lost. Her screaming was heard, far off, by a camp of men gathering chicle in the dense forest to the west. They paused for a moment at their work on the trees and listened. The screaming was coming their way.

CHAPTER X

CONSULTING THE BURSAR

I

At the hour of dawn when Isie was awakened in the
temple by the oriole, those who had been searching
for her in the forest, were assembled in the hall of the
Villa Maya. Discouraged by failure, shaken and wet
and fatigued from their encounter with earthquake
and storm, shivering with nervous exhaustion, they
were inclined to look on the dark side, as, indeed, is
usual at dawn. The tale brought by Mr. Piper and
Benet was received by Lady Cradock with horror and
hope.

" Oh, if it's money they're after, they can have all
they want," she said, with chattering teeth. Sir
Richmond, however, considered that this was an over-
statement.

" We must hope to frighten them into bringing her
back. We must use threats. Once we yield to the idea
of ransom, it will be all up, and they may go on extort-
ing for ever. Yielding to blackmail never answers."

" I don't agree," said Adrian. He sat on a bench,
sallow and soaked and fevered. " People have continually been captured and returned for ransom.
Savages are ignorant and easily satisfied ; they haven't
the cunning of European blackmailers. We must pay

what they ask. We can't risk refusing. It might come off, or it mightn't, but we can't take a chance on it."

" If only they do ask. If only Mr. Phipps is right," Belle moaned.

" Now, dear, you had better go and lie down for a little. There is nothing you can do by staying up. In fact, we had all better go and get into dry things. A night like this is most fatiguing. We shall need our strength to-morrow . . . to-day, that is."

" What shall we need our strength for ? " Julia asked. Querulous with fatigue and oppression, she was still enquiring.

" Naturally for looking for Isie," her father replied.

" And for bargaining with Indians," Benet added, faintly. He was draped over a chair, like a wet dish-cloth in colour and attitude. What a night it had been.

" Well," said Mr. Piper, " I don't reckon there's anything more to be done at this moment, I shall turn in." He went out into the dusk of the storm-wrecked morning, walking stiffly and heavily.

They all went to their rooms.

2

Catherine felt it strange to be again in a rose-pink bedroom in a rococo palace, after the wild Guatemalan night of kidnapping, terror, earthquake and storm. She thought, as she peeled off her soaked clothes, of Isie ; the jolly, tranquil, robust-fibred young tomboy, who seemed after all to be no such thing, but a neurotic, excitable creature who dashed away alone into the forest from wounded feeling. Poor little Isie,

who had become in a night a figure of tragedy and
doom, like a young actor who has suddenly been
given a star part in a tragic drama, having hitherto
only acted comedy.

The question was, what other people had parts in
that drama, or was it only of Isie's own spinning ?
Catherine, the greedy interest of the novelist tempered
by the pity and sympathy of the nice young woman,
hoped now one, now the other. She would have liked
to talk to Claudia about Adrian and Isie and that
whey-faced little rake, Julia. But did Claudia ever
emit illuminating womanly confidences ? Catherine
failed to imagine it. Benet might prove more fruitful ;
or Julia herself. Or, likely enough, Belle, the distraught
mother.

What a pig I am, thought Catherine, getting into
bed. Isie is in the hands of Red Indians, and all that
matters is to get her safely back. It is safety that
matters, not love and anger and jealousy. We invent
all these, and can think them away, but physical
danger and pain and Red Indians are real.

The image of Isie tortured by fear among Lacandones
in the wilderness wavered before her, a wraith of
nightmare.

3

The day had climbed into a warm and steaming noon.
Sir Richmond, standing in the patio talking to Mr. Piper,
saw Mr. Phipps ride up the path from the forest.

" Can he have heard any news, yet ? " Sir Richmond
wondered.

" I think he has news, Judge," Mr. Piper replied.

Watching Mr. Phipps as he waved his panama hat at them, Sir Richmond thought so too. He hurried across the patio to meet him at the gate-post where horses were left. Mr. Phipps, fresh and natty as usual in white drill suiting, was dismounting.

" Well, man, well ? " Sir Richmond, gaunt and haggard by contrast, urged him impatiently.

" Well, Judge, I'm delighted to be able to tell you that a message has come through. It's as I thought ; the girl is with the Lacs, and safe up to now, and they're after ransom."

" A message ? Who brought it ? Where's the messenger ? You've got him shut up, I presume ? "

" No, Judge, the messenger wasn't so soft as to come to me in person. He left the message in the village, with one of the Indians, who came to me with it."

" Hell," said Mr. Piper. " I told those Indios to freeze on to anyone who came."

" Well, they didn't. You can't expect it, you know ; they will stick together. We must use them as go-betweens, and not bully them too much, or they'll refuse to take messages. The point is that we have the Lacs' terms."

" Well, what are they ? What do they want ? "

" They want——" Mr. Phipps mopped his head with his silk handkerchief. " Shall we go in here and talk in the shade, Judge ? "

They followed him into the coolness of the temple.

" It's warm after the storm," said Mr. Phipps. " I'm afraid you were caught out in it, Mr. Piper."

" We'd like to have that message, if you don't mind, Mr. Phipps."

" Well, Mr. Piper, the fact is that it's really for the Judge's ear alone. It seems that they stipulated that."

" Nonsense, man. Piper manages all our affairs. I suppose they're scared of him, and think that without him we shall be more easily plucked. In any case, how should they know you've told him ? Get on with it, please, Mr. Phipps."

" As you like, Judge, as you like. Well, now, without beating about the bush, what the Lacs want is treasure."

" Treasure ? " Sir Richmond, frowned. " What d'you mean, treasure ? Money, I presume ? "

" It isn't money they said. It seems there's a tradition among the Indians round here that there's a box of treasure hidden away somewhere by the priests in the days when the place was a monastery. Gold, jade, and copal taken from the Indians, and all kinds of church ornaments, gold candlesticks, vestments, cups, and all that. That's what the Indians say, and it sounds likely enough. Anyhow, that's what these Lacs want for ransom—a share of the treasure."

" But this is intolerable. Demanding treasure that can't be found. . . . I mean, that probably never existed, or has been stolen long ago."

Mr. Phipps was watching Sir Richmond closely.

" You've not come on it, then, Judge ? "

" No, sir, I have not."

Mr. Phipps sighed.

" If I may suggest, we better all search, for Mrs. Rickaby's sake."

" But, good God, they daren't do anything to her. We should turn out all the soldiery of Central America on them. They aren't the only ones who can send threats. Their friends can take that message back to them."

Mr. Phipps shook his head. " It won't be any use, I fear. They're ignorant men, and have one idea at a time. If you send a message like that, the next message we should have might as likely as not be one of that poor girl's fingers. They think they're safe, in those jungle swamps of theirs. You can hunt them afterwards, Judge, but till we get the girl back we're in their hands."

Sir Richmond frowned still more heavily. " You've been reading melodrama, Mr. Phipps. Piper, what do you think of this abominable nonsense ? "

Mr. Piper shrugged lean shoulders, expressionless.

" What I think, Judge, I'm goin' to get hold of that Indio who gave Mr. Phipps that message, and make him sorry he didn't do as I told him and freeze on to the messenger. S'what I think, Mr. Phipps."

" You'll only do harm that way, Mr. Piper, believe me. If we had detained the messenger, Mrs. Rickaby wouldn't have been safe. We certainly must put that poor girl's safety top."

" What d'you think, Piper ? Is it just bluff, or will they dare to hurt her ? "

" I wouldn't say," said Mr. Piper, gloomily, " but that those damned Lacs mightn't do anything, once they set their minds on something they think they want. Same as any other gang of thieves might. No, I wouldn't say they mightn't, if it was only to scare us."

" But look here, suppose there is no treasure. Supposing no treasure is to be found, what then ? "

" Then it may be the worse for Mrs. Rickaby, I fear. We must search, Judge."

" Search, hell," said Mr. Piper. " Judge has been searching these three months and found nothing."

Now, thought Sir Richmond, annoyed, how does Piper know that ?

" Then," said Mr. Phipps, " you knew about this treasure, Judge ? "

" This alleged treasure," Sir Richmond corrected. " I had certainly heard a mention of it, but I can't say I attached much importance to the rumour. Such traditions easily arise in old houses. Like the tradition of ghosts and secret passages."

" Well," said Mr. Phipps, " there *are* secret passages in this hacienda, aren't there ? "

Sir Richmond said he did not know about secret ; the whole household used them regularly.

Mr. Phipps said, " Well, as to the treasure, if we all get busy searching, we'll soon discover whether there's any treasure or not. By the bye, Judge, how did you hear of it ? "

" It was alluded to," said the judge, " in a document, a bursar's note, which I found when going through an old chest full of monastic papers. I can't say I attached much importance to it, though I have kept it in mind while working at the uncovering of the carvings. But I suggest to you that it has probably been found and removed long ago. We must remember that, after the priests left the hacienda in 1830, it was in the hands of Spanish ranchers for eighty years or so before Mr. Higgins bought it. I put it to you that it is most improbable that, through all that time, a collection of valuable objects, whose presence was suspected by the neighbours, would lie concealed on the premises."

"And I put it to you, Judge, that it's up to us to make sure in the next two days whether it's to be found or not."

Mr. Phipps looked so solemn, and so determined, that Sir Richmond was impressed by the truth of what he said.

"We will certainly search," he said, "though I confess it would go against me to hand over any considerable quantity of valuables, should we find them, to these scoundrels. However, it would, of course, be without prejudice to the carrying out of a punitive raid later on."

"You've said it, Judge. And now, if you'll show me that note you say the monks left about it, we'll get busy with the searching."

"As you like," said Sir Richmond, somewhat vexed that he was no longer going to have his treasure hunt to himself for he was a rather proud, rapacious man. "It is in a chest in the cellar."

They returned to the patio. Lady Cradock met them at the hall door, distraught and entreating. "Dickie, Dickie, what news ? "

Dickie told her, with kind discretion.

"Treasure ? " she exclaimed. "Oh, all the treasure in the house ! Would my pearl necklace do, if we can't find the treasure they want ? It's worth two thousand dollars."

"Or mine," Catherine suggested, for they were now in the Villa, surrounded by the family, "which is worth two guineas. It's unlikely that in the Lacandon forest the difference would be observed."

" If the Indians have a fancy for getting their own ornaments back again," said Sir Richmond, " it is wiser to gratify it, anyhow partially, and not to cast before them pearls for which they may not care."

So saying, he led the way down to the cellar, whither the company followed him.

4

Sir Richmond, having unlocked the ancient oak chest that stood in a corner of the cellar, carefully and delicately turned over the piles of brittle parchment and faded yellow paper with which it was stuffed.

" There are some extraordinarily interesting manuscripts here, from the eleventh century on. The monks must have brought the chest and its contents with them from Spain when they came out. It is apparently about all they did bring, in the way of literature ; there's no trace of a library. Half of these papers, you know, are medieval monastic writings, tales of saints and illuminated prayers, inscribed over what look like erased pagan writings. Who knows what lost classics may be hidden here ? Stray pages from the lost books of Dion Cassius, or Livy, or Polybius, may, for all we know, lie hidden behind these scripts . . ."

" Papa, you're immoderate," Claudia impatiently protested. " Surely we have already enough, or even too many, books by these persons extant. What do we want with more ? What we do want is the bursar's account of the treasure."

" Well, here it is." The judge fished out a small, thick, vellum-bound book, and turned the yellow pages. " This seems to be a kind of general note-book kept by the bursars, or tesoreros, of the convent from 1796 to 1830, when the monks left. This is the entry—it is dated June, 1830, just when the troubles with the Indians were getting serious, and just before the abandonment !

" ' Una caja que contiene muchas joyas de oro y de jade, dadas de vez en cuando por los Indios, y tambien varios ornamentos de la yglesia, hemos escondido dabajo la piedra suelta.' That's all. He goes on then about something else. They were in a hurry, you see, storing away their valuables as best they could, surrounded by insubordinate Indians and the Mexican soldiery who had been sent to keep the Indians down, and who for a year after that used the Convent as their barracks. Possibly, if the tesorero had not been in such a hurry, he would have been either more definite or more obscure in his description of the hiding-place of this box. ' Hidden under the loose stone——' that is very vague. The loose stone of what ? I have made all kinds of investigations, but so far in vain."

" Well, for heaven's sake ! " Lady Cradock exclaimed. " So that's what you were doing all this time, when I thought you were hunting for inscriptions."

" I was doing both," the judge, still rather annoyed, explained. " Naturally, if I have any reason to believe that valuables may be concealed in my house, I look for them. I am human, I presume."

" But you kept it so quiet, Dickie ! "

" I certainly tried to do so. Obviously the fewer

people knew about the bursar's story, the less talk there would be. But it seems I needn't have troubled, as it is common gossip in the neighbourhood." Sir Richmond looked a little severely upon Mr. Phipps, as if *he* had been the common gossiper.

" Gold, jade and copal," Mr. Phipps said, with the look of satisfaction that the contemplation of these precious substances give to the face.

" Copal ? There is no mention of that. ' Oro y jade,' the tesorero says. Gold and jade. Where do you get copal from ? "

" Oh, the Indians say copal. And they are likely right. It was a favourite offering. The gift of balls of copal was a common penance for the priests to exact from their penitents."

" That's quite true, of course," Sir Richmond agreed. " It is a very frequent entry in the tesorero's book, almost as frequent as eggs and laying hens. Though he says nothing of any copal being in the hidden box." Sir Richmond had a fleeting wonder as to where Mr. Phipps, hat merchant in a Middle Western town, got his knowledge of the ways of Guatemalan priests with their flocks. He must have a quite remarkable touch with Indians, to obtain so much information from them.

" Look here," Adrian impatiently broke in, " are you proposing that we shall spend our time hunting for this absurd box of treasure, instead of for Isie ? What we must do, obviously, is to rouse all the Indians, ladinos and white men for miles round, and make a raid into the Lacandon country. The thing is to frighten these people at once by showing them we're not sitting down under their threats."

S.W.R.   K

Mr. Piper intimated that he, too, favoured this policy.

"Of course, of course," Mr. Phipps agreed. "We certainly must do that as well. But remember that such a hunt may be a lengthy business, and that we have to work against time. We may be too late. We must try, meanwhile, to lay hands on that treasure, as, if we find it, it will be the speediest way. I suggest, Judge, that you and I and the ladies search in the villa and grounds to-day, while Mr. Rickaby and Mr. Piper and Mr. Benet organise this raiding expedition. But I must warn you, Mr. Rickaby, you may have quite a bit of trouble getting the peons to help you."

Mr. Piper said, grimly, "I'll see to that. I'm going out to talk to them now."

"The loose stone," Belle wailed. "Oh, do someone find the loose stone! It surely must be somewhere, among all these hundreds of stones!"

Mr. Piper turned at the cellar door to say, "Ask Jacinto to help look."

"Jacinto! Will he be useful? He always seems such a stupid man."

"When it comes to seeking out treasure," said Mr. Piper, "a ladino is just about as useful as a terrier seeking out rats. Instinct, they have, and that's a sight more use than reason sometimes. . . . Ask Jacinto what he knows about the hole in the temple floor before the altar."

CHAPTER XI

LOOKING FOR TREASURE

I

THE parroquin was having his siesta, while Mixa, his wife, cleared away the mid-day meal, when the youngest, the palest and the most voluble of the Englishmen from the Hacienda del Capitan knocked at his door. Mixa opened it, smiled with her usual affability, and called the parroquin, who came drowsily, for the night had been ruined by earthquake, storm and prayers, and he was very tired.

" Good day, Father," the young Englishman began in his fluent, book-learnt Castilian with its English accent, that was so comically different from the Spanish of Guatemala that the cura could not always follow it. " I hope that you and the Señora did not suffer in the earthquake, nor any of your family nor your property, and that to-day you enjoy the best of health."

Father Jacinto returned these good wishes without enthusiasm, in his melancholy ladino voice. " Will you come in, Señor ? My house and all that is in it is yours."

" You are very courteous," said Benet, and came in and sat down. Father Jacinto trusted that he would not spoil the afternoon by staying long, and offered him a glass of pulque.

" Listen, Father," the youth began, after declining this drink, which was in fact very loathsome to him.

147

" We want you to have the kindness to help us in a very urgent matter. You have heard, perhaps, that one of our ladies, Mrs. Rickaby, has been abducted by Lacandones and taken we do not know where."

" So the peones told me, Señor. It is an unusual misfortune, for the Lacandones are in general very mild men, though not Christians. I think the lady will suffer no harm."

" I am glad you think so. But they say they will not restore her unless they are presented with some objects of value which they believe to be hidden somewhere on the hacienda since the days of the Dominicans. We cannot find any such things, and we hoped that perhaps you might be able to help us."

" Sir, I know nothing of any objects of value. I have no objects of value in the world, only those." Ironically he indicated with his hand a troop of his offspring who played outside the house, and whom, in point of fact, he tenderly loved.

" Oh, we didn't think you had the objects," Benet quickly explained. " But that you might perhaps be good enough to assist us in searching for them."

The cura looked as devoid of hope as he felt.

" They will be ornaments belonging to the church," he suggested.

" No. There may be also those, but what the Indians have asked for is some gold and jade which their ancestors gave as offerings of religion to the monks."

Father Jacinto looked somewhat brighter. " Ah, gold and jade. But, as to that, the ancestors of the Lacandones gave nothing to the monks ever, since they have always been of the Maya religion."

" Well, then, the ancestors of the Christian Indians. I do not suppose the Lacandones said their ancestors presented them. The fact is that they want them, and they say they are concealed somewhere on the hacienda, and, unless we can hunt the abductors down, which seems difficult, they will keep Mrs. Rickaby until they get them."

" It is a sufficiently odd affair," the cura observed. " But, yes, without doubt I will come and assist in the search."

" Ten thousand thanks, Father. Will you then do us the favour to come at once ? "

" You search in the mid-day heat, then, is it true ? "

" Yes, it is true. We waste not a moment."

The priest sighed a little, and abandoned his peaceful afternoon. Life is so restless. First God agitated the night, then the gringos the day. He pulled himself together and followed the young man, who irritated him rather, out into the blazing afternoon.

" You know that large hole," said Benet, as they walked up the forest path to the hacienda, " in the floor of the ancient temple before the altar."

Father Jacinto looked stupid. " I think I have seen such a hole."

" Well," said Benet, " do you know what was in it, in former days ; and how long it has been empty ? "

" Of that I know nothing, sir."

An inquisitive and prying young man. All these gringos were meddlers. What concern was it of theirs ? The Dominicans had not hidden away the silver candlesticks, images and ornaments of their chapel for gringos to steal. They belonged to the church, and to the priests of the church. It had been a fortunate and blessed day in which he himself had, in looking about that heathen temple five years ago, before the arrival of the ubiquitous Piper, discovered, hidden beneath a great slab of stone, that cache of ecclesiastical treasures, never intended to fall into the hands of heretics. Willingly now he would help them to look for the Indian treasures, though he had supposed that any such objects must have been unearthed long ago by the successive dwellers in the hacienda during the past century. By good rights any such treasure found should belong to the church, as they had been offerings of religion. Alas, those were the good days ; the Indians, poor children, had little to give their priests now, beyond an occasional fowl or turkey, a little maize, fruit or cacao. One had to give then their absolutions and their masses almost for nothing, poor underpaid little ones. If he should have the good fortune, while assisting in this grand search, to find anything, some of it would rightly be his portion. His heavy steps quickened a little. At heart he, like many ladinos, was a romantic child, and when he considered a treasure hunt, it was as if angels played to him on their harps a little magic tune.

2

To go over every foot of floor and wall of that part of the Villa Maya and its grounds which had been once a Dominican priory, testing each stone to see if it were one of those stones that, on occasion, move,— such was the strange task of half of this deranged household through that hot afternoon and evening,

while the other half betook themselves to the sending
of messages for assistance, and to that occupation
known as rousing the neighbourhood. As regards the
Indian section of the neighbourhood, it was a somewhat discouraging task, for they showed themselves
apathetic, and unwilling to be roused, telling Mr.
Piper that it was a useless expedition he demanded
of them, for none knew where the kidnappers were,
and none could find them.

Less discouraging was the task of the treasure-seekers,
for those who seek treasure are ever full of hope,
seeing in every crack a possible hiding-place, in every
stone and panel something which may be induced to
move and to reveal a yawning cavity gold-stuffed,
like the hole in a tooth. To Catherine, languid after
the night of so much activity, the drowsy gold of the
afternoon flickering in through the trellis of vines onto
the pink stone pavement of the loggia seemed lovely
and remote, and she bathed in a warm dream that had
no part in life, standing on the shadowed terrace and
tapping its wall as if she had been a diviner, with Julia
kneeling not far off and rapping on the pink-washed
slaps of the terrace pavement.

Glancing now and then at that slim, crouching form,
so intent upon its task, Catherine wondered what was
in the little creature's mind, what load of conscience
and of self-reproach weighed down the sleek, ash-blonde
head, that bent from a slim neck like a smooth yellow
fruit from its stalk. Calm enough, she seemed, and a
little languid, for now she paused to yawn, and sat
up and addressed her companion.

" Catherine, have you hope ? "

" Of discovering, you mean, treasure behind these
stones ? Not very much, I am afraid."

" Nor I. I tap and tap, like one of those men who
are for ever deranging the streets of London, but all
seems firm and fixed. I fear no miracle will occur to
me. I wasn't born to find treasure ; I always lose it.
. . . Papa is the one who will find anything that
is to be found ; he was made by the Lord for riches and
splendour. Papa or Phipps, for Phipps was made for
riches too, I think. As to poor Jacinto, I hope someone
is keeping an eye on him ; if not, he will certainly find
something, even if not buried treasure, and whatever
he finds will return with him to the vicarage. Of course
he would be right ; one is told not to muzzle the ox
that treadeth out the corn. . . . But how perverse of
poor Isie's kidnappers to set their hearts on just what
we can't find for them ! Had it been jewels, now, that
they had had a fancy for, or money—— As it is, I
feel that what papa, who is so clever and so patient
and so determined, has been looking for all these months,
you and I, Catherine, won't find in an afternoon.
If only papa had set us all looking long ago. But he
was so very discreet and judge-like about it. Though
of course one suspected that he was looking for *something*."

" Did you ? I thought it was just inscriptions and
carvings."

" Partly, of course, it was. But what gave him his
great ardour and perseverance was treasure. Treasure,
you know, even when buried, gives human creatures
a peculiar glint in the eye and firmness about the mouth,
that even Maya inscriptions don't give. And papa is

a very human creature. Perhaps you despise him, for being so human, and for being a judge. But papa on the whole, and as judges go, carries it off well. I mean, he is less of a bully, and less unfair, and less preposterously archaic, than many of them."

" I am sure he is," Catherine agreed. " I don't mind judges, especially, I think. After all, it is a job someone has to do. I don't know that they are worse than people in other professions."

" I fear they are worse," Julia sighed. " For you see, they must be worse, as they are allowed, and even encouraged, to speak evil of and to the people whom they are judging, and no one is allowed to speak or write evil of them, however unfairly they behave. It makes a position which only an angel could adorn. Alas, they are, they must be, to some extent bullies and cowards. But, as I was saying, papa is only that to a trifling extent. I mean he is so much better than Jefferies was, or Bacon, or Pontius Pilate, or Coke, or any of the infamous judges of history that Claudia speaks of—myself, I don't read history, so don't know these eminent men. But I have a feeling that any of them could have found any treasure that was at hand, so possibly papa will find this."

" I hope so," said Catherine, running her fingers round a mortared crack. " Though it seems not much of a hope to trust to, for Isie's safety. I wish there was some better thing we could do."

She thought, Julia, who caused the trouble, takes it too lightly. Does she feel remorse ? If I were in her place, I think I should never feel happy again.

Julia sighed. " I wish so too ! Perhaps Mr. Piper

and Adrian will succeed in frightening those men into
setting her free. Poor Isie ; how could she have plunged
into the forest like that ? Should you have dared,
however sad or angry you were ? I never should,
I'm sure. The forest is so astonishing and shocking ;
such dreadful things lurk in it."

" She *was* sad and angry, then ? " Catherine thought
that she would stop being a gentlewoman for a time,
till she had learnt more about this affair of Isie and
her troubles. Being a gentlewoman all the time is
cold and comfortless, and leaves you too uninformed,
too much out in the dark, for satisfaction either as a
novelist or as a woman. And, after all, with Julia,
who was, surely, a gentlewoman so little of her time
as to be negligible in that capacity, it could not matter
greatly. Had it been Claudia, it would have been
different. So, with a helpful, enquiring inflection,
Catherine said, " She *was* sad and angry, then . . ."

Julia had the grace to sigh. " Oh, yes. Indeed she
was. . . . You know, Catherine, how complicated and
difficult life is."

She leant back on her two hands, looking up at
Catherine with her head a trifle on one side, considering
difficulties, complications, and life.

Catherine said that she did know this.

" And you must, of course, have observed the situation here, all this time you have been with us."

Catherine said that she certainly had observed
something.

Julia nodded. " I thought you must have. I thought
so all the time. Nothing is hidden, I often think, from
female observers, when it's a question of affairs of the

heart. That is our great gift ; we see all. Well then, there you are, Catherine ; you know it all."

But Catherine did not feel that she knew it all.

" They've been married such a short time," she said. " Adrian can't have stopped loving her, Julia. He must have loved her when they were married ? This, this other, is just a passing distraction, that doesn't matter . . . ? "

Julia replied, after a moment, " But I'm afraid unfortunately it is Isie who is the passing distraction and doesn't matter. You see, the other came first ; years first."

" Years first ? "

" Oh, years and years. And out here it came back again, though we had all thought it dead. It revived, and was worse than ever. And now they are both fallen into love and sunk in it, stuck fast as if they were in a bog and couldn't get out. Claudia meant to go away weeks ago, but he wouldn't let her, he said he would follow her."

" Claudia . . . ? "

" You see, Adrian has loved her, on and off, for ten years and more. It began during that war. . . . They were engaged for a time, when she was nineteen and he was twenty-five. But she broke it off quite soon, for she fell in love with someone else, whom she loved for years. Claudia has so much love, you see ; she must always love someone ; she enjoys loving, as a pastime. Now I don't really feel that love is necessary, or even the most amusing kind of sport ; I could be happy a virgin. Though I hope that I shall marry, when I've done with being a virgin, some nice, quiet, contented

man, and live in the country in a small, very comfortable
white house, and have five children, two servants, a
garden and a cat. You see I am ordinary, and not
excitable in my affections. Claudia isn't ordinary ; she
is a great sentimental lover ; I feel she was made to be a
mistress of kings. She has met no kings ; but she met
other men who loved her, and some of them she loved.
And Adrian loved her in a way all the time, but to her
he was only a friend. And he was ill, and shell-shocked,
and could only love, I think, in a dead, unexcited kind
of way. And then he met Isie abroad, and he fell in
love with her for being so beautiful, and Claudia was
taken up with someone else, and Isie and he got engaged, and we all thought, and Claudia and Adrian
thought too, that his old feeling for Claudia was quite
dead and over. But when we were all out here together,
and planning the villa, it woke up again, and he began
to love her more than ever before (you see he had got
used by then, I suppose, to Isie's being so beautiful,
and her nerves tired him—Isie's nerves are exhausting,
of course, sometimes.) And then Claudia seemed to
fall in love with him too, after all those years. I don't
know why, except that they were suddenly so much
together, and she had no one else at hand. Perhaps
it would have happened at any time, if they had seen
as much of each other, and if no other men had been
near ; or perhaps they had to get through with other
people first, before they knew how much they wanted
each other. Anyhow—it was most perverse—they
began to look at one another and speak to one another
as if they were all alone in a world in which no one else
existed. So very unfortunate, because, of course, they

weren't ; Isie did exist, very much. They did really try,
I think, but oh, dear, Love is so strange and selfish, it
seems to drown people, go right over their heads so that
they can't see or think. Anyone who knew them well
must have seen it—Isie didn't know them well, and
didn't see it at first ; but, of course, she soon did, for un-
luckily you can't hide Love. And there they both were
in the middle of the forest, and neither could easily go.
I think Claudia thought it would pass away, when we
all left here, and leave Adrian and Isie none the worse ;
and Adrian—oh, I don't know what Adrian thought,
except that he wanted Claudia. He tried to hide it
from Isie, and to be so kind to her that she would guess
nothing ; but, you know, Isie isn't a fool. Not, at
least, in that way. She is in another way, for she
makes scenes. She flies into passions and storms, and
I think she did that with Adrian, and storms frighten
him since the war. Poor Isie, she is like a wild cat,
scratching and spitting when she is vexed. It was
partly that, I think, that put Adrian out of conceit
with her at first, and made him want Claudia so
much again. I don't know what happened between
them, for, of course, Adrian never said a word, and Isie
never did either. Not even to Belle. Belle didn't know,
I think, what was happening ; I'm not sure that she
knows now. Or, if she does, she doesn't think it serious,
only a lovers' quarrel. She adores Isie so that she could
never suppose anyone else really preferred to her. I don't
know if she guesses what Isie said in that note she left."

" What did she say ? Did you see it ? "

" No, indeed. No one saw it but Adrian, and he
would never say. But I can guess."

" Yes, one can guess. . . . Oh, dear, Julia, how can it all end ? "

Catherine, in her surprise at listening to this drama, so different as to one important member of the cast from that which she had imagined, had forgotten to look for treasure and had ceased to tap the wall. She felt that she owed Julia an apology, which she certainly could not make. Both Julia and Claudia had surprised her.

" Only in disaster," Julia replied, with a shake of the head. " Well, I suppose we must proceed with our search," and she bent again over the pink stone floor.

" It's odd," Catherine commented. " Claudia seems not like a lover. She seems as if all that would bore her. The celibate type : aloof, remote and detached. A spinster."

" Type ? " Julia glanced up at her, puzzled. " You've used that word before. I don't understand it. Are there types ? What type am I, or papa, or any of us ? It seems to me that there are only people, not types. But I expect you are right, Catherine, since you are much more intelligent than I am. Anyhow, Claudia is a great lover, and always has been. A spinster—why, yes, of course, so far. But spinsters and bachelors are surely often lovers."

" Of course. But you'll admit that Claudia doesn't seem *like* a lover. That she hasn't the air."

" Oh, like . . . What *are* lovers like ? Like every-one, I think. You are original, Catherine, with your ideas of dividing people up into types. Does it help you to write about them ? "

" Well, after all, people have characters ; they *are*

like this or like that, and different from one another."

" Are they ? I wonder if they are . . . like this or like that I mean. I expect you are right. But I can only see them as being just anyhow, and like nothing at all."

" You mean that anyone may do anything ? That must surely be nonsense."

" Perhaps it is. I don't know. Or perhaps we don't know enough about them to guess what they'll do. I never try to. . . . You must get a lot of surprises, Catherine, arranging people as you do. . . . I just take them as they come. Yours is the tidy, intelligent way, of course. I expect your novels are full of people all with the characters you give them and all keeping beautifully to them. They must be wonderful."

Catherine, who had already some reputation as a novelist of human character, felt a little disappointed that Julia should not be more aware of it.

" I do write about people," she said, " and about their characters. They interest me more than anything else."

" And I am sure you are right," Julia warmly agreed.

" But how," she went on, " we are idling, with all the loggia to search, and not a loose stone found yet. Somehow, Catherine, I *feel* there are no loose stones in the loggia, and no treasure. I wonder how papa and Claudia and the rest get on. Should we go and see, in case something may have been found and they have forgotten to let us know ? "

" Oh, we must go over all the loggia first." Catherine, though equally lacking in hope, was ever conscientious.

Julia, sighing, acquiesced.

3

Lady Cradock came out on to the loggia. She was red-eyed, and had the appearance of a disconsolate bird.

" Girls, girls, haven't you found *one* loose stone yet ? "

" Not yet, dear Aunt Belle."

She collapsed into a chair and rocked herself to and fro, her hands pressed to her temples.

" Oh, what's the use of looking ? There *aren't* any loose stones, and there is no Indian treasure. Treasure ? Why it wouldn't have stayed here quietly all this time, what with Mexican soldiers and Spanish ranchers and your Uncle Heck all in the house in turn, not to mention all the Indians about, and the priest—however well they'd hidden it, it wouldn't."

It did indeed appear to Catherine and Julia highly improbable that, when all these persons had failed to enrich themselves, such as they would succeed, and they could find little comfort for the distraught parent.

" Where are the others looking ? " Catherine asked, and Julia, " I hope someone is with Jacinto."

" Oh, Jacinto. All *he's* done is to find a secret panel in the chapel sacristy, that's empty but for a few pieces of old paper. I wish he hadn't, for those old papers have gotten Dickie so excited he's almost forgotten the treasure. He says he thinks they're bits from something that's been lost centuries, or that never was found at all, and that lots of people think never was written, and I'm sure I wish it never had been. Jacinto knew nothing about the papers, but Dickie says he went right to that panel like a cat to milk, though he said he never knew of it, but found it by chance just now, looking about the

sacristy. It's my belief he'd found it by chance some
other time, and took what he fancied out of it, whether
it was gold and jade or something else. What I
mean is, you can't *trust* Jacinto, not like one ought to
be able to trust one's clergyman. Anyhow, now he's
hunting about the patio, with Mr. Phipps at his heels,
and Dickie's in the chapel, hoping he'll find more secret
panels with lost works in them, and Claudia's hunting in
the refectory, though I'm sure that's been so altered and
done up that no treasure could have escaped the workmen. And Piper and Adrian and Benet are out, getting
help for a search raid. I told them to promise my pearls
for ransom, but Piper thinks the Lacandones wouldn't
get any kick out of pearls, though Mr. Phipps thinks it
certainly would help."

"Well," said Julia, " we have been all over the
loggia—haven't we been all over it, Catherine ?—in
vain, so I shall go and begin on the hall."

" One of you girls had better just look in and see how
Meg is, on your way down. I can't go in, I should fret
the child."

4

Meg was in bed, with one of her temperatures, and
was not to be excited ; she had not been told of the
kidnapping of Isie. Catherine looked into her room,
the little square room which was the only unaltered
monk's cell left in the villa. She was sitting up in
bed, playing solitaire. The unfortunate child had to be
perpetually guarded from brain-fever, a disease of which
she had once been sick.

" All right, Meg ? " Catherine asked her, with the cheerful kindness that made her so useful with invalids.

" No," said Meg, after a moment's consideration.

" Well, what is it, dear ? "

" I want Tray, please."

Catherine cast her mind about among the hacienda menagerie, endeavouring to identify Tray.

" That's one of the monkeys, isn't it ? "

" No. The baby armadillo. Please, might I have him in bed ? "

" Darling, I don't think one has armadillos in bed. They'd be so uncomfortable."

" Tray's not uncomfortable in my bed. He likes it."

" Uncomfortable for you, I mean."

" Oh, no. He's not. He's a very cuddly armadillo. Please, may I have Tray ? "

" Well, I don't know where he is, at the moment. In fact, I don't know where he ever is. And everyone's rather too busy this afternoon to go looking for him. Shall I bring you the cat instead ? "

" No. If I can't have Tray, I won't have anyone. . . .. Why is everyone busy this afternoon ? Is Isie back yet ? "

" Not yet—I expect she's coming in soon. Would you like a drink of lemonade ? "

" Yes, please." Meg accepted the drink of lemonade as a pis aller. One must have some consolations in bed.

" Now I must go. You've got the bell by you, haven't you ? Ring for Amy if you need anything. But don't send her to fetch Tray ; that would be a mistake."

" All right." Meg, bored and hot, pushed away the solitaire-board, and lay back with a sigh. One would certainly have thought that when a person was ill in bed, lying all alone, perhaps about to die, they might be allowed a baby armadillo in bed with them. Yes, one would certainly think that.

" And so it was to end here, her brief, inglorious career," Meg murmured, when alone. " Let this be her epitaph, for she has no other : Here lies one whose name was writ in water. She might have been a great poet if she had lived, but fever took her in a Central American forest, and only a few brief lines from her pen are left us. They are strangely good lines, some of them, and no doubt if she had lived she would have written lots more and much better. But it wasn't to be. . . . Oh, I do want Tray in bed with me. I'm quite *well* now. I want to get up."

5

" Well, papa, how are you getting on ? " Claudia entered the chapel sacristy, where her father was searching for more secret panels. He looked up from his task.

" No treasure so far. That is to say, no gold or jade. But, Claudia, just look at these, that were in a recess behind a panel in here."

He carefully took up half a dozen pages of parchment, on which were inscribed in monkish script what appeared to be a life of Saint Jerome.

" You see—it's tenth century script, written on the top of something only partially erased. Classical Latin, I think of the first century A.D. The title of the fragment is quite distinct—' De causis corruptae eloquentiae.'

" A copy of Tacitus's Dialogus de Oratoribus, then ? "

" No," said Sir Richmond, " it's certainly not that. The style isn't that of Tacitus. Enough of it is legible to show that it is far more polished and graceful. The name written under the title of this work is M. Fabius Quintilianus. Of course that is no proof, but I am inclined to believe that it actually *is* a copy of Quintilian's lost book on the Causes of the Corruption of Eloquence. You remember the passage in the Institutions where he alludes to such a book : ' sed de hoc satis, quia eundem locum plenius in eo libro quo *causas corruptae eloquentiae* reddebamus, tractavimus.'— and how people were led by this at various times to assign the Dialogus de Oratoribus to him, as no copy of such a book of Quintilian's has ever turned up. Well, there's at least a chance that this is a fragment of a copy. These monks seem to have brought out with them a small but miscellaneous collection of books and manuscripts from their convent library at Valladolid, which must have been a remarkable one. . . . Oh of course it's only a chance, but *what* a chance ! A fragment of a lost book of Quintilian's that the world has searched for in vain for five centuries. The question is, is the rest of it scattered and destroyed, or somewhere in the Valladolid convent library, hiding beneath the lives of other saints, or under some scriptural treatise ? I must write to Cochran about it."

" Exciting," Claudia murmured, examining the pages. " I wonder if it was a good book. Still, one has to remember that that doesn't really matter and is not the point. . . . In some cases I feel it must have been very right and judicious of those monks who mislaid books or covered them up with other writings. I don't know why it's not more done now. It might be a very beneficial industry for monks and nuns, to cover up large quantities of contemporary literature as it comes out."

"From the fragments I can decipher, I should say that this book is in Quintilian's most graceful style."

"Well, that's a pity, if now we shall have to think we've lost something good. I have always decided that lost books were probably bad. . . . There was nothing else behind the panel, then?"

"Unfortunately not. There may once have been, however. Jacinto found the panel remarkably rapidly."

"Oh, dear. I fear it's no good, papa. Who are we to find treasure, after all these more experienced searchers have covered the ground? No doubt Jacinto wouldn't care particularly either for Saint Jerome or for Quintilian, so would have left the manuscript where it was. I feel, however, that leaving things that he finds must be quite unusual with Jacinto. . . . Papa, it's no good."

"No, dear, I'm afraid not. I must say that it is getting to seem to me something of a wild-goose chase. When first I came on the tesorero's entry, I thought the chance of finding anything so long after was remote, though I from time to time amused myself by looking about. But the more I think of it, and especially now that Phipps says the buried treasure is a tradition among the Indians, the fainter I feel the chance to be. I fear we must give it up, and concentrate on bringing these people to reason by threats. Piper has gone over

to Phipps's ranch to impress on the villagers that any
messenger purporting to come from the Lacandones
must be kept. But I fear, from what Phipps says, that
Indian feeling is not with us. . . . To say the truth,
it's mainly to satisfy poor Belle that I go on looking
for this alleged treasure. She's pinned her hopes to it.
. . . Claudia, has Adrian told you any more than he
told us all about that note the child left ? "

" No, no more."

" Had they had a quarrel, do you suppose ? "

" I don't know."

" I suppose they'd had a quarrel. Some tiff or
other. Isie is very impetuous, isn't she ? Easily
upset ? "

" She is, rather."

" Well, I suppose they'd had a row, and off she flew
in a passion, not stopping to think what she was doing.
Young women are really very foolish sometimes.
Unbalanced. Dashing off like that, not troubling about
her mother and husband and everyone being off their
heads with anxiety. In fact, I suppose that would be
her object. Well, poor girl, she's been punished enough
for it. She'll have learnt her lesson, that's one
thing."

" It's we who are doing that," Claudia murmured,
and went out into the courtyard with a lost look in
her eyes.

5

Mr. Phipps and Father Jacinto were examining a
corner of the patio, with the concentration of terriers

hunting for rats. Mr. Phipps, pausing to wipe his perspiring face, addressed Claudia as she passed.

" Hot work, Miss Claudia, and no luck yet, except that the judge has gotten some papers that he gets quite a kick out of. I hope Lady Cradock is not too prostrated by her anxiety ? "

" I hope not, Mr. Phipps."

" I certainly do understand a mother's feelings in this terrible predicament. I've a little daughter myself, and I surely would hate to have her taken by Indians. Yes, I certainly would hate to think of Ada in any such predicament. But won't you tell Lady Cradock we're doing our best to find that ransom, and if we can't lay hands on it we'll maybe try if those pearls you spoke of will do, so she's not to worry too much. Are the other young ladies searching inside ? "

" I believe they are."

" Well, we surely must keep up our spirits, even in this discouraging emergency. . . . Que hay, padre ? "

Father Jacinto crouched a few yards away beneath a statue of Saint Dominic, and seemed to Mr. Phipps, who kept a keen and attentive eye on his activities, to be thrusting his hand into a hole. However, he withdrew it empty, and shrugged his shoulders with a disappointed " Nada."

" They say," said Mr. Phipps, " that the padre is a little on the slack side as a parish clergyman. Just the same, when it's a question of looking for treasure. I'll tell the world he's a real conscientious hustler."

CHAPTER XII

FINDING TREASURE

I

THE afternoon wore on. Old Amy brought Meg her
tea. Meg now felt quite well, as one does after tea, and
wanted to get up, but was not allowed, for she still had
a little temperature. She was bored with bed and with
the books she was reading. She thought of writing a
letter to Pamela Morris, in England, but decided that
this would be troublesome. She also considered going
on with the poem she was writing about a humming-
bird, but did not feel inspiration, so refrained.

Still, she must have some amusement, something to
distract her mind and console her for being ill, and for
having, whenever her mind strayed that way, cold and
horrid thoughts about last night, about how Isie had
been lost in the forest in the dark and had not come
in all night.

Meg sat up. She would be a princess, she decided.
This occupation was her last bulwark against the chill
tides of reality when they threatened to submerge her.

Dizzily she stumbled out of bed, and into the tiny
alcove where her washstand stood. This alcove was
unplastered ; its walls were of grey stones. Meg, who
loved it, called it her treasure-room.

Reaching up at arm's length she groped about the

wall for the familiar yielding. She found it ; a stone
moved, pushed in ; a thin, flat stone like a huge coin,
that swivelled round on its axis and disclosed a long
dark hole behind it. Pushing in her hand, Meg pulled
out a narrow cedar box, with something of the exquisite
thrill with which she had, a month ago, first done so.
She left the alcove, hugging the box in her arms, and,
comfortably again in bed, laid it beside her.

" What shall I wear to-day for the assembly, Dinah ? "
she enquired of one of her retinue of black slaves.

" I think your majesty had better wear them all
to-day, because it's a very good assembly, with a lot of
foreign kings and queens and emperors," Dinah replied.

" Oh, all right, Dinah, if you think so. Give me my
gold crown, then."

She fitted a circlet of thin gold round her head.
" And my emerald necklace." She put about her neck
a golden chain hung with green jade ornaments.
" And my emerald brooches and earrings. And my
ivory bird."

The carved, white jade bird she put on her head,
supported by the circlet. " And I'll have some of the
gold coins with me, for largesse. Now I am ready.
Show in the foreign potentates."

The door opened, but what came in was not a foreign
potentate, but Mr. Phipps.

2

The two stared at each other, startled and round-
eyed. The jewelled princess was scarlet with a blush
beyond that of fever.

"Hullo," she managed to ejaculate, preserving an appearance of sang-froid amid her confusion.

Mr. Phipps advanced into the room, quietly closing the door behind him, and collected his wits.

"Well now," he said, "isn't that fine! I'll say I never knew you had so many pretty things."

"Well," Meg replied after a moment, "I don't really see how you could have known what things I had."

"No, quite so, my dear. No, to be sure I couldn't. Why, you never put them on for me, so how could I have known? Now you'll let me see them, won't you? . . . Why, isn't that nice! They're real lovely, aren't they. Now, suppose you were to tell me all about them—where you got them, and that."

Suppose I weren't to, thought Meg, pulling off her adornments and sulkily eyeing this intruder into her private realm, this gate-crasher at her royal party, this grown-up visitor who had caught her out and made her look a fool. Suppose I jolly well don't tell you a thing. It's not your business, anyway.

Mr. Phipps caught the obstinate look in the small, stolid, freckled face.

"Listen, now, Meg. I'll tell you why I want to know about these jewels. You know Isie's lost?"

A little flicker stirred the stolidity.

"Well, she's been stolen and kidnapped, by wild Indians in the forest."

Meg gasped.

"Yes, she has. And they won't let her go till they get some gold and jewels they say are hid somewhere in this place and that belonged to them long ago. So we've all been searching for these gold and jewels all day, but can't find a thing. Now it looks to me like you've gotten the very goods right here. Say, honey, where'd you find them ? "

Meg jerked a shaking hand at the alcove and replied, hoarse with emotion, " In there. In a hole in the wall. there's a loose stone. I found it ages ago—before Christmas. I keep them to play with. I didn't know about Isie. Please will you take them to the Indians quickly."

She was gathering the treasures together and thrusting them into their box. Then cupidity overcame her.

" Do they want them all ? " she enquired. " I suppose I couldn't keep the ivory bird ? "

Perceiving that the ivory bird was of white jade, richly wrought, Mr. Phipps replied that she could not.

" You see," he explained, " that bird might be the very piece those Indians have set their hearts on, and they might refuse to let Isie go without it."

" Oh." The bird was dropped quickly into the box.

" Well, do you think they'll need all the balls, or that I could keep one of them ? "

The balls were of a hard golden brown substance, with a resinous smell that made them very agreeable.

" Why," said Mr. Phipps, " aren't those cute ! Why yes, you can surely keep a ball. They won't need all the balls. Well, I'll take these right along. Now isn't that nice, you having found them, so as we can get your sister back."

" Isie's not my sister."

" Why no, of course not. Your stepsister, isn't she ? Anyhow, you want her back, don't you, and as you've found these ornaments so cunningly, we shall have her in no time. I shall take them over with me right away. But I first must break the good news to Lady Cradock. Where's she, honey? "

" I don't know."

" Well, I'll find her. She'll be tickled to death at the good news. Now, I'll say good-bye and be off."

3

Mr. Phipps met Belle in the gallery, as he came from Meg's room, the contents of the cedar box in the spacious pockets of his coat.

" Lady Cradock, I'm delighted to have fine news to give you. I've gotten the treasure for the Indians. The child found it ; months since, she says. And now I'm off right away with it back to my place, to be in time for that messenger when he comes. I won't stop even to tell the judge, for I daren't delay. It may be a question of seconds."

" You've *gotten* it, Mr. Phipps ? The treasure ? Oh, thank the Lord for that. Dickie, Dickie, where are you, Mr. Phipps has gotten the treasure ! "

But Mr. Phipps was hurrying downstairs and through the hall and out into the courtyard to the stables where his horse was. Sir Richmond, standing by the chapel entrance, saw him go by.

Phipps seems in a great hurry, he thought. Fussy little chap. You'd think he'd be too fat to race about as he does in the sun.

A minute later he heard the patter of a horse's feet

on the path that led to the forest, and the horse seemed
in a hurry too.

Lady Cradock went into Meg's room to hear the tale.
A few minutes later she went down to the hall.
Father Jacinto was coming out of the refectory as she
passed.

" You have heard the news," she cried to him, in her
loud and fluent Spanish that, picked up in Guatemala,
was more like his own than was that of the rest of the
party.

The parroquin, looking shy and uncomfortable,
replied that he had not.

" Oh, did not Señor Phipps tell you ? The treasure is
found. The little girl found it in the wall of her room,
and Señor Phipps has ridden off to give it to the
Lacandon messenger when he comes to-night. Is it
not good news ? "

The clergyman had no time to comment on it, for
Sir Richmond, with his daughter Claudia, had come
in from the patio while his wife spoke.

" What, Belle ? What's that ? The treasure found ?
Phipps gone off with it ? Did you see it ? Why was I
not told ? "

" I suppose Mr. Phipps was in too great a hurry,
dear, and didn't meet you. You see, he wanted to be
back at his ranch in case the messenger came ; he said
it might be a question of seconds."

" What do you mean, it might be a question of
seconds ? What might be ? "

" Why, his being in time for the messenger. But of
course the messenger would wait a bit, wouldn't he ?
And now it will be all right, and they'll get their

treasure and send Isie right back.—Oh, Dickie, I do trust they'll send her right back. . . ."

" Very odd and irregular of Phipps, going off by himself like that. The things weren't his, and he should at least have shown them to me. Did you see them ? "

" Why, no. I met him coming out of Meg's room with his pockets full of them, and I didn't delay him wanting to look at them. Meg told me what they were like ; they must be real lovely. It seems the child found them a month ago in a hole in the wall of that alcove off her little room. You know, the room's the only one up-stairs that hasn't been altered and enlarged since the monks' time ; I dare say it was the tesorero's own cell, and that's why he hid the treasure there."

" Do you mean that Meg has known of this treasure for over a month and not mentioned it ? Very secretive behaviour."

" Why, Dickie, the child meant no harm ; she kept the things to play with. You know what children are, and how they just love secrets. And she never knew we were looking for them, till Mr. Phipps told her. I surely feel too thankful she did find them to scold her about it. Why, where's the padre gone ? How quickly everyone does go off to-day, to be sure ! "

" He hurried across the patio, with his pockets full, like Mr. Phipps," said Claudia.

" Were they full ? "

" I am afraid they looked so, but I didn't like to ask him what he had found, it seems so suspicious."

" Dear me ! How long was he hunting in the dining-room by himself ? I'm sure I thought someone was seeing after him. I wonder how much he found. Do go and look what's gone, Claudia. No, never mind, I'm sure I don't care."

" It is really rather annoying," said Sir Richmond, " this not being able to trust any of one's neighbours. I must say I thought I could have trusted Phipps to consult me as to what action should be taken, should this so-called treasure be found. He had no business to take matters into his own hands like that. Even in the event of our deciding that any bribe ought to be offered to these ruffians, it would be a question how much. I suppose I must ride over to Phipps's place now and try and catch him before he takes any action."

" I'm afraid you will have to ride rather fast," said Claudia, " I think Mr. Phipps was in a hurry."

" Phipps is a fool," the judge impatiently and angrily commented.

" A fool, papa ? No, I don't think that. Nothing so bad as that. Racah, perhaps."

" Well, well," said Sir Richmond, too vexed to split hairs, and was turning away, when Adrian and Benet came into the hall. They were tired and hot and gloomy after their day's fruitless search, but cheered by the news of the discovered treasure. Mr. Piper, they said, was over at Mr. Phipps's ranch ; he had intended, it seemed to stay there until the Lacandon messenger came back to the village, in order to seize and retain him.

" Quite right," the judge approved. " If Piper is there, he will do the sensible thing about this ransom business. With any skill, the jewellery could be used as a bait to entrap the kidnappers. Phipps is too much inclined to give these criminals what they ask for, without a struggle—a deplorable idea. Piper will manage to outwit them, with any good luck. After all, they are only savages, and likely to be rather simple. I shall ride over there myself at once, before it gets dark.

" I shall go too," said Adrian.

Benet said, " Well, I don't see that it would be any special use my coming. I shall stay here. After all, they may send a message here, I suppose. But if they do I don't believe anyone in the village will keep the messenger for us, in spite of all Piper said to them about it. They seem such apathetic people. No pep."

" Well, I shall go right down to the village," said Belle, " and stay there. I certainly am not going to have messengers from Isie slinking in and out without my seeing them. I shall stop off at Jacinto's as I go by, and get him to watch out, too."

" Wouldn't that be tactless ? " Claudia suggested " He might be showing his family the treasures he found in the villa."

" All the more reason why I should pop in unexpectedly. Jacinto oughtn't to be let keep the things he takes. It's not right ; not for a priest. Such an example in the parish. . . . And then I shall go round the village seeing people. One of you girls might come with me. We could take some soup along."

" Soup ? "

" Yes, that's what's right to take villagers, whatever colour their skins are. I'm sure your mother used often to take soup around the village, Catherine, didn't she ? Though, of course, it's a right awkward thing to carry.

I ought to take some to Jacinto's really ; Amy says there's another baby there."

" Are Indian babies allowed soup ? It oughtn't to have pepper or chili in it, I should think."

" You'd better take some chicha," said Benet, " if you want to get on the right side of the villagers."

" Oh, they've too much of that already. I surely don't want to make them stupider than they are. There are those two riding off to the Phipps ranch. Oh, if only we hear before morning ! Now, which of you girls will come down to the village with me ? Benet, dear, you'd better come too ; we'll maybe need a man."

" To make the babies drink the soup, you mean ? Yes, I expect you will. All right, Belle, I'll come. Shall we have some sandwiches or something first ? Adrian and I have eaten nothing all day but plantains, and I don't suppose you've even eaten those."

" Plantains—no, I've been too busy hunting around for the treasure to eat any plantains. Yes, of course, we'll have sandwiches and coffee. I just begin to feel I can eat again, now we've gotten that ransom safe."

CHAPTER XIII

CALLING ON MR. PHIPPS

I

WHEN the two gentlemen arrived at the Hacienda del Rio, it was already dark. Sir Richmond, who did not care about riding in the forest by night, was annoyed by the swampy, slippery paths, the insect life, and the vampire bats, which repeatedly settled both on him and his horse and sucked their blood. He was vexed with Mr. Phipps for having dashed off by himself with the treasure like that, and was, in fact, in no agreeable mood, and neither was Adrian, when, tired, muddy, and bitten, they were admitted by the old negress into the house.

"Mass' Phipps jess goin' to dine, sah," she told them.

"Dine, is he? Well, that'll be something, after a ride like that. At least we can dine. . . . Apparently Piper is here, too. Isn't that Piper's voice?"

"Mass' Piper jess done look in, sah, to see Mass' Phipps."

"All the better, to find Piper here. Now we can all discuss what is to be done together."

In the dining-room they found Mr. Phipps and Mr. Piper drinking cocktails. Mr. Phipps, standing at the sideboard, looked like an elated cherub; Mr. Piper,

178

bestriding a chair, glass in hand, seemed as gloomy as usual.

"Well, Judge; well, Mr. Rickaby!" cried Mr. Phipps gaily. "That's fine, your coming over. Just in time to join Mr. Piper and me in celebrating the happy event. You'll have a cocktail, Judge, and then we'll dine."

He passed them drinks, and the soothing, heartening, syrupy stuff, with its gay cherries, cheered them up and made them feel kinder.

"You were very quick away, Phipps," said the judge nevertheless, "with that jewellery and so forth. We must think very seriously what is our best plan of action before we do anything hasty."

"Why, Judge," began Mr. Phipps, and Mr. Piper broke his grieved pause with "Mr. Phipps has done something hasty already, Judge. He did it quite at once, before he got home. He'd done it before I met him at the gate."

"Sure," Mr. Phipps agreed, "I met a Lacondon in the forest as I rode over from your place. He'd been waiting around for me, to know if we were going to send what they asked; he said if he didn't get back to-night with enough treasure to satisfy them, they'd surely send us a sign."

"A sign?"

"An ear," Mr. Phipps explained. "That's what the Lacs call a sign. Now I couldn't face the idea of that poor girl's ear—or it might be a finger—coming along to-morrow just because we'd delayed sending the ransom till we'd considered it all round. No, Judge, I could *not* face that. I will admit I'm pretty squeamish when it comes to a woman's ears. I didn't feel I could trifle or dawdle any, so I sent him right off with the goods and they'll send the poor girl back complete by to-morrow night. Was I wrong, Judge? Was I wrong, Mr. Rickaby? "

" Yes," said the judge and Mr. Rickaby. " Completely wrong. Good heavens, man," cried Sir Richmond, " are you crazy? Trusting all that gold to one stray Indian to deliver, and trusting the others, if they ever get it, to keep their word. Why the devil should they? They'll only ask for more. Don't you see, we should have used the treasure as a bait, and trapped them. Why didn't you keep the fellow till we came? We could have got together a party and gone back with him ; we could have captured the lot of them, and rescued the girl ourselves. Don't you realise, man, that you've simply thrown in our hands and handed them the game? "

Mr. Phipps soothed him. " It would have been no use, Judge, to accompany him. He'd never have led us right, he'd have died first. These fellows are as obstinate as the devil. I tell you, our only chance was to keep the conditions the Lacs laid down, and one was that the messengers must come back alone. I tell you, I didn't dare play any tricks with the situation. I may be squeamish, when it's a matter of——"

" Oh, shut it," Adrian rudely stopped him. " The point is, what are we to do now? Is it your idea that we all just sit and wait till to-morrow evening, to see whether she comes back or not? "

" Why, Mr. Rickaby, there's not a thing else we can do. Not a thing, believe me. It'll be all right, you'll see ; before this time to-morrow she'll be with you at the hacienda. That treasure is all they wanted of you, and now they've gotten it. Believe me, my dear sirs, you don't need to worry any longer, you surely don't. These Indians, they're men of their word."

"Nonsense," Sir Richmond said crossly. "Why in the world should they be any such thing? Most improbable. Scarcely anyone is. No, no, Phipps, you've made a very stupid blunder, and put us in a very bad hole, and you'd better face facts. May I ask if you made an inventory of the jewellery, or know in the least what you gave the fellow ? "

"Well, no, Judge, there wasn't exactly time to take inventories. I just handed him the bunch of stuff."

Sir Richmond turned up his eyes to the ceiling and seemed to pray that, in the incalculable mercy of heaven, Mr. Phipps might somehow and at some time find forgiveness.

"All that stuff," he said, when he found words, "that I have been searching for, day and night, for months, handed over, without a word, to a set of damned Red Indians. My *good* sir. I ask you. And I understood that you were a man of business."

"Now, now, Judge. We white men don't get any good of recriminating one another, at a moment like this, when we need to stand together against the savage races. Blame me if you don't get Mrs. Rickaby back by to-morrow night, but don't blame me now. What it is, we've all had a hard twenty-four hours, and we're all a little upset. You'll feel a lot better when we've dined, Judge."

The judge supposed that he would, and was gratified

to see Gladys the negress entering the room with a large tray. The gentlemen, who were all hungry, fell to with appetite, and temporarily forgot their troubles, for Mr. Phipps kept an excellent table.

2

" Well," said Sir Richmond, when they had finished their wine and cigars, " I shall go home now. I am sorry our coming here has been to no purpose, but since the damage is done, it's of no use to stay on. You're coming back with us, Piper, I suppose ? "

" Yes, Judge, presently. But I think, if you're agreeable, we'll first make that little inventory you mentioned."

" An inventory ? How can we ? Mr. Phipps has told us he unfortunately has no idea what he gave to the Indian."

" Indian, hell. Mr. Phipps has a very good idea what he's got in his pockets at this minute. And we're going to get that idea, too, inside of thirty seconds. Put your hands right up, if you please, Mr. Phipps."

Mr. Phipps, looking in embittered surprise at the revolver presented towards his waistcoat, then at Mr. Piper's saturnine and unchanging face above it, mustered a smile as he put up his hands. " Scarcely my notion of an after-dinner joke, Mr. Piper."

" Nor mine, Mr. Phipps. Cover him, please, Mr. Rickaby ; he's as slippery as a snake. Now, Judge, will you turn his pockets out on the table—joolery *and* guns. Guns first."

" Very extraordinary," said Sir Richmond, and laid

down his cigar and approached his host. Half apologetically he plunged a hand into one of the deep pockets of Mr. Phipps's white coat, and drew it out full to the thumb of glittering prizes.

" Good God," he said, and dropped them on the polished mahogany table with a jingling clatter.

" Get the guns, Judge. We can sort out the trinkets later."

Sir Richmond's hand plunged into another pocket, and returned with a small revolver, which he passed back to Mr. Piper, who laid it on the table before him.

" Go on, Judge. All the guns first."

" You keep saying guns, Piper," Sir Richmond complained, " but I really don't think Mr. Phipps has any more guns. Have you, Phipps ? Well, I suppose you don't have to answer that. . . . Yes, you were right, Piper ; here *is* another." He drew it from a trouser pocket and threw it across the table.

" Right," said Mr. Piper. " Now we're ready for the joolery display. Don't miss any pockets, Judge. Billy the Banker should have at least ten."

" That his name ? " Adrian enquired, as the judge fished in their host's pockets and produced therefrom handfuls of bright baubles, as if he were dipping into a bran tub at a Christmas party.

" Yeh," said Mr. Piper. " Least, it's one of them. It's what the boys in Texas used to call him, fifteen years back, when he ran a bank for them to put their money in. Later, he left the place in a hurry, bank and money and all, and became Billy the Bunker instead. It was only to-day I remembered where I'd seen him, though his bun face has been fidgeting me for

months. You wouldn't remember me down at Pinty's
Ranch, in 1912, Billy, would you. Not likely, for we
never spoke, so far's I know."

" I'm afraid I don't follow you, Mr. Piper. My name
is Phipps, and always has been."

" Fancy that, Mr. Phipps. Now, I call that quite
unusual. When I was a boy to Brixton-on-Sea, my
name wasn't Piper, by any means. Still, call yourself
what you please ; it makes no odds. Got the lot,
Judge ? "

" It seems so."

" Then we'll tie him up while we talk business. If
you'll take my place with the gun, Judge, I'll attend
to that. I brought some cord along, thinking we'd
maybe find it useful."

" Listen, Judge." Mr. Phipps turned on Sir Richmond an outraged and reproachful face as Mr. Piper
approached him. " Are you going to stand for this ?
What harm have I done, I'd like someone to inform
me ? Merely practised on you a trifling and harmless
deceit for the time being. I had to tell you I'd parted
with the stuff already, as I knew you'd never let me
send it at all if I didn't, and I was quite resolved to
rescue that poor girl. I was going to send it along to
the Lacandones directly their messenger turned up ;
that's why I kept it on me, all ready. You don't need
to point your gun at me and tie me up as if I was a
bandit myself, you certainly don't need to do that,
Judge."

" That will do." Sir Richmond frowned at the prisoner
as if he were on the bench and Mr. Phipps in the dock.
" It is quite obvious what your intentions were ; you

meant to appropriate all, or the greater part of, these valuables yourself. Whether or not you meant to use any of them for ransom to the Indians is doubtful."

"Ransom hell," said Mr. Piper, tying knots with zest. " I will say this for Billy, he's not such a fool as that. He'd have to give a small reward to whoever's doing his dirty work for him, but he wouldn't go further'n that in the giving line. Turn around, Billy. There you are. You can sit in this chair, if you like."

Corded hand and foot, Mr. Phipps sat resignedly down in his own arm-chair at the head of the table.

" You mean to suggest," said Adrian, " that the whole thing—the kidnapping and the messages and the demand for treasure—was a fake ? "

" I do mean to suggest it. I consider that they certainly were."

" Do you mean," asked Sir Richmond, " that the Indians don't know about this treasure, and never demanded it at all ? "

" I can't find an Indian that seems ever to have heard of it. I've been enquiring around a good bit to-day. If hidden treasure at the hacienda is an Indian tale, it's not one they seem to tell much."

" Then how did Phipps know of it ? "

" That's what he's going to be so good as to tell us. . . . What's that you've got, Judge ? "

Sir Richmond, who was turning over the jewels, was unfolding a piece of paper that lay among them.

" I suppose I turned it out of his pocket with the things. It's—why, it's a list of them : one gold circlet, two gold snake bracelets with jade eyes, one gold and jade necklace, and so forth. . . . So, after all, Phipps, you had time to make that inventory. No, though, by Jove, you didn't. This isn't a new list." He held out the sheet of paper, discoloured and worn, written over with faded ink.

" It's his writing," said Mr. Piper. When did you write it, Billy ? And where'd you copy it from ? It's not a bit of good you sitting there so smug and saying nothing while you invent a good yarn, because no yarn's going to do you any good now, and you'll get off cheapest by spitting out facts. Now, where'd you get that list of joolery from ? "

" I certainly will tell you the truth, gentlemen. I've no reason to be ashamed of the truth. Those jewels are rightly my property. Yes, sirs, they rightly belong to my family. That list you hold in your hand, Judge, I copied from one my mother had, and she got it from her father, and he was left it by *his* father, my great grandfather, and my great grandfather, gentlemen, was a Dominican monk and had been the tesorero of that convent. When the monks left it in 1830, they went to California, and after a time the community was broken up, and there my grandfather was born, of an American mother. His father didn't do a lot for him it seems, but he did, when he was dying, pass him over a list of the goods he'd hidden away in the convent when they left it in a hurry, so as he might get hold of it if ever he was that way. I suppose my great grandfather's mind troubled him about the boy he couldn't care or provide for, and he thought to make it up to him that way. He seems to have been a very decent kind of monk. Those monks, they were grand old fellows, some of them, doing kind acts to the folks round about, even after they'd gotten all scattered and homeless. Anyway, my grandfather kept that list of goods, and had it in his mind, I guess, to go there one day and see if he could get hold of them, but he never could get so far—he was a vine-grower in Imperial Valley, and never made any money. When he died, my parents found the old list among his things, but he hadn't made a note of the hiding-place his father'd told him of, only that it was somewhere in the convent. My father kept the list, and always had it in his head that he might one day get to those parts and look, but he never did, and he didn't really suppose it was likely to have stayed hidden all that time, either. But he and my mother brought me up on that old tale, and how all that gold and precious stones hidden away belonged rightly to our family——"

" A very odd notion for you to have had," the judge interrupted. " It was in no sense the property of your great grandfather."

" Well, he hid it, and saved it from the plundering Indians and Mex soldiery, so in a manner that made it ours in the sight of heaven. Anyway, that's the way we've always looked at it in my family. And I dare say some of it was given to him personally by the Indians ; and anyway the convent's broken up and can't have it. You know, gentlemen, once you come to look close into the ways families have gotten their property, there certainly doesn't seem a lot to be said for any of them, does there. I guess ours was as good as most others."

" But not quite so effective, so far," Adrian said, spitefully.

" Anyway," Mr. Phipps went on, " when I'd made my bit in business in Oshkosh—(no, Mr. Piper, I never was in Texas, so it must be someone else who kept that bank you referred to ; I've been busy in Oshkosh, Wis., the last twenty years)—when I'd made a bit I got a notion of coming to these parts. I'm a sentimental kind of guy, I suppose, and I just had a feeling to see the old convent where my great grandfather had lived a hundred years ago. I tried to buy it, as you know, but Lady Cradock wouldn't sell. So I came down here and took this little hacienda and looked around, with the notion of seeking out the treasure, just for the interest of the thing, if ever I got the chance. You'll ask, Judge, why I didn't mention it to you, and have you look for it."

" Not at all," said Sir Richmond. " It would not occur to me to put such a question."

" I see you appreciate, Judge, that to pass over my secret to others would have robbed my search of its romance, and I will admit I am a romantic man. So I kept it to myself, and waited my chance to search. When that poor young girl was taken away like that it seemed to give me just that chance I wanted. I won't lie to you gentlemen ; I did invent that story of the messenger that had come to me asking for the treasure. What the messenger asked for was money. And to-night I sent a message back that they should have gold and jewels directly they sent the young lady home. I meant to hand them over some of the stuff, when they brought her back. The major part I meant to retain, as I regard it as my property. I may say that my views on the matter are not altered, gentlemen, by your peculiar attitude and behaviour since dinner, which I am willing to overlook on account of your worry and anxiety. And now I must ask you to release me, if you please."

" No use talking big, Billy," Mr. Piper said. " You never were a fool, that I know of, and you know as well as we do that you're up against it."

" You have been guilty," said Sir Richmond insultingly, " of deliberate fraud and theft, of a peculiarly heinous kind. You have traded on the grief and anxiety of an unhappy family for your own ends, and attempted the appropriation of property of value to which you had no claim. It is odious and outrageous conduct, for which you will certainly pay the penalty the law inflicts."

Adrian, who disliked the judge's uncivil habit of moralising to his victims, interrupted.

" The only thing that matters in all this is, is he speaking the truth about the messenger ? Did he really receive or send a message at all, either this morning or to-night ? Or has he made the whole tale up ? Mr. Phipps, I don't want to be inquisitive about your own affairs—that's not my business—but I do want to know the facts about these messages. You see that we must know, in order to take the right steps about my wife's disappearance."

" We must certainly know," said the judge with severity.

" Spit it out, Billy," said Mr. Piper. " We can make you, you know. Though you do seem to have quite forgotten Texas and the boys there, you'll maybe remember that much, if you try. So there's no point in wasting time over it. You framed Mrs. Rickaby's disappearance yourself, didn't you ? "

" Certainly not, Mr. Piper. I would never dream of playing a low-down trick such as that."

" Dream, hell, Mr. Phipps. You played it. She called on you that night, and you thanked the Lord for what he'd kindly dropped into your mouth, and had her taken off somewhere by Indios. You told 'em to keep her till you gave the word; that was it, I guess. Was it ? "

" No, Mr. Piper. It was not. I have told you so."

" Well, Judge, I reckon we've got the rights of it. Now then, Mr. Billy Phipps, have you sent that message to them yet to let the lady go ? "

" I told you before that I had."

" I'm not enquiring what you told us. You've told us the hell of a lot to-night. I'm asking what's the fact. *Have* you sent that message to-night ? "

" I certainly have."

" Where did you send it to ? " Adrian asked.

" I don't know, Mr. Rickaby. The messenger knew where Mrs. Rickaby was ; I do not. But when he reaches her, he surely will bring her back straight away. There's no need for any anxiety on that head, I assure you, gentlemen. She will be with you to-morrow evening."

" In fact, sir, you admit to having played this outrageous trick on a lady, endangered her safety, caused her acute discomfort and fear, and her family deep anxiety, for your own fraudulent ends. It is one of the most abominable things I have ever come across, and I hope you realise it."

" I have played no outrageous trick, Judge. But it certainly is useless for me to repeat that, if you insist on believing Mr. Piper's accusations against me, which are quite unsupported by any evidence whatsoever. I say I was not responsible for Mrs. Rickaby's abduction, and that to say I am is a slander you can't prove. You can believe me or not, but as a British judge, and acquainted with the laws of evidence, you can't assume me guilty without proof."

" Oh, yes, he can," said Adrian.

" The question is," said Mr. Piper, a practical man of action, " what we're to do with the little skunk now. Lock him up somewhere, I presume."

" We must, of course, send to the nearest police headquarters as soon as we can and give him in charge," Sir Richmond said, " for attempted theft and for abduction."

Mr. Piper shook his head.

" I wouldn't do that, Judge. We wouldn't get any good of that. A lot of trouble ; and besides, though I'd like all right to see Billy safe inside a Yank gaol, I don't stand for 'letting these half-breeds shut up a white man in one of their stinking holes. It's a long sight easier to get into them than out, and I wouldn't want even Bunking Billy shut in a Guat gaol for years. No, Judge ; we'll deal with him ourselves, I think. And when we do let him go we'll warn him out of Guat for life. But first he's got to get Mrs. Rickaby back for us. If we don't get her safe, he don't get away safe either."

" Rather informal justice," said the judge, doubtfully. " I agree that the Guatemalan penal system leaves a good deal to be desired ; still—— And when you say ' deal with him ourselves,' Piper, I hope you don't intend to imply any physical violence. That I certainly could not sanction. It would be highly irregular."

" Life in Guat," said Mr. Piper, indifferently, " *is* highly irregular. Anyway, compared to what it is in London, or Brixton-on-Sea. It was a trifle irregular in Texas, too, when I was that way. . . . Say now, Billy, listen. A thing we'd like from you is a little more news from that grandpa of yours. Seeing how he was the convent bursar, he maybe put away some other valuables besides those Indio jewels. Wasn't there some plate and church ornaments ? "

" Gone," said Mr. Phipps, briefly and morosely.

" Gone ? Where were they put ? " Sir Richmond asked, disappointed.

" Why, in the hole in the temple floor, and the panel in the sacristy wall. That's where the monks hid what they couldn't take. Yes, gentlemen. There was gold plate, and silver candlesticks and a large-size silver statue of the Virgin Mary, and gold cups, and golden vestments—I take it they're the clothes the priests wore in church—and I don't know what else. Yes, sirs. My great-grandfather wrote them all down for my grandfather, and I've got the list. But every article is gone. Someone's cleaned up on the lot. I will admit it's natural, after all this time. Maybe Jacinto knows something. I certainly don't trust Jacinto."

" No, no, why should you ? " Sir Richmond agreed. " No one in their senses would do such a thing. But,

of course, these ecclesiastical valuables may have been
plundered immediately after the departure of the
monks, by the Mexican soldiery, or, in fact, at any
time since by anyone."

" It don't matter who," Mr. Piper said. " Point is,
the goods are gone, so that's that. Now, Judge, I
reckon we'd better make ourselves comfortable here
for to-night, and get back to the hacienda directly
it's light, taking this guy along with us. We'll shut
him up in some room where there ain't nothing he
can steal, till we've done with him."

Gladys the negress came in with a tray, to clear the
dinner table. She stared at her master tied up in his
chair, at the three visitors sitting opposite him, and
at the jewels and fire-arms that strewed the table, and
sunnily and toothily grinned.

" You play game, gen'lmen," she told them, and
rocked with mirth. " You tie massa up."

" Quite right," said Mr. Piper. " Nothing escapes
you niggers, does it. Well, Gladys, your master's
kindly invited us to stay to-night, so you might bring
us a few blankets down here. No reason why we
shouldn't all be comfortable."

" I presume you'll allow me to pass the night in
my bed, Mr. Piper ? "

" Bed hell, Mr. Phipps. You'll stay where you are."

" I think," said Sir Richmond, a not unkindly man,
" that we might allow Phipps to lie down on the floor
with a blanket, if he remains tied."

" As you like, Judge. It's up to you. If you want to
pamper the little thief, pamper him. It's all one to
me, so long as he don't give us the slip. But, just the

same, we'll have to mind him ; he's slippery as an
eel. Ain't you, Mr. Phipps ? "

" Why, Mr. Piper, I wouldn't say that. No, I certainly don't think I would say that. In fact, I will
tell you quite frankly that I have no intention of leaving
you until this affair of Mrs. Rickaby is cleared up. I
should take no opportunity of doing so, even should
one present itself, Mr. Piper."

" You needn't worry, Mr. Phipps. It won't."

Sir Richmond was storing the treasure carefully
away in his pockets, after comparing it with Mr.
Phipps' list.

" Whom does it actually belong to, in law ? "
Adrian asked.

" Undoubtedly to the owner of the house in which it
was discovered," the judge replied. " The house,
with all contents, was purchased by Mr. Higgins and
now belongs to Belle. There is no question as to that."

" Why, isn't that nice," said Mr. Phipps, who,
having resigned himself to circumstances, was now
bent on making himself agreeable.

" That'll be enough from you, Billy," said Mr. Piper.
" You talk the hell of a lot too much for a man in your
peculiar position, and that's a fact."

" Why, Mr. Piper, you surely don't need to be so
disagreeable ; we may as well act like gentlemen, even
if I am tied up and the Judge has pouched my
joolery."

" Gentlemen hell, Mr. Phipps. You'd need to be an
even better actor than you are—and I'll allow you act
pretty good—to get away with *that* part."

" Well," said Adrian who was very tired and cross,

and hated wrangling and fuss, " don't let's talk any
more, shall we."

Since the war, he had often thought how nice it
would be to have peace, but he had not yet had it
anywhere, and did not seem at all likely to have it
to-night. He had mislaid peace long ago, and strayed
blindly after it, always taking wrong roads. Possibly
he would have been the better for one of those pamphlets
that religious people leave in trains, called ' Have you
found peace ? ' which, I suppose, explain inside how,
if you have not, you can do so. But, of course, it is of
no use even to look for peace so long as your wife is
in the hands of Red Indians who may or may not be
bringing her back complete or sending her back in
parts. It was all oppressive and dreadful, and Adrian
felt that blank, sullen rage and despair that often
assailed him for far less cause than this.

3

In the morning Gladys came into the dining-room,
beamed with surprise and pleasure that the game with
her master was, apparently, still progressing, and
brought a message which someone from the village
had given her when she had gone out into the garden
to pick some fruit for breakfast. The message was that,
unfortunately, the Indians who had taken away the
lady could not return her as ordered, for she had run
away from them the night before last, during the
earthquake, and had not been seen since.

" Why now," cried Mr. Phipps, pale and tousled

after his uncomfortable night, and turning paler still as he met Mr. Piper's eye, "why now, if that isn't unlucky! Why, gentlemen, I wouldn't have had a thing like that occur for the world. No, Judge, no, Mr. Rickaby, I surely would *not*."

"God," said Adrian thickly, and sprawled over the table, his head on his arms, like a last night's drunkard who is about to be sick.

CHAPTER XIV

FINDING ISIE

I

THE day was spent in searching the forest, with the help of the peons of several villages, for it quickly got about that a reward was offered for the finding of the gringo señorita, and volunteers rolled up from miles round. Mr. Phipps, promised his freedom if the young lady should be found alive and unhurt, rode a horse tied to Mr. Piper's bridle rein, and was active in urging his mozos on. They found the wreckage of the palm hut where the Indians had rested with their captive two nights ago, but they did not know this, for the storm had obliterated all traces and tracks.

North of this place, the forest was so wild, trackless, and dense that no one thought it likely that a young lady could have pushed through it. So they did not follow her into it, and never, therefore, set eyes on that elegant temple in the heart of the jungle which had been her sanctuary, and which Sir Richmond, anyhow, would have found such solace in beholding.

When darkness suddenly submerged the forest, Mr. Phipps, who now felt that Isie had certainly been murdered or devoured by wild beasts or had died of something, and that his position, in this event, would be very sad, took advantage of Mr. Piper's being occupied in searching a tangle of bush on foot to hurry away with both horses towards his own home. When Mr. Piper, hearing scampering, hastily struggled out from the bush, Mr. Phipps and the horses were out of sight, and there was no rider at hand to pursue them. Mr. Piper swore, for here he was stranded on foot in the forest ten miles from home with night coming on, and Billy the Bunker had bunked once more, and would, Mr. Piper felt sure, have collected his belongings and fled over the Mexican border before he could be stopped.

Mr. Piper and the two peons with him made their way on foot to Mr. Phipps's hacienda, reaching it after three hours. At first they thought the house was dark, empty, and deserted, but as they stood in the garden they saw lights moving and heard voices, and the two peons observed, not without envy, that some of their fellow countrymen were engaged in appropriating such of Mr. Phipps's abandoned belongings as they fancied.

Mr. Piper hammered on the door, and Gladys shuffled up and opened it and peered out, smiling, her mouth full of supper.

" Mass' Phipps done gone away, sah. He not coming back."

" Well, I know that. So you and your friends are clearing up his leavings, are you ? "

" Yes, sah. Mass' Phipps, he take what he want with him."

" Took a lot, did he ? "

" Sho, sah. Mass' Phipps take two big bundles on his other horse, sah."

" His other horse—hell. He took my horse along, did he ? Any horses left here ? "

" No, sah."

" Well, I'm coming in here for the night, Gladys. Maybe I might fancy some of Mr. Phipps's things myself."

" Mass' Phipps ain't done left much, sah. He done take all the little things he bring home when he go over to Cradock hacienda, sah."

" The hell he did. Did he often bring home little things from the Cradock hacienda ? "

" Oh, yes, sah. He always bring some little thing that Mass' Cradock done give him. Very pretty things, sah. He took them all away this evening."

" He would. Well, bring me something to eat, Gladys. I shall sleep here to-night."

Mr. Piper was tired and discouraged, and abominably bitten by insects. As he sat in the ravaged dining-room, waiting for food, hearing the exclaimings, quarrellings, and jubilations of Gladys's peon friends, now joined by his own two, as they scuffled about the house, his thoughts were of Mr. Phipps, who had circumvented him, but whom he thought he might yet, with sufficient ingenuity, in the end circumvent. He forgot, in the ardent interest of his thought, Mrs. Rickaby : that poor young foolish creature seemed to him to be for ever lost.

2

While Mr. Piper thus mused in the abandoned house of Mr. Phipps, a large party of kind and rapacious chicle-gatherers were delivering Isie at the Villa Maya, remarking that they had found her in the wood, that she had been having jungle fever for a night and a day, that with great assiduity and care their female friends had nursed her, feeding her lavishly with invalid foods, and they had now lost a day's work in order to conduct her to her home. A day's work among the chicle trees is a costly thing, they said, and they trusted that Lady Cradock would not forget this.

Isie, sallow and hollow-eyed, submitting passively to her mother's embraces, said, " They've been very good to me ; give them a lot of money and send them away. They scared me to death, looking so and talking so, and crowding around. Oh, dear, I certainly did think I'd gotten into hell, when first I saw them. But they were good to me."

So Lady Cradock (the judge being still out) poured money into the chicleros' hands, and sent them to the kitchen for refreshment. It struck her that a rather large number of chicleros seemed to have been considered necessary to convey one young woman through the forest, and that they would make rather a crowd in the kitchen. She spared from her joy over her restored child a fleeting hope that the servants would keep their eyes on the guests and not leave them alone with the silver. Then she dismissed them from her mind and took Isie up to bed, twittering unceasingly over her and not pausing for reply.

" Why, honey, you certainly are sick ; your hands are hot and dry, and you're shivering like a leaf. What you've been through, lovey, the Lord knows ! And that Mr. Phipps, it was he had you taken off by

Indians; can you beat it? He seemed such a kind amiable man, and all the time he was laying schemes to rob us, and at last he thought of this dreadful plan. Yes, you shall hear all about it to-morrow, when you're better. And you shall tell us all about your adventures to-morrow, but to-night we won't say a single word ; you shall drink off this nice hot milk and go right to sleep, and when Adrian comes in, I shall tell him he isn't going to see you till to-morrow."

" No milk, mother. You know I hate it."

" Well then, pet, you must take your quinine in water. . . . Now, what for goodness' sake made you rush off that way and scare us all to death? Poor Adrian—he's been looking as sick as a ghost, I've been quite frightened for him."

Maternally, Belle placed this picture in her child's mind as she had been used to pop a sweet into her mouth to go to sleep with, ten years since.

Then he did mind, he did, Isie feverishly thought, and this agreeable consolation exalted her nightmare-ridden soul, joining with the exquisite happiness of lying safely in a soft bed at home and not in a forest temple or a chicle-camp hammock, to make her forget that she was a mass of insect bites, scratches, bruises and fever, and to conduct her into a deep and stupefied sleep.

3

Sir Richmond, Adrian, Claudia and Benet came in, dejected after a day's fruitless searching, while Belle was putting her daughter to bed, and Julia informed them of the news.

" It seemed to be practically a whole chicle camp that brought her back," Julia said. " That is what you hear in the kitchen."

" Dear me," said Sir Richmond, hearing them. " I think they might perhaps go back to their work now. They work by night as well as day, these chicleros, and it would be a pity if they were to lose more time. . . . Well, this is certainly a great relief ; a very great relief indeed. I am very glad."

He sat down in the hall, tired out with all the riding about and searching, and looking for treasure, and unmasking Mr. Phipps, that he had been doing continuously for the past two days and nights, and that was really quite too hard work for a judge of nearly sixty.

" Poor child," he added. " She must have had a terrible time. I hope it will be a lesson to her—and a lesson to all you girls—not to go too far into the forest alone."

" And not only the girls," Benet added. " It's been a lesson to me not to go far into the forest, alone or not. I definitely now dislike the forest ; in future I shall stop about the grounds, then no one will be anxious about me. By the way, Piper was wrong about those chicle men. He said they wouldn't be nice for Isie to meet, but it seems they were. People seem nearly always to be wrong about what other people are like."

Adrian went upstairs to his room. He did not go to see Isie, but dropped onto his bed and lay there, exhausted. He had scarcely ever been more tired, even in France during the war. His mind, as well as

his body, seemed emptied of all power, and all emotion.
Fear and anger and grief, that had chased one another
horribly across his brain for forty-eight hours, stood
back now, exhausted, and left him cold and dead.
Isie was safe ; he had not driven her out to her death ;
that was all of thought or feeling that survived in him
now that the strain was relaxed. The shocking incident
was closed. He had no desire to see Isie, the persistent
storm-maker ; he desired only quiet. It seemed that
between him and Isie no quiet could be ; they needed
a shock-proof screen between them, to deaden the
assaults of each on the other's strained nerves. A
neurotic tied to a neurotic ; what disaster for both !

4

Later, the night was full of the revelry of the
gatherers of chicle, who, politely taking their leave
after supper, reeled off into the forest, pausing on their
way back to work to appropriate a few of the fowls
from the poultry run of the absent Mr. Piper.

CHAPTER XV

SOOTHING ISIE

I

Isie lay in an exquisite and radiant peace. Her temperature was normal ; the lovely morning flowed in upon her as she woke in her own soft, beautiful bed, the double bed with its four slender posts and blue damask canopy, and the pillow for Adrian on its right-hand side. Now that he had so all but lost her, Adrian might occupy that pillow more often, she thought.

A golden oriole fluted very sweetly just outside the window, and reminded her of that strange happiness and hope with which the oriole's song had pierced her sad heart as she lay in the jungle temple in the dawn. The oriole had been right ; she had got safely home, and now he was without doubt promising her further happiness and love.

In spite of the nightmare memories of fear that still besieged her brain, she was triumphant and glad ; her stroke had cut the tangle in which her life had seemed snarled, and cleared her path to happiness. It had—it must have—shown Adrian what he had been doing to her, how he had almost lost her, and how he would utterly lose her unless he took heed ; and the shock of that would have cleared his eyes of their blindness and his mind of the dark unlove that had obsessed it of late like a disease, rolling, an evil miasma, between herself and him. He, who had forgotten how he loved her, how he had caressed and worshipped her loveliness, how he had smiled on her caprices tenderly, as on a pretty child's, would remember it all again now that fear had so shocked him, and the evil dream of unlove would be over. It had been like dying ; she had had the pathetic advantages of sudden dying, without its great and everlasting drawback. She had, in fact, established herself again in her lover's heart.

This gratification combined with the physical pleasure of returning strength to make her smile delightfully at her various visitors ; first her mother, then Amy bringing a tray with chocolate, then her stepfather, who said that he was not going to ask for any account of her adventures until she was quite strong, but that he hoped she would presently be able to enlighten them. She told him about the temple, and now, with his mind full of ease and joy concerning the treasure that had rewarded his long and single-minded industry, he was able to feel that he would much like to see it, and all the other buildings that must be scattered about the thousands of miles of jungle, and that had hitherto seemed to him of such minor importance.

" But I'm afraid you may find it difficult to find it again," he said.

" Oh, I hope I never will," she agreed.

2

Adrian came in. Her heart seemed to swell and choke her. He looked pale and tired. He bent over the bed and kissed her. She clung tightly to him, till he gently released himself and sat down in a chair by the bedside, enquiring after her health.

" Oh, I'm all right now. I'm fine. I'll be quite fit in a day or two."

" You must have had a hellish time."

" It was pretty bloody. Did you worry after me, darling ? "

" Well, of course. What do you suppose ? "

" I'm sorry, sweetie. Are you mad with me for going off like that ? I expect you are. Do you forgive me ? Kiss Leopard and say you forgive her."

" Forgive . . . that's nonsense ; that doesn't apply. I'm only sorry you had such a frightful time, and thankful you're safe back."

He seemed a mile away, his tired voice coming gently from across a chasm of mist.

" Adrian, I couldn't help going away. I was so miserable, I just had to."

" I'm sorry." Nervously he seemed to be fending that misery off. " But it wasn't your fault that you got taken by Phipps's paid kidnappers. You couldn't help it."

" No, not that. But it was my fault I went. I didn't mean to come back, you know. I was so miserable, I didn't care what happened to me."

Her voice was shaking. It had that little ominous break that she knew frightened and annoyed him, and yet that she could never control. From childhood the barrier between herself and the ocean of tears had been frailer than that which preserves most female creatures,

and at any strain it broke and precipitated her into
those sad seas. It was a physical and nervous weakness
that she could no more control than sneezing when she
had a cold. She knew that when she cried Adrian hated
her, and she was not surprised, for anything more dis-
gusting than a weeping adult she herself found it hard
to imagine, but still when he hurt her she must weep,
unprotected and lost. Did Claudia ever weep ? No ;
she would never suffer that misfortune ; and so Adrian
was never frightened of her ; he could trust her to be
composed and calm. If he should say to Claudia those
unfair things, those rough, angry, lacerating things
that struck on her own heart like blows, Claudia would
smile it off, seem indifferent, change the subject, or
merely leave him until the weather was smooth again.
Claudia understood him, and what the war had done
to him. Claudia was older, and had poise and ease and
a harder shell. Isie, having known through her brief
years nothing but pampering, had come to her war-
shocked husband as a lamb to the slaughter.

He winced now from the quivering voice.

" You mustn't be miserable," he said, gentle and
kind.

" I couldn't help it, Adrian. . . . I told you, in my
note. . . . Did you read my note ? "

" Yes. I read it and tore it up. We won't speak
about it, or think of it again."

He was burying the note from sight, as the lapse
from sense and good taste that it had undoubtedly
been. In his view he was giving her and himself a
chance to recover and go ahead without a noise of
breaking ; in hers, he was dragging them both blind-

fold past the opening she had made for understanding and she pulled him up with a jerk.

"But, Adrian, I meant it. It was true. You *were* stopping loving me, and I couldn't bear it. . . ."

The interview was turning out all wrong. The contrast between the remorse and love that she had hoped for and expected and the tired aloofness that she met, suddenly stabbed her sharply and drew tears. She turned her head from him and silently wept.

He pushed his chair sharply back and got up.

"It's no use my staying if you cry. It's bad for you. Why must you drag up these things again and again ? I've told you before, I'm sorry for everything ; sorry I can't make you happier, or feel all you want me to feel, and sorry for all the times I've hurt you. I've told you I've a cursed temper, and we're not good for each other, we're both much too nervy. But for God's sake let's get on as best we can, unless or until we decide to end it all. At any rate, I can't see what we gain by writing notes, or running away, or having scenes. . . . And now I've hurt you again, and I'm sorry. Of course you won't believe me if I say I do my best ; perhaps it's not true, either, but, in heaven's name, what *am* I to do ? If only we could get on quietly. . . . Oh, my God, stop that crying."

"I c-can't. I'm *trying* to. Christ ! I don't *want* to cry. You think I cry on purpose, but I don't. It's hellish, crying."

He became gentle, with an effort suppressing his own rising hysteria. He bent over her and touched her dark, averted head with his hand.

"Look here, dear. You really mustn't go on like

this. It'll make you worse. You must keep quiet.
We both must. . . . Now we won't talk any more ;
we'll just forget everything, and go ahead and try to
do our best. Shall we ? I'm sorry I ever got you into
this mess, but still, here we are, and I'll try and not
make it worse than I need, if you will too."

But that was no way to talk to one who desired only
to hear " Darling, how nearly I lost you ! It has taught
me that I love only you after all ! " Isie stuffed the
sheet into her mouth ; she was afraid of screaming.

" Go away," she sobbed. " Oh, I wish I'd never
come back. I wish to hell I'd died in that damned
jungle. Go away to Claudia. It's her you love, not
me."

To Claudia. To peace, to civilisation, to comprehen-
sion, to quiet. To that white, clear face, that sweet,
dragging, ironic voice which he had loved through the
long, turbulent years, which were twined about the
deep roots of his soul. Go away to Claudia, his friend,
from this stormy, sobbing, nerve-racked, nerve-racking
child, to whom neither he nor life would ever bring
content, this crude, beautiful, vehement feminine thing
who for ever needed scenes and whirlwinds, who
rasped his every nerve and made him cruel—that
seemed such good advice that he had to bite down
a cry of " By God, that's the truth. I will."

Having bitten it down, he said, stiffly and unnatur-
ally, " Need we discuss that again now ? " fighting so
hard for restraint that he did not know how his words
struck her like a whip and broke the last link that was
binding her to sanity. He only saw how she flung back
the sheet and sprang from bed and rushed to the door

and tore it open, and ran out into the corridor, sobbing,
" Mother, mother, mother ! " like a desperate child.

When he got to her she was in Belle's arms.

" Why, honey, why, baby. . . . Why Adrian, for the
Lord's sake, what have you been saying to her ? Why,
lovey, you don't need to take on like that ; mother's
gotten you all safe, and you're coming right back to
bed. Why, the idea ! Crying like that, when you're
safe and sound at home after all your trapesing. . . .
Whatever is the matter with her, Adrian ? Couldn't
you have kept her quiet just for that little you were
with her ? "

Keeping Isie quiet ; that had been one of Belle's
tasks for twenty years. She did not consider that
Adrian was doing his share of it. She took her child
back to bed, shook and smoothed her crumpled pillow,
tucked the sheet about her, gave her a drink of lemonade, and sat down at her side. Really, men were too
clumsy to be allowed in a girl's bedroom (except, of
course, when the girl was well). Belle's strong partiality
for Adrian had long been assailed by maternal dis-
pleasure. He wasn't making Isie happy ; he was
treating her badly. Isie needed gentleness and spoiling ;
Adrian seemed always to be snapping at her, hurting
her, making her cry. Besides, anyone could see that
Isie was jealous of his affection for Claudia, and, that
being so, he ought to modify his affection for Claudia.
Belle had herself thought lately that this affection,
however long-standing, seemly, and respectable, was a
little aggravating, a little much. She had sometimes
thought of giving Claudia a hint, or of getting Julia
to give Claudia a hint. But giving Claudia hints was

an enterprise that one did not approach with confidence.
. . . And, in any case, the symptoms of over-great
affection were not shown by Claudia, but by Adrian.

Meanwhile, Isie was on the edge of hysterics, and
had to be soothed. To her cries of " He hates me, he's
cruel, I wish I was dead," Belle returned, " Why,
honey, he just dotes on you. Of course he does. He's
crazy about you. Why, pet, you mustn't cry like that.
Whatever will Adrian think you look like, with your
eyes all swollen up ! Now you lie quite quiet, and I'll
read you out of a nice book, and Amy will bring you
some broth."

For twenty agitated years she had been thus soothing
her distracted child. To her consolations Isie presently,
between hiccupping sobs, gave a response which she
had not, in all the twenty years, given before.

" I think I'm going to have a baby," she said.

3

Adrian went downstairs, and out into the patio
among the placid statues. The tears and cries of his
wife were strident in his ears, like the shrieking of the
blue jays in the trees.

" God ! " he muttered—" I could scream myself."

He felt drawn tight, like a wire, as he had felt all
those years ago in France, when shells were screaming
round him. He was as bad as Isie, he supposed ; as
hysterical, as nervy, and worse-tempered. There was
only one person who could loosen and relax his brittle
tautness, cool the fever of his temper. He wandered

about looking for her, as, in these days, he was always half consciously looking for her. He found her in the grotto, with Catherine, and perceived with annoyance that she read a book about the architecture of Yucatan. He sat down at her side, in the cool green shadow of the trickling rocks.

Catherine, who was (good guest, as always) writing letters, asked how Isie was this morning.

" Not up to much yet," he answered. " The fever's gone, but she's rather over-wrought."

" She must be. I should think so ; poor Isie. I wonder if I might go and see her now."

" Well—Belle's with her, and I shouldn't think she'd better see people any more this morning, perhaps."

He said it reluctantly, for certainly Catherine had better leave the grotto, but still, he did not want her to go and talk to Isie at present, and hear her lamentations. Rows were damnable enough, but, at least, let them keep as long as possible a decent secrecy.

" All right," said Catherine. " I'll wait, then. I'll go and see what Meg is doing instead."

For go she must, being the soul of tact, when lovers sat together in the grotto and she made the third.

" If only," said Claudia, looking at pictures of rich sculpture, " if only I had an aunt in Yucatan . . ."

" Who bought a python from a man," Catherine, who could be relied on to continue quotations, added as she left the grotto.

" I would propose myself for a visit. As it is, I shall have to stay in inns, if Yucatan has inns."

" How do you propose to get there ? " Adrian asked, roughly. " You know quite well you can't."

Claudia's eyebrows went up. " My dear, why not ?
By sea from Livingstone, of course. Do you think
Catherine would come too, or would that bore me
rather ? I own I'd rather take Benet or Julia. Only
neither of them enjoy roughing it, and one knows that
Yucatan is rough. Papa might come, now he's got
all the treasure he can hope for out of the villa. He
might find some more Dominican priories in Yucatan,
with more hidden treasure."

" Or Belle might go," said Adrian bitterly, " or Meg,
or Piper, or Amy, or, in fact, anyone in the house but
me."

" Well, obviously *you* can't. That wouldn't be
proper."

" Look here, Claudia. Don't go on like that. I'm
through. I'm sick to death of it. I can't stick it any
more. We've got to get away together. For God's
sake let's get back to Europe and leave all the fuss
behind. I loathe this morbid forest ; it's as unwhole-
some as hell. Let's go to Spain, then Venice, then
Vienna and Prague. The very smell of all these trees
makes me see yellow. I mean, all this vegetation . . .
it's obscene . . ."

" Well, of course it is. Vegetation shouldn't be in
enormous masses. It's like salad. And it grows over
the buildings and smothers them. It's certainly
obscene."

" Foetid. Unhealthy. *Lush.*"

" Yes," said Claudia. " We've said so. Still, there
it is. We can't stop it."

" We can leave it. You and I must go away. To
Europe."

" I shall go to Europe. Or Yucatan. Not with you.
I keep telling you that."

" Look here. I can't stand it any more. And Isie
can't stand it any more. I make her wretched. She
makes me wretched. Well, there you are. The only
thing is to end it. We'd much better do it at once,
and save trouble all round."

" Isie doesn't want to end it."

" She doesn't know what she wants ; she's no sense.
She knows I make her miserable. She'd be much
happier if she were free of me. Look at the way she
ran off into the forest. I don't make her happy, and
she can't make me happy, and we shall never mend
that ; I'm damnably sorry for her, being married to
me, and damnably sorry for myself. We make each
other furious half the time ; we've both rotten
tempers and no self-control to speak of. When she
goes off the deep end, I could be sick. When *I* go off,
she has hysterics. When I suggested to her just now
that we should try and rub along together as well as
we could, she screamed for her mother and ran out of
the room. That's a nice marriage, isn't it. We should
never have married ; we both need someone *peaceful*.
. . . She says I bully her, and tell lies."

" So you do. When you get excited and angry you
do tell lies."

" Perhaps. . . . I don't when I talk to you."

" Oh, yes, sometimes. Not much, because you don't
so often get angry with me. And anyhow, it doesn't
bother me particularly ; I just wait till you're calm
and accurate again. Isie's more particular than I am.;
she's an idealist. I'm old enough to take people as they

are, I suppose. And you're so much nicer than I am,
anyhow."

" Oh—no one's nice. What does it matter ? There
are people who need each other, and people who don't,
that's all. You and I do. You know we do."

" We certainly do seem to love each other," Claudia
admitted. " It's all most unfortunate. As to need,
that's a word I don't understand. It's surely a relative
verb, and wants completion. Need each other for
what ? For happiness, I suppose. Well, so we do, at
present, or at any rate, so we think. Once you thought
you needed Isie ; and as for me, I've supposed myself
at one time or another to need at least three people
besides you. This needing—it's not a final, absolute
thing, like the way we need food in order to keep living.
It's a thing one can control, and deal with."

" Why *should* we control it ?   When everyone all
round will benefit by our not controlling it ? All this
damned repression. Life seems to consist of nothing
else. Can't we be ourselves, for a change ? Why must
you talk like a prig ? "

" While you talk like a text-book on psychology.
Repression—well, of course repression *is* damned ; it
must be ; one has read so. But—just think of it—
suppose there was no damned repression among human
creatures—life would be as lush and as obscene and as
murderous as the forest. Repression is damned, but
unrepression is more damned. Of course as we know,
human life in general is, on the whole, damned."

" Well," said Adrian sulkily, " I think we talk too
much about it. I'm not interested in human life.
Except that I think every one ought to get through it

in the most decent and civilised and bearable way he can. And when two people have got tied together by mistake, and drag one another day in day out through a bog of unnecessary, unintelligent, meaningless emotion and anger—well, it becomes simply silly. I tell you, I can't work, I can't think ; I do nothing but feel, in a kind of irrational, stupid chaos. You've never been married ; you don't know its *continualness*. It never lets up. There's no *sense* in such a relationship as ours has become. No hope, either, because it rises out of the way we're both made. We ought to end it, if only out of pity for each other and ourselves."

" Probably you ought, when you can both agree to. The sooner the better, I should say. But till you are agreed on it, I don't see that you can leave a sobbing young woman in the lurch. It would *look* so extremely bad, for one thing. What would Belle and papa say ? "

" I know all that. You don't suppose I haven't thought about that. But these things have to be done somehow, after all. One of the two has to make the break. Isie'll be glad very soon. After all, it's not as if she were older. To be set free at twenty, when her life's still beginning—it gives her every chance in the world to find the right man. She'll be luckier next time. I hope so, anyhow."

" I hope so, too. Though one doesn't feel that Isie will ever be very lucky. . . . Anyhow, there it is. I've never yet taken a husband from a wife who wants him, and I don't feel I could carry off the position gracefully. Give Isie a chance to get so sick of you that she wants you to leave her. When she gets back to civilisation, she'll probably meet someone she prefers

to you. Then you and she will be quits, and can come
to an arrangement by which no hearts are broken.
It's only a question of time and patience. Meanwhile,
I shall go——"

" Oh, to Yucatan. Yucatan hell, as Piper would say.
Where you go, I shall go ; that's clear, whether it's to
Yucatan or Europe or Chicago."

" Darling Adrian, one might as well waste words on
a goldfish. You apparently haven't even been listening,
all this time I've been talking. I do wish you would
be less abstracted, and sunk in your own reflections.
Do I have to say it all again, my piece about not
running away with you ? But I can't say it just now,
because here is Belle."

Belle was hurrying across the garden to them,
excited and hot, with Catherine in tow. She entered
the grotto, looked at them both with the triumph of a
player who plays a trump card, and said, " Why,
Adrian, what do you think now ? Isie says you're
going to have a baby ! Isn't *that* a surprise ? "

" Why ? " Adrian asked, very reasonably, though he
turned red, and anyone could see that he was vexed.

Claudia remained pale, and no one could have
guessed that she was vexed.

" Belle," she said, " you are like the London newspapers—' Baby Surprise Bomb Shell.' That Adrian
and Isie are to be parents seems to me to be all
that there is of the most natural."

" Of course it's natural," Belle sat down, and fanned
herself, erect and jubilant. She was like a mother hen
with her feathers on end. " Nature's way ; that's
what it is. Just the same, it doesn't seem to happen

so much as it ought, these days, and I'm real pleased. So'll Isie be, when she's feeling less sick. Adrian, you shouldn't have upset her the way you did just now. Whatever made you ? What did you say to her ? "

" Nothing whatever. I merely tried to keep her quiet."

" Well, you didn't succeed. No, you certainly did not succeed in doing any such thing."

" Did you ? " Adrian gloomily asked.

" Well—I will admit she's still quite a bit worked up, but no wonder, with all she's been through, and then this baby coming on the top."

" Surely not . . ."

" Oh, not yet, of course : don't be silly, Adrian. Why, you need to give babies time. But she got thinking about it, and of course it fussed her. Now listen, Adrian. She must be kept soothed from now till that baby's right here. Yes, I don't say it's easy, keeping Isie soothed, poor lamb, but we all must try and do it."

The picture of Isie, her taut nerves tautened by that extra turn of the winch that coming infants give, her temperamental hysteria reinforced by the physical hysteria of the expectant mother, painted itself sharply on two imaginations. The expectant father's disturbed and brooding face might have suggested that he was one of those fathers who suffer from couvade.

To be a father. There perhaps has been too little thought and written by the world about this state ; (Walt Whitman believed so) ; perhaps, on the contrary, there has been enough. Fathers, of course, are less frequent than mothers ; they are often, on the other

hand, more prolific. Their importance in the joint
enterprise is equal, their responsibility for it usually
greater, their retribution considerably less. Yes :
fathers on the whole deserve more attention than they
have received.

These were Claudia's reflections, as she gently
looked at Adrian's downbent face. Poor Adrian, to
be in the family way when he had so little expected
it. Poor Isie ; to be carrying the child of a husband
who wanted neither the child nor her. Poor child, to
be born of quarrelling, nerve-sick parents into a home
of strife. And poor Claudia, to be obliged to go to
Yucatan all alone but for Catherine, Benet, Julia, Meg,
Mr. Piper, and Amy the negress. For it is apparent
that, even if one can go travelling away to Europe and
Yucatan with the husband of a lamenting wife (and
Claudia did not see that one could) one cannot well
travel as far as either with the father of the lamenting
wife's infant.

" We had better all go back to Europe," said Adrian
gloomily, " before it's too late."

" It won't," said Belle, " be a bit too late at the
end of March, the date we'd fixed to leave. It can't
happen before August. But Isie swears she's sick to
death of Guatemala, the forest scared her so she won't
be happy staying around it any more, and she's just
crazy to travel about and see something new and get
it right out of her head. She wants you to take her
some place, Adrian, right now. Take her travelling
about, and distract her mind ; that's what I'd say you
should do. Keep her happy, and nature will see to the
rest. I don't care how you do it, but it's certainly a

fact that we must have Isie's mind distracted between this and the summer. Now Adrian, don't look so downcast ; the girl will be all right if we look after her well. I certainly think this baby will do her good, she always was crazy about anything new. You go right up to her now, and tell her how tickled you are. I shall go and find Dickie and tell him he's to be a grandpa. Oh, he's with Piper, is he. Well, it maybe is early for telling Piper, particularly as he's not a married man—at least, not so far as he's ever mentioned, but then I always call Piper so reserved."

" Well," Claudia suggested, " we might tell Father Jacinto instead."

Bent on telling someone, Belle hurried away.

" If Isie really wants to travel," said Adrian to Claudia and Catherine, " we'd better make up a party. It will be more cheerful for her than being alone with me. We had better all go somewhere together."

" That would be very nice," said Claudia, " but I have to get back to Europe. The rest of you can go. Catherine will, I'm sure ; and as for Benet and Julia, they will always go anywhere, provided they can get hold of the fare."

Adrian did not speak. Catherine felt embarassed, not knowing whether to go or stay. While she hesitated, Adrian got up himself and went away, without a word or look.

" Ought we really, do you think, to make up a party to travel ? " Catherine asked Claudia, doubtfully.

Claudia, looking negligent, was eating a guava.

" Certainly you ought," she replied. " It's your duty, Catherine. Isie needs soothing. To be alone with

Adrian wouldn't soothe anyone. Belle says she needs distracting, too, but she seems to me quite distracted enough already. You are a very soothing person, Catherine, and you must certainly travel with them, wherever they go. So must Benet and Julia. I am not soothing to Isie, so I shall go off by myself. Besides, I'm tired of the Americas ; I want Europe. Let's come and talk to the others about it at once."

5

Benet and Julia were together, examining the jewellery which their father had locked in a drawer of a cabinet. He had left the key in the most secret recess of the escritoire, so that his children had readily been able to find it.

"Oh, here's Claudia," said Benet. "The question is, Claudia, (a) how we shall all divide the booty between us, and (b) whether we shall dispose of it for cash out here, or take it home. Julia and I think we ought all to choose the things round, turn by turn. There are one or two I should like to have very much, but I see very little chance of my getting them, as I don't come high up in order of age. I think the family all have equal rights in them, anyhow, don't you ? And certainly Piper ought to have the most, as he got them for us from Phipps. I suppose Meg thinks she ought to have more than the rest of us, as she found them, but she doesn't really deserve any, as she was a selfish little swine and kept them to herself."

"And meanwhile," said Julia, "papa says they are

all Belle's, as Mr. Higgins bought them with the house and left them to her. So it's not the least good our making plans about them, and fancying this or that for ourselves. Claudia, you would look very well in this jade necklace, and so should I, but papa means neither of us to have it. Nor Isie either. He will keep them all together and show them to people as a priceless collection of Maya jewellery."

" He will be quite right," Benet said.

" Listen, children," said Claudia, " a plan has been made for you. You are to go on a pleasure tour with Adrian and Isie, who are to have a baby in the summer, and so must be distracted and soothed. I myself shall return to Europe and Civilisation."

A baby! thought Julia. How discouraging for Claudia.

" A baby," said Benet, " well, they will come. . . . Where do you think of looking for civilisation, my dear ? And what kind ? "

" Oh, wealth and fashion and wit. All the things that the poor Maya lack. Where, I don't know quite. Neither do I know where the soothing and distracting tour means to go. Possibly Yucatan."

" I thought," said Catherine, " that it was you who meant to go to Yucatan."

" Oh, I've given that up. The civilisation there lacks life ; it perished nearly as long ago as the civilisation round here. And the landscape is still more barbarous, they say. I feel now that cities call me. I should like to get off with a president, or a prince, or an ambassador, or a film or pork king."

" The place you seem to require, in that case, would

be Washington, Rome, Palm Beach, Chicago, or Beverley Hills. We had better all try and get some money out of Belle for our expenses. Isie's being about to have this baby will make her so happy that she will give us anything, even more than usual."

"It seems rather sad, though," said Catherine, "to be leaving Guatemala and the hacienda. I don't feel I've got to know the Guatemalans yet. I would like to know the Indians better. They are so small and gentle and dignified and attractive. I feel they must be nicer than the Mexican Indians."

"Well," said Julia, "we needn't know the Mexican Indians. I hope we shan't linger in Mexico. D. H. Lawrence says that's a pity and only leads to depression and lethargy, if not worse. Is Adrian thinking of Mexico?"

"I doubt if Adrian is thinking of anywhere."

"If we knew where Mr. Phipps had gone to," Benet mused, "we'd go after him and recover papa's gold watch, my snuff-box, Claudia's jade necklace, and the other trifles he has with him. However, I feel Phipps is too clever to allow himself to be caught up with, though Piper says he means to catch him in the end. As for our expenses, we might all give lectures en route if we can't raise enough money from Belle. Americans listen to lectures, don't they?"

"Do Mexicans?" Catherine asked.

"Oh, I dare say. Oh, yes, I believe they listen to anything."

"But will they pay? Anyone can listen, of course."

"Oh, I expect they'll pay according to their means and the Latin temperament. Centavos, you know.

Well, I mean, we must make some money somehow to get about on, or we can't get about."

6

Catherine thought, perhaps if we travel together, I shall get to know them at last, for so far I have been all wrong, and they have turned out different to what I thought. How is one to know what people are like ? I wonder what Julia would say. Perhaps one can never know ; perhaps people are uncapturable, and slip away like water from one's hand, changing all the time.

But still, as a novelist of human character, she felt that she must try to understand it. After all, there it is ; people must be like something, if only one can discover what. How does one penetrate through the idea they give of themselves into the elusive spirit behind ? Can it be that one never can do that ?

CHAPTER XVI

TRAVELLING FOR PLEASURE

I

THE S.S. Eugenia, 18,000 gross registered tons, 687 feet long, 74 feet wide, is one of the most comfortable liners that runs between Panama and San Francisco.

This elegant boat, with three large decks devoted to passengers, has been completely rebuilt to provide the greatest possible degree of personal comfort for every traveller at extremely moderate passage rates. An unusually large number of beautiful public rooms reproduce authentically some of the supreme periods of architecture from world-history. In the main social hall, of Louis XVI. design, on A deck, the woodwork is selected chestnut, hand-carved and ornamented in gold ormulu. The color scheme gives harmonious beauty without ostentation. In the center of this great room is dancing space for a large number of people. When this space is not used for dancing, it is covered with specially woven Oriental rugs. In this room arrangements have been made for Divine Services, regardless of creed, with Altars so contrived that their purpose is only discovered when ready for use.

The main dining room, of Louis XV. design, seats 274 people, and chefs provide a world-famous cuisine which is unequalled on the ocean.

So (and much more) says the booklet issued by the S.S. Eugenia about itself, and it should know.

It was this admirable Crichton of a vessel that was boarded at San José, Guatemala, by Mr. and Mrs. Adrian Rickaby, Miss Julia and Mr. Benedict Cradock, and Miss Catherine Grey, one afternoon towards the end of February.

It was a hot day, with a south wind. Little marcel waves lapped at the Eugenia's white sides as she lay at anchor in San José harbour. After the slow, hot, somewhat jolting train journey from Guatemala city, the travellers felt, as they boarded the boat, like birds who had escaped from a cage into the unsteady open spaces of the ether. They had travelled on mules and rivers out of the forest to the railway that took them to the capital, and had spent a few days in that agreeable city, visiting its surrounding mountains and lakes, and the remains of the former capitals which, abandoned, lie so charmingly strewn about the landscape. Then they had travelled to the pleasant little port of San José to catch the Eugenia on its way north to the Pacific coast. They intended to leave it at San Diego and visit California.

Isie was already better ; each mile they had come from their forest home had taken some of the edge out of her querulous voice, restored roundness and colour to her pale cheeks. Already, thought Catherine, she is happy again, with herself and Adrian travelling west together (even though in a crowd) while Claudia travelled east alone.

They steamed out of port in the warm noon hour, with all the fifteen hundred inhabitants of San José waving their adieux from the jetty, excepting those who were diving for coins in the muddy harbour water.

" Filthy dagos, how can they ? " Isie commented. She was such a clean young woman that she found a great many things filthy, let alone diving in San José harbour. She would probably soon be finding the boat's cuisine filthy, as she found that of the other liners and hotels wherein she stayed.

" Oh, I suppose they're used to it," Adrian replied. " They're clever, too. Look at that chap. There, he's got it—no he's not, he's down again—there, he's got it between his toes. That's what they do, grab it up with their hands and stick it between their toes as they come up."

" If only they knew," said Benet, " it looks even less well there than between their fingers."

" It looks just terribly silly in either," said Isie.

" Oh, I think they're brilliant men," Julia cried, leaning in ecstasy over the side. " Don't you think they're brilliant, Catherine, like fishes ? "

" Very brilliant. Look, it's going to be a marvellous journey, half the passengers are Guatemalans or Mexicans, and a lot of the stewards."

" Well, really, Catherine, I should think the honest-to-goodness white stewards will be more use to us on the boat than all these dagos. It's going to be as hot as hell. I shall go and put on something cooler. Come on, Adrian, help me unpack."

" Not just now. It's too hot to be inside."

The ship's photographer was running from place to place with a camera, taking the shore crowds. Every time he took a photograph he squeaked loudly twice, and the boat and shore population all laughed.

" How merry people are," thought Benet. " What a bright voyage we shall have. Everyone will be bright except Adrian. We are what used to be called ten years ago ' a cheery crowd.' (Benet's sense of period was abnormally acute). " There will be sports and dancing and sweepstakes and gala nights and flirtations and mirth, all the way to San Diego. But the voyage will be superb, in spite of everything."

2

The afternoon was occupied by the usual hurrying about the boat, complaining of state-rooms, reading of passenger-lists, talking to the purser, and unpacking. As, on this line, all the state-rooms are outside, the most usual topic of complaint to the purser was eliminated. Everyone could see, as they lay in their beds, the daylight, and the rippling, marcelled sea.

At dinner they all looked at the other passengers, at the waiters and at the food. Half the passengers were brown-skinned ; the men tucked their napkins into their collars, the women rustled fans. They were from South America, Honduras, Nicaragua, Costa Rica, Salvador, Guatemala and Mexico. The liquid Spanish of the Americas rolled about the room. The women were exquisitely padded with fat and decorated with powder. Many of the men were fat too, but others were lean and lithe, like iguanas. There were a great number of Mexican generals. They all ate largely, and particularly of sweetmeats and dessert. Of the white passengers, some were American planters or business men from Central or South America, some were Californians going home after a business trip, a few were European tourists. There were, as always on boats, the man who seemed an English colonel and his daughter (for, wise colonel, he leaves his wife, who is elderly and not strong, at home).

Those who sat at the captain's table looked, Isie scornfully remarked, duds.

" You would be sure to call them that, whatever they were like," said Adrian, not lifting from his plate his eyes that must be, judging by his voice, gloomy and malevolent. " You always do."

" Well, just look at the women," Isie said, " I ask you. Did you ever see such freaks ? Look at that head-dress. And that one with the fat arms. . . . You can't say they're a smart bunch, Adrian."

Adrian said, " I don't want to. I don't care in the least whether they're smart or not. They're not doing me any harm, nor you. Why do you let them get between you and your dinner ? "

Well, dear me, thought Catherine, there doesn't seem much hope, if he is as annoyed as all that by her, and speaks to her in that voice. What an idiot she is to criticise people's clothes to him ; if she's not learned yet that that bores him, there's no hope for her, poor Isie. Or is she trying to annoy him, out of spite ?

She seemed to be doing so, for next she said, still looking at the captain's table, " Most of the women seem to have dipped their faces in a flour-bin. They look too awful."

" My dears," said Benet, " there's the *most* surprising man two tables to our left. Really too sinister. Don't look. . . ." and carried the conversation away from the table of the captain and the clothes and make-up of the female passengers.

Julia, having looked over her shoulder at the surprising man, said " I do think fat is ravishing. I mean sleek, tight, Latin fat, that doesn't sag. If I were a man I would have a great passion for some fat woman. Catherine, have you ever had a fat lover ? "

" Well, no, not really very."

" Fat can look pretty cute on women," said Isie, who knew for certain about such matters, " but on men I call it just contemptible. If Adrian grew fat, I'd leave him right here."

" You're so commonplace, Isie," Benet told her. " You, no doubt, adore Gary Cooper, and the other lean film beauties. You probably say you like *line* ; as if lines were any the less lines from being curved. For my part I think fat a superb adornment."

So, in idle chat, the evening meal was consumed ; after it the passengers went, for the most part, on deck, and, reversing the expected behaviour of the different races, the Nordics lay in chairs and talked, while a number of the Latin Americans walked to and fro like prisoners in a yard, or caged beasts.

The stars, huge and golden, pierced the violet sky ; the ship's lights twinkled up again from the dark blue sea ; the night lay warm and sweet on the world like a huge and velvet-petalled flower ; even the uneasy smell and voice of an ocean liner was somehow caught

up into the gentle embrace of a temporarily rational
and God-ennobled universe.

" Life must, for all of us, be somehow good," thought
Catherine, falling easily into that old snare. " Yes,
life must be working towards a goal . . . why not ?
Many people at all times have thought so."

Isie, lying in the starlight, her clear face in repose,
her naked young arms and breast exquisitely paled
by night, had the loveliness of a poem or a dream ;
she shook the senses. At a little distance, Adrian stood
by the rail, staring down at the wake of phosphorescent
spume that gushed back, a lit fountain, from the ship's
keel ; he brooded, doubtless, on Love, Marriage, and
the mistakes by which men make havoc of their
lives.

" Nothing," thought Catherine, " will keep him
and Claudia apart for long. They might just as well
fly to one another at once, for they must do it in the
end. It will be better for them all, for Isie will soon
recover and love again. How we bungle and protract
our agonies ! "

Music struck up in the saloon, and Isie reared upright
like a snake who heeds the call of the charmer.

" Where's that Peruvian ? " she enquired. " There
was a Peruvian who liked me before dinner, and we
fixed to dance. . . . Hullo, Señor, yes, let's go in
right now."

The handsome pair went in. Through the saloon
windows they could be seen taking the floor. Adrian
watched them sombrely.

Meanwhile Julia searched for the stars, calling them
all by names not theirs.

" Benet, should you take that for Herculis ? "

" No, I should take it for Algol. Does it matter ? "

" Oh, very much. Oh, everything matters on such a night as this, in the Gulf of Tehuantepec. Look, there is Sirius."

" Can you be right ? I should rather call it Betelgeux. What do you say, Adrian ? "

" That ? I should say it was Atair."

" Still," said Benet, " I don't know that their names are of any consequence. I know a man at Cambridge who always said " It's of no consequence " when he was asked his name, and he was really quite right.

Adrian went into the bar and drank a little whisky, and thereafter played bridge in the smoking room with two Californians and a Chinaman.

Catherine, who had, as Benet told her, the bibliomania, went to see what the library contained. It contained, among other three-year-old novels, one by herself. Gratified, she watched an American lady take this volume out, sit down on a sofa, open it and read two pages. After that the lady ceased reading ; she said to her husband that she thought she would go and watch the dancing. She left the book on the sofa.

I don't believe my books are interesting, Catherine reflected. Certainly they hold no one's attention for long.

She selected a volume of Proust (translated) and went to the saloon, to make acquaintance with her fellow passengers.

3

The dilatory voyage was enlivened by little incidents. The Eugenia put in at various ports on the Mexican coast, such as Santa Cruz, where a whirlwind that overtook the passengers as they strolled in the sandy streets carried away the mistress of one of the Mexican generals and flung her into the harbour water ; and Acapulco, where the company promotors from California eagerly sniffed the oil-laden air and the ladies bought pearls from the oyster. At Acapulco and Manzanillo many passengers left the Eugenia for Mexico city, and others embarked in their stead. Among the new first-class passengers who came on at Manzanillo was a small plump American gentleman with several large suitcases, whom Benet, meeting him that evening before dinner going to his bath, recognised as their friend Mr. William Phipps.

The recognition was reciprocal. But neither had time, at that moment, for conversation ; the bathroom door closed behind Mr. Phipps's small violet-silk-dressing-gowned form even as Benet perceived him.

Benet, who was returning from his own bath, called at Adrian's state-room on his way back. Adrian was lying in undress on his bed, doing accounts. (The family had decided, sympathetically, that when Adrian did accounts he was seeing once more whether he could afford to go in for a life of paying alimony or not, and discovering afresh that he could not.)

" I owe you twenty-eight Mex dollars," said Adrian.
" Do you want it in Mex, to spend at the next landing
place, or will you have American ? "

" Anything you like." Benet shut the door behind
him and sat on the end of the bunk.

" Phipps is having a bath," he said.

" ? "

" Yes, really. He went in as I came out. He must
have come on at Manzanillo. He saw me, but we hadn't
time to speak. We shall see him at dinner, I expect ;
he can't get off the boat now, and he knows I saw him,
so it would be no use his trying. He must have all
the stuff he looted from us with him ; he wouldn't
have sold it in Mexico."

" He got off with a lot of things, didn't he ? "

" Yes ; we made a list of some of the missing objects.
Papa's gold watch and chain, the enamel clock from
the saloon, the Louis-seize snuff-box Belle got in New
Orleans and gave me. Claudia's jade necklace, quite
a lot of silver, and other trifles. Of course, Jacinto
is probably responsible for a few of the things, but
after all he didn't get much chance at them, and Phipps
was about the place every few days, filling those great
flap pockets of his. I must say I should like my snuff-
box back. I've never had anything I liked better."

" Well, I wonder what we'd better do. Wireless the
police at San Diego and have him arrested there,
I suppose."

" My dear, he won't stay the course to San Diego,
now he's seen us. He'll probably land at Mazatlan
and flee into the depths of Mexico and hide there
till the danger is past."

" We can stop that. We'll watch him. We'll speak
to the captain about him."

" Could we have his baggage searched ? I should
like my snuff-box."

" I don't know that we could. It would be merely
our word against his, and the captain has got no reason
to believe ours. Phipps looks so respectable always.
I wouldn't mind betting he turns out to be an old
acquaintance of the captain's and sits at his
table."

" Probably he will. In that case, he'll poison the
captain's mind against us. Perhaps we'd better get
hold of some of the Mexican generals and employ
them, for a suitable fee, to break open his suit-cases
and recover the goods."

" The Mexican generals might recover the goods ;
we shouldn't. No, I'd prefer to proceed in an ordinary
and legal way, and land Phipps in gaol. An American
gaol, not a Mexican ; as even Piper has admitted,
that would be heartless."

" I wish Piper were here. We need him. I feel that
Piper would somehow manage to get inside those suit-
cases. Once we had the goods back there'd be no need
to jug Phipps."

" But I would like to jug Phipps, very much. I
shall wireless the police all up the Californian coast."

" Meanwhile it's dinner time. Don't tell the girls ;
it will be amusing to see it dawn."

Benet strolled away to his own room.

It was an unexpected gift of fortune that Mr. Phipps
should be hurrying from his bath along the same
corridor at the same moment, so that the two dressing-

gowned figures almost collided at the corner by Benet's room.

" Oh, how do you do, Mr. Phipps ? " enquired Benet.

Mr. Phipps beamed at him, affable. but surprised.

" Pleased to meet you, sir, but I think you are making an error. My name is Van Tilden."

" Oh, is it ? I'll try and remember. I think it's a very good name. All the same, how do you do ? "

" I see, sir, you still are under a delusion. You take me for some old friend of yours. But I surely would recollect it if I had met you. May I enquire your name, sir ? "

" Oh, don't be silly, Mr. Phipps. I mean, it's really no use, you know. Of course I'll call you Van Tilden if that's your present name ; but you surely needn't be absurd about it when we are alone."

" I see," said Mr. Phipps, " that I must humour you, sir. And you certainly don't have to tell me your name if you feel reluctant. Are you travelling alone, if I may enquire ? "

" Not now I've met you, Mr. Van Tilden."

" Why, that's mighty friendly of you. We certainly must see something of one another between here and San Francisco, if that's where you, like myself, are bound. Are you on a pleasure trip ? "

" Yes."

" Well, you can't do better, if you're looking for beauty and romance, than to seek them on this wonderful old Pacific coast, and in these romantic Mex ocean cities. For my own part, I am investigating the mining industry. May I enquire if you stopped off at Acapulco ?

" Oh yes."

"A rising port with a great future, now they've completed that new Mexico-Acapulco highway. I certainly can't say much for Mex highways, but that really is the genuine article for once. Just the same, it needs paving, as I was saying to the Alcalde. What it is about the Mexes, they won't spend on roads, though they are aware that they will never attract the tourist till they do. They won't do it, because they know every revolutionary army that marches along a road will tear it up, just to spite the rival army. That's what's wrong with Mexico, they've gotten no public spirit ; each faction for it's own hand. But I mustn't keep you standing in the passage while we discuss Mex politics. We will resume our pleasant conversation when we've both gotten a few more clothes on."

The gentlemen parted.

"You just wait," Benet murmured, as he entered his cabin. "If you think you've gotten away with my snuff-box, Mr. Van Tilden, you're under a delusion."

4

Adrian had been right ; Mr. Phipps dined at the table of the captain.

Naturally Isie, the most assiduous looker-about, saw him there before she finished her grape-fruit, and said, "Why, Adrian, why look, why if that isn't Mr. Phipps."

"If that isn't Mr. Phipps it's Mr. Van Tilden."

Benet, whose neat taste disliked unfinished sentences, thus completed Isie's.

" Why, what do you mean, Benet ? It's surely Phipps ; why, I'd know him five miles away. Adrian, it certainly is Phipps, isn't it ? "

" Certainly," Adrian agreed. " Phipps is on board He came on at Manzanillo."

" I met him in bath attire," said Benet. " Twice. The second time he said his name was Van Tilden, and that he didn't know mine. He thought I was travelling alone, I think. He'll get a nasty shock when he sees the whole family. We'll waylay him after dinner and chat with him. I'll introduce you all."

" He's surely got a nerve," said Isie. " When you think that the last time he and I met he had me kidnapped by Indios. Good*night*, what a man ! and here he is, as cool as ice-cream, enjoying himself at the captain's table. What are we going to do about it ? "

" Wireless to San Diego," said Adrian, " and have him arrested."

" What name do you think he's got on his passport ? " Catherine speculated.

" Oh, my dear," cried Julia, " he must have thousands of passports. Men like that do. And to think of the bother we have getting only one."

" No doubt," said Benet, " he'll get past the American Immigration Officers long before we do. We, as British subjects, shall have to contend with superhuman difficulties. Phipps will speed through like a homing pigeon to his native land."

They were all gazing fascinated on Mr. Phipps, while they waited for iguana cutlets to be brought them

(for they all chose this little reptile when it was featured
on the menu, finding it delicate, if surprising, food).
Mr. Phipps, drawn, and no wonder, by the attention
of ten eyes, turned his own in their direction, and saw
them all at once, this party from his so recently
abandoned life, this polite, yet no doubt aggrieved
and vindictive family, from the Guatemalan back-
woods. A composed man, Mr. Phipps did not blush
or blench ; he merely focused for a moment on the
table of his old friends a bland, uninquisitive regard,
then turned his amiable beam on their next neighbours.

" He's seen us now," said Benet.

" He certainly," said Isie, " has a nerve. Just the
same, he's shaken. You can see he's shaken."

" We'll all recognise him at once," said Adrian, " as
he comes out from dinner, and call him by his name.
He'll be more shaken then."

" I think it would be yet more effective," said Julia,
" if we each met him and called him by his name
separately, one after the other. And each in the presence of a group of other people ; so that by the time
we had all five done it, the whole of the passengers
and crew would be convinced he was who we said,
and not who he said himself. Catherine, you meet
him first ; you look so truthful and moderate, no one
will suspect you of inventing a name and career such
as Mr. Phipps's has been."

" But do I recount his career to him, as well as
calling him by his name ? To his face, and before
people ? That would be to go too far, surely. After all,
I always used to like Mr. Phipps."

" Oh yes, you'd like Mr. Phipps, you certainly would, Catherine, if he'd had you kidnapped by Indios and lost in the jungle two days. You certainly would love Mr. Phipps if he'd done that to you."

Sarcasm comes but heavily, as a rule, thought Catherine, from people who are still under twenty-five, and particularly from expectant young mothers, who are so often over-strained. Saint Clement of Alexandria was wise, recommending these not to utter words in public, but to brood in quietness over the trouble which is so soon to overtake them.

" Well, Catherine," said Benet, " if you've finished dinner—or even if not—perhaps you'd better go and wait just outside one of the doors. Julia, shouldn't you be at the other, so as to make sure he runs into one of you ? Adrian, you go and stand on guard by his state room. Ask the purser which it is ; I know it's B deck. Isie and I will sit here and eat fruit and stare at him."

They ordered themselves thus. Mr. Phipps came out from dinner talking to the captain, who seemed, as Adrian had predicted, to be a friend of his. He passed through the door at which Julia waited. She stepped in front of him with a soprano cry of pleasure.

" Why, it's Mr. Phipps ! What a surprise ! "

Mr. Phipps explained to her, kindly but firmly, her error. She followed him, not heeding his words, but crying out her astonishment and delight in thus encountering an old acquaintance in mid-ocean. She told the captain about it. " Just fancy, Captain, meeting Mr. Phipps on your ship like this, when we last

saw him in Guatemala. He had the next hacienda
to ours, you know, and he was always in and out, but
he left us quite suddenly and never said goodbye.
Oh, *isn't* the world small ? "

The captain, who was American-Dutch, replied with
a deliberating nod, " Dat is so." But he was thinking
more about his forthcoming game of bridge than about
the size of the world, this garrulous and presumably
foolish young female, or Mr. Van Tilden, whose agreeable acquaintance he had made on previous voyages.

Catherine, seeing that Mr. Phipps had gone out
through Julia's door, had hurried up the stairs and
was waiting on the landing outside the lounge. As
the taciturn captain, the ejaculatory Julia, and the
gently denying Mr. Van Tilden, reached the landing,
she came forward with outstretched hand.

" Mr. Phipps ! Well ! How are you, Mr. Phipps ?
We couldn't think what had happened to you, after
you left Guatemala so unexpectedly. Mr. Piper and
all of us were quite worried about you."

It is possible that for a fraction of a second a hunted
look flitted across the placid moon of Mr. Van Tilden's
countenance. But he recovered himself in an instant,
and, with an amiable laugh, remarked to the captain
that he appeared to have a double somewhere.

" Dat is so," the captain noddingly agreed.

Glancing behind him, Mr. Van Tilden saw Benet
and Isie, side by side ascending the stairs. At the
sight of Isie the faintly hunted expression flitted again
across his face. What that young woman might say
to him, he could guess, but preferred, it seemed, not
to find out ; he made abruptly for the corridor that led

to the B deck state-rooms. Turning a corner, he was
in sight of his own room, half-way along a passage, and
of a lean, fair-haired man who waited outside his door.

As swiftly and silently as a hunted lynx, Mr. Phipps
slipped into the gentlemen's lavatory on his right, and
bolted the door.

What a family! But they could not reach him in
here. Here, at least, he was temporarily immune from
their inane greetings, and had a breathing space in
which to take thought. He wiped his forehead with a
towel and wished that the Eugenia's lavatories were
not kept so hot.

The next moment someone tried the door, and Adrian
Rickaby's voice called through it, " You can't stay
in there all the evening, you know, Phipps. You'd
much better come out and face the music."

" Dear me ! " called back Mr. Van Tilden. " Another
of these curious mistakes, I suppose. But really, you
must let me wash my hands."

" Why ? " asked Adrian.

As Mr. Van Tilden turned the cold tap into the
basin he looked forward with melancholy appre-
hension to a voyage in which at every moment of his
usually agreeable days and nights, a Cradock or a
Rickaby would start up in his path and denounce
him to his face with stories of the old plantation.
What kind of a voyage was that, for a man who
liked things pleasant and cheerful ? It wasn't safe,
either . . .

" Well," Adrian was saying, outside the door,
" you've washed now. I heard you. And here are
all kinds of people wanting to come in. You know

quite well, Phipps, that you can't occupy the place all the evening."

"Why ? " Mr. Phipps gently retorted.

However, to avoid further hubbub, he presently emerged. Adrian stood alone in the passage, looking at him with the morose pleasure with which a cat watches a mouse-hole.

"Really, now," said Mr. Van Tilden, "this surely is most peculiar behaviour. If I am annoyed further, I shall feel it my duty to complain to the purser."

"Do," said Adrian. "And we will too. In fact, we thought of doing so in any case. You know perfectly well that you carried off a lot of things belonging to us ; no doubt you've got most of them on board with you."

"I got things belonging to you on board ? My dear sir, what in hell can you mean ? "

"Look here," said Benet, coming up, "we'll make a bargain with you, Mr. Phipps. If you give us back our things that you've got—including my snuff-box—we may let you go without further proceedings. What do you think, Adrian ? "

Adrian nodded. "All right. I don't particularly want a fuss."

"There you are, Mr. Phipps. What about it ? If you won't produce the goo s—including my snuff-box—or if you've sold them already, but we feel sure you haven't, in Mexico, we'll have you arrested at the first American landing-port. Well ? "

Mr. Van Tilden gently shook his head. "I can't reason with you, gentlemen ; you're too obstinate. I'm going right to bed now, for you've certainly gotten me tired out. But, first thing to-morrow, I speak to the captain and purser about you."

"That's your answer. Very good. Go to bed, then, and have it your own way."

They watched him into his room, then went back along the corridor and up to A deck, to join the ladies.

"He'll give us the slip if he can, of course," said Benet. "Where do we put in next?" he enquired of the second officer, who was flirting with Isie. "Mazatlan?"

"No, we don't fool around the Mex coast any more," said the second officer. "We go right out to sea now, and the next place of call is Ensenada in Todos Santos Bay, Baja California. Three days run from here."

"Ensenada," said Adrian. "That's only about seventy miles from the States frontier. We must look out there; he might slip off."

He went away, to have a drink and to leave Isie and the second officer the more free to enjoy the lovely evening.

CHAPTER XVII

FOLLOWING MR. PHIPPS

CATHERINE, who was sleeping on deck, drowsily opened her eyes in the great warm violet night to see that the stars were dim and that the moon was dipping beneath the port horizon. It would soon be dawn.

The Eugenia was slipping through the dark and now starless ocean ; surely very quietly, thought Catherine, who had dropped asleep to the churning and vibration of screws. She slept on the forward A deck, and could see the dark sea and sky stretching limitlessly ahead. Yet did they now stretch limitlessly, or was that a shadowy spur of land ? Catherine sat up and looked more intently. Yes : it was land, and looked now quite near. It was the end of a long promontory or peninsula, and on it a tiny cluster of lights blinked.

The tip of Baja California, of course. But were they skirting it, as the second officer had said ? The Eugenia seemed to be moving straight for the cluster of lights, which must be a little port, and certainly she was slowing.

Catherine, bent on missing nothing, got up, thrust her feet into slippers and her body into a dressing-gown, and went to the rail and looked. One or two deck sleepers were doing the same.

Someone said, " Putting into San José del Cabo, it seems. I thought we were to run right up to Ensenada now without a call."

Someone else grunted, half-asleep, " So we were. This is a new idea since last night. Hope we don't stop long. I suppose someone wants to land. Though why the hell anyone should want to land on the toe of this God-forsaken peninsula . . ."

But Catherine knew why someone might want to. She suddenly knew for certain that it was Mr. Phipps who had persuaded the Captain to put in at San José del Cabo, that he might make his quiet and private getaway in the night. She turned from the rail and made for the door that led into the state-rooms and nearly collided into Benet coming out, his fair hair hanging into his eyes.

" We're putting in somewhere, aren't we," said he.

" Yes. San José del Cabo. Benet, I believe Mr. Phipps arranged it, and he'll get off here. What can we do if he does ? "

" Get off too, I suppose," said Benet, sleepily. " We can't let him get away with the goods. Let's get dressed, then we'll watch for him."

Catherine went back to the state-room which she shared with Julia, and began to dress. Julia woke. Catherine said, " Yes, we're making for the port of San José. Benet thinks we had better get dressed, in case Mr. Phipps disembarks there."

" Yes, I should think so indeed," Julia murmured, and shut her eyes and rolled over on her other side.

" Julia," said Catherine after a moment, " shall you

dress, too ? In case we have to pursue Mr. Phipps to shore, I mean."

" Yes, of course. I am getting dressed now," said Julia. " I'm nearly done."

Catherine pulled the sheet off her.

" Do wake up. You'll be sorry if you miss Mr. Phipps, you know you will."

Julia sat up and yawned, a fair plait over each shoulder, her eyes shut.

" Oh, how slow we are going. Oh, dear, Catherine, we must be all but in. *What* port did you say ? Oh, I must certainly get up and watch Mr. Phipps trying to land."

She tumbled out of bed and pulled off her pyjamas and began to wash.

" *What* port, Catherine ? Oh, dear, I thought there would be no port for days."

" San José del Cabo, at the end of Lower California. A tiny place, it looked. Hurry, Julia, we must be nearly in."

The Eugenia had almost ceased to move.

Someone knocked at their door.

Catherine looked out, and Benet stood there dressed.

" Are you both ready ? Bring your passports and money ; we may have to land."

" But, Benet, she probably won't wait long enough for people to have a trip ashore in the middle of the night. She will probably just drop anyone who's leaving the boat here, and go straight on."

" Well, of course. But we may have to leave the boat here. If Phipps does, I shall. He's got my snuff-box."

" Leave the boat, with all our luggage and everything, and be stranded at the bottom end of Lower
California ? Surely . . ."

" Well, don't if you don't want to. I don't see why
you should, really, now I come to think of it. Only
that it might be amusing, chasing Phipps. As to our
luggage, Adrian and Isie can see to that."

" Have you told them ? "

" I told Adrian we were putting in here and that I
expected Phipps would get off. He was sleepy. He
only said ' let him, good riddance.' In any case, he
can't very well leave Isie alone on board, and Isie'd
better stay where she is. We can get the next boat on to
San Diego, after we've cornered Phipps and got the
things off him. We can each take a small suitcase
with things for the night."

" Oh, I think it will be lovely, following Mr. Phipps,"
Julia said, her voice muffled in the dress she was pulling
over her head.

" Hurry up, we've stopped now," said Benet, and
left them.

Catherine and Julia, having each stuffed a few trifles
into a small case, hurried on deck.

2

The Eugenia was seen to be lying a quarter of a mile
from a dark shore, and a boat was coming out to her.

In the dark dusk of the pre-dawn little of San José
was visible but a few lights from the shore and some
fishing boats lying off it. Back from the shore rose
dark and shadowy mountains against a paling sky.

Seeing the three passengers looking so ready for disembarkation, one of the crew told them that this was no time for a shore expedition ; they were not going to wait longer than it took to drop into a lighter a passenger who wished to leave here.

" That's all right," said Benet. " If we land, we shan't come back. You needn't wait."

The sailor assured him that they would on no account do so. The three stood back in the shadow and watched, while a ladder was let down to the shore boat.

" We must keep our heads," Julia whispered. " If the disembarking passenger should not be Phipps, we must on no account leave the ship. . . . Good God, Catherine ! There's a clutch of stewards coming on deck, in case any of their prey should be slipping from their hands. Have you money ready ? "

" No—yes—but we don't know yet that we're landing . . ." Catherine felt hysterical ; stewards en masse affected her like that.

" Look ! There he comes ! " Benet whispered, as if he saw a fox. And, sure enough, Mr. Phipps stepped quickly and firmly across the deck to the ladder, accompanied by stewards carrying portmanteaux and cases.

The Cradocks and Catherine followed him, furtive and swift.

Seeing them come forward, the stewards surged towards them ; they flung largesse into outstretched hands as they stepped over the ship's edge.

" Why, I didn't know you were getting off here," said someone. " What in the world are you going to do here ? Dive for pearls ? "

They said nothing ; they scrambled after one another down the ladder and dropped into the tug.

The ladder was drawn up, and the tug, which smelt of oil, fish and tomatoes, and was manned by three Mexican fishermen, steamed for the shore.

" Good-morning," said Mr. Phipps blandly, to his three young friends. " Or is it still good-night ? I didn't know that I was to have fellow passengers landing with me, in this little port. Do you plan a long stay in San José ? "

" Our plans," said Benet, " are not yet settled."

" Well, it's a secluded locality, but if you wish to see fine scenery and quaint unspoilt Mex towns, you can't do better than Baja California. Maybe you are interested in sport ? On those mountains back there you'll find bob cat, sheep, lion, deer, hog, goat, javelina, quail and dove, and all along the coasts I'm told there are turtle, tortoise, shark, sword-fish, tuna, sail-fish, cabrilla, toros, sperm-whale, otter, seal, yellow-tail, sierra, bonita and albicore. Yes, you could have a mighty nice time hunting or fishing in Southern B.C. only that it doesn't happen to be the shooting season just now. I am planning to stay here a few days myself, looking into the argentiferous resources of the country. This country round here needs developing. I'm told it offers wonderful opportunity to a man with a little capital. Here we are at the jetty. San José has no harbour, you see, though it is quite a little port for entry and for shipments. Just a shore and a jetty ; the town is two miles back, way up a valley."

They landed on the jetty, and were confronted by two little officials in green uniforms, who, blinking drowsy eyes, were preparing themselves for the treat of rummaging in luggage.

Perceiving that Mr. Phipps's bags were about to be opened, the Cradocks watched with eager eyes, hoping that they, as well as the customs officers, might make acquaintance with the contents. But Mr. Phipps courteously waived his turn.

" I surely mustn't keep you waiting while they peek into all my baggage, when you've only gotten but one small grip apiece. The officers will no doubt have the goodness to pass you through first, so that you can go on to the Immigration Officer."

" Not at all," said Benet. " We had rather wait."

But Mr. Phipps was already explaining to the gentlemen of the customs the advisability of the order he had suggested.

" For my baggage," he pointed out, " will take long, since I have much."

All the more reason, the officers were doubtless inclined to think, why the other arrivals should wait, since the night would thus agreeably be occupied for all. But, on catching Mr. Phipps's eye, they agreed, and after enjoying a hasty hay-making among the slumber-wear and toilet necessities of the English, they passed them through and concentrated on the more promising American. Nor could the English linger near, for they were required a few yards further on by the Immigration Officer. Getting into Mexico at any point whatsoever is a considerable feat for the British race, though not so hard as to get out of it again. Compared with this last achievement the transit of a camel through a needle's eye is a journey de luxe.

Catherine, Benet and Julia spent twenty minutes explaining their British passports, the London Mexican Consular visas thereon, why they wished to visit Mexico, how long they intended to remain there, and why they thought they were entitled to enter it again, after already having visited it at Salina Cruz, Acapulco, and Manzanillo.

Having endeavoured to clear up these points, they were informed that they had, actually, no right to be in Mexico again, that their visas, though granting them a year's visit, only permitted of one entry, and that, if now allowed to remain for a while, they came on sufferance and under suspicion, and must keep in touch with the San José police.

By the time this understanding had been reached, and inscribed upon their passports, Mr. Phipps, his luggage, interesting though it had been, done with, caught them up, showed his passport, and was stamped and passed through with charming brevity, while their cases were still under discussion.

3

Leaving the wharf, in the still faint light of dawn, they picked their way up the beach between crates of tomatoes and piles of sharks' fins, to a dusty sandy road bordered with coconut palms. Three small open carriages drawn by mules galloped down on them in clouds of dust, their drivers uttering the wild war cries of their race. One driver captured Mr. Phipps, another his luggage ; both galloped off with these into the dusty dawn.

Into the third carriage leaped the English party, and galloped after, their chariot bumping fiercely along the bumpy track.

So, after a couple of miles up a valley road, they arrived in the little town of San José, and drew up in a plaza full of orange trees and palms and set about with low adobe houses and a pink church. A nice little town, but smelt sharkey, on account of the fins and oil of sharks, which seemed to stand about in considerable quantities.

In the plaza there were two two-storied hotels, at opposite sides of the square, the Hidalgo and the Miramar. The Hidalgo was of yellow-ochre adobe, the Miramar of blue.

Mr. Phipps's vehicles had deposited him at the Miramar, and at the same hostelry the cochero of his pursuers drew up.

But the drowsy proprietor appeared at the door, full of apologies. Not a room, not a bed, remained in his hotel. The Hidalgo opposite would doubtless be able to accommodate the señores.

Mr. Phipps appeared behind his host.

" My, isn't that a pity," said Mr. Phipps. " I must have taken the very last. But I guess the Hidalgo will be much the same. Are you acquainted with small-town Mexican hotels ? No ? Well, well, we all need to get our experience. Good morning, folks ; we shall surely run across one another to-morrow."

He went into the Miramar.

" I suppose he's taken all the rooms," said Benet. " Well, I dare say we can keep an eye on him nearly as well from the inn opposite."

They crossed the little plaza to the yellow Hidalgo. On the whole it looked even a little more decayed and small-town than the Miramar.

Having aroused the proprietor, they rented a double and a single room. Only the double one looked on to the plaza ; Benet's faced on to a narrow street. They were fine large rooms, with enormous beds, painted ceilings and several capacious spittoons set about the brick floors.

" God help us, Catherine," cried Julia, " the spittoons have not been emptied. . . . Oh, horror, *nothing* has been emptied. This is more than we can endure, even for Mr. Phipps."

Catherine pushed in vain the electric bell, which appeared not to be in action. Julia ran to the head of the stone stairs and called down them in voluble and inaccurate Spanish, mentioning the cuspidors.

A sleepy mozo appeared, came into the bedroom, and politely indicated that there were already three cuspidors. Julia cried that he was to empty everything, everything, and prepare the bedroom for occupation.

" Ah, by God," the mozo with an enlightened smile agreed. " One has overlooked various things. A tiny moment, and everything shall be achieved."

Benet came out of his room.

" I'm not going to bother about mine," he said. " It's irredeemable. Besides, I can't watch the Miramar from it. I shall go and find out when the next boat leaves here for anywhere, in case Phipps goes by it. He may or mayn't, but we must watch it."

" For how long," Catherine sighed, " is life going to be like this ? I suppose we *are* sure Phipps is worth it ? "

" Yes," said the Cradocks, firmly.

Catherine was seeing them with new eyes, these fragile, butterfly beings, grown so determined, so one-idea'd, so tenacious in pursuit, so avaricious of their goods.

" We had better all go down to the beach," said Julia, " in case Phipps should be catching a boat quite soon."

" In that case," said Catherine, " we must, I suppose, pay our bill here and say good-bye."

" I don't see," said Julia, " why we should pay a bill, as we've done nothing beyond complain about the cuspidors. Still, no doubt it will be expected of us. You pay, Benet, and say we may be coming back for the rest of the night or we may not."

" Perhaps," Catherine suggested, " they might know here when the boats go."

" Why, to be sure, I suppose they might," Julia agreed, and asked the mozo, who was now emerging from the ladies' bedroom with an air of triumphant accomplishment.

" When the boats go ? " he repeated. " About noon a boat carrying oyster shells goes to Mazatlan. A few days later there is a fruit boat to La Magdalena. Next Monday or so the steamer for Ensenada touches. You will observe that San José, being a very celebrated and important port, maintains a continuous service of boats to all the world. You can go anywhere, at any moment, from San José."

" But not till noon to-day," Benet complained.

The mozo looked as if he thought this unreasonable.

" The señores have only this minute arrived," he

pointed out. " They have not yet slept. Look, ladies, how I have made the room extremely elegant and convenient for you—I wish you a very good rest . . . . . . Without doubt," he added, after a pause during which nothing occurred, " you will see me to-morrow about the little gratuity."

" Without doubt," said Benet, bored.

" Well," he speculated, " I wonder what Phipps means to do. He won't go to Mazatlan with the oyster shells, surely ; he could have got the Eugenia to put him off there if he'd wanted. Perhaps he really does mean to stay here for a while and look at mines or something. How light it's getting."

" Yes," said Catherine. " I think I shall go out for a walk, in spite of our room having been made so elegant and convenient. Somehow I don't care much for the look of the bed."

" A walk," Julia exclaimed. " What odd notions you have, Catherine. This idea you have of what you call *walking* on all occasions, is one of the oddest. As for the bed, I don't much care for it either, no one could, but that won't drive me to a walk. I shall lie on the outside of it and finish the sleep you interrupted."

" I'm not sleepy," said Benet. " I shall come out with you, Catherine, and look round, and see what attractions the neighbourhood is likely to have for Phipps."

4

It was a little before sunrise, and promised a hot day. Catherine and Benet strolled through the little town, where in the plaza stalls were already being set out for market, heaped with glowing piles of ripe tomatoes, oranges, strawberries, bundles of sugar-cane, coconuts, maize, spring vegetables, fish, turtle, sharks' fins, tortoise shell, coral, sponges, pots and pans, sweetmeats, and all kinds of wearing apparel.

Peons were arriving from the country, with tiny burros loaded with fruit, vegetable, and canes for market. San José lies at the mouth of a fertile valley and the ranches round it are well cultivated.

Catherine and Benet, walking down the valley road along a prancing river, were surrounded by fields of cane, maize, tomatoes and asparagus, orange gardens, and orchards of blossoming and ripening fruit. Above the valley on either side the hills rose sharply, terraced with cedar groves, sugar canes, and banana plantations. It was the foot of the long cordillera that runs down Baja California from north to south, but here, in the peninsula's southern end, the lower slopes of these savage mountains had been tanned, and blossomed into gardens. In the faint and dewy dawn, with the shadow of night yet lying across the little valley, the wild tropic land seemed gentle and benign, and smelt sweetly of strawberries.

The walkers—and strange it seemed to Benet that he should have been seduced by his vigorous companion into going a walk—climbed up from the sheltered valley by a winding path that led between terraced orchards to the top of a spur of hill. From here, looking south, they saw the little gardened valley, with its singing river running between patches of green, squares of ruddy gold, and strips of pale wavering blossom, and along the valley road they saw the string of laden burros trooping into market, with their owners walking behind, or sitting in little carts, or perched behind the panniers on the tiny creatures' backs.

Below them spread the little ramshackle, gaily-coloured town. They could see the market, with its splashes of bright colour, and the pink tower of the church, and, two miles down the valley, the little port with its fishing-fleet slipping home with the night's catch.

Beyond the port the Pacific spread, pale blue grey and shadowed like a dove's wing. Limitlessly it spread to west and south, but far to the east the horizon was shaded as by the ghost of a distant world, as if it were a dream that the mainland of Mexico lay there.

Above that faint blue dream golden fingers reached up, and the dove's breast of the ocean glittered with a thousand shining feathers. The sun tipped the horizon, swung up, and Baja California jutted into a Pacific grown golden and blue.

Lazily the two fatigued European travellers lay on the hill, beneath a banana tree. Lulled by the husky whispering of the tree's ragged and wind-torn leaves, soothed by the enchanting morning air, and exhausted by their strangely broken night, they lay half asleep, or quite asleep, for close upon an hour.

They were roused by a sudden clangour of bells,

springing up from the town. The pink tower in the
plaza was lifting up its voice, calling the pious of
San José to Mass.

The sun was now climbing high. The bay was full
of fishing boats moving·before a little morning breeze.
Anchored three hundred yards out there was a small
steam boat, being loaded with fruit by shore boats.

" A fruit boat," said Benet, " in act to depart. My
mind misgives me. It would be just like Phipps to
be on it. We must go down and make sure."

" Well, we can't catch it now," said Catherine ;
for even as they watched the last shore-boat rowed
away, and the steamer lazily hooted several times and
began to move.

" That mozo was deceiving us," said Benet, " in
order that we might spend the night and stay to breakfast. There *was* a boat leaving early after all, and
that was it. I wonder where it's going."

" It seems to be bearing north-east."

" The question is, is it bearing Phipps ? We must go
down and find out."

" All right. But we can't catch it now, even if it was."

" No, but we can follow it. It's going up the Gulf,
obviously, not up the Pacific coast, so it's not for
Ensenada."

They hurried down the hill path and down the shady
valley towards the sea. As they walked, the clamour
of the bells in the town behind them filled their ears,
then ceased. The faithful were at Mass, and the less
faithful chaffering among the market stalls outside.
The eager Europeans turned back for neither church
nor market, but hurried to the shore, where sallow,

black-eyed fishermen were unloading their last night's
haul upon the little beach.

" Pardon me, sir, but that steamer which lately
departed," said Benet to a fisherman who lounged
upon the beach stringing abalone shells together. " Did
an American gentleman go in it ? Small, fat, and with
much luggage ? "

" Yes, yes, sir, surely. An American from the Miramar, and with much luggage."

" There," said Benet to Catherine. " I knew it.
Where, sir," he asked the Mexican, " was the boat
going ? "

" To La Paz, sir. It is a boat that carries fruit up
the Gulf at various times. To-day it went to La Paz
only. It is called La Purisima Santa."

" And when will the next boat go to La Paz ? "

The Mexican's spread hands indicated vagueness.

" Who knows, sir ? It will be La Purisima Santa
again, and it had first to come back. It may be back
to-morrow, the next day, any day. Then, when there
is a cargo, it goes again."

" Carramba," said Benet, annoyed. " Dear me," he
translated into English. " Well, hell, Catherine, as
Piper would say, we've certainly messed it. I suppose
Phipps has gone to La Paz after pearls. If so he'll stay
awhile there. Curse that mozo. Look, sir," he addressed
the fisherman, " we wish to go to La Paz immediately.
Can we get something to take us, either by sea or land ?
An automobile perhaps ? "

" The road," said the fisherman, " is not so good
for automobiles just now. Part of it is washed away.
There are donkeys and mules. But they take some

days, perhaps a week. It is over two hundred kilo-
metres."

" Too long. Is there no other boat going with cargo
which will take myself and two ladies ? "

The fisherman conveyed lack of knowledge on this
point, but a bystander (a little crowd of these had
collected and were listening with interest) contributed, " The other American young lady has already
departed for La Paza in La Purisima Santa, with the
American gentleman."

" Truly ? Very good. Then it is only I and this
lady here who need passage. I'm glad Julia caught
it," Benet added with satisfaction. " She'll keep an eye
on Phipps till we get there. I suppose she saw him
leaving his hotel from her window, and gave chase.
Very smart work."

Catherine thought so too.

" You are really a most surprising family. I should
never have thought Julia would have had so much
determination and dash. I thought she was going to
sleep, on the outside of the bed."

" Oh, well, I daresay even the outside, when she came
to look closer. . . . Anyhow, I'm glad she made that
boat. She won't lose sight of Mr. Phipps. She's of the
bull-dog breed—very tenacious, avaricious and vindictive."

" Oh, should you say that ? Julia ? "

" Why not ? Julia and I both are."

" Well, I do hope she'll be all right, Benet. I mean
chasing Mr. Phipps all by herself. . . . After all, I
suppose he is a desperate criminal, though he doesn't
look it."

" Oh, I suppose so. But he can't very well murder Julia on the tomato boat, or on shore with all La Paz looking on. Besides, he's not afraid of us. He doesn't think we can do anything to him. And I'm not sure that we can, so long as we are in Mexico. Particularly now that those suspicious remarks are written on our passports. Of course we might try going to the American or British Consul at La Paz. But I feel it would be useless. No one would believe us against Phipps."

" Then what *do* we mean to do ? "

" Wait till he tries to get into the States, then have him arrested forthwith for theft and fake passports. The immigration people are already warned. Meanwhile, we must catch up with him. We will now enquire further into travel facilities."

Information as to these was not lacking. Everyone on the beach told them of a different boat sailing to La Paz at different hours. As there appeared to be considerable difference of opinion as to whether more tomatoes for La Paz were about to depart within an hour, immediately after the midday meal, at six o'clock that evening, early next morning, on the following Wednesday, or in a week, they concluded that the best course was to collect their suitcases and remain on the beach until they could bribe some vessel to make the voyage.

" This life is passionately tiring," said Benet, as they sat outside the Hidalgo, and waited for coffee. " We both begin to show it. I suppose really I ought to shave before we appear on a fruit boat, among all those fresh tomatoes."

"What we both need," said Catherine, "is a hot bath, two cocktails apiece, and a little face massage. But I don't suppose San José can supply any of them."

Benet shuddered. "My dear, how British and bracing. You'll be suggesting kippers next. Cocktails! How I loathe them. But I admit they are very tonic at times. Well, we must make do with coffee and Mexican bread. We may have a strange and enervating day before us, tossed on the Gulf among tomatoes. I suppose Julia and Phipps are having it now. I wonder if they are conversing, or if Phipps is pretending not to know her. He is really in many ways a rather silly man."

"Because, I mean," Catherine amplified, "it must be so obvious by now to every one on these coasts that he does know us."

CHAPTER XVIII

VISITING LA PAZ

I

AFTER a day and a night's outing on the heaving waters of the Californian Gulf, during which five sword-fish, three tuna, and several tarpon were captured, the steam fishing boat San Miguel rounded Punto Coyote and rode into La Paz bay, and finally disembarked two cream-cheese-faced English tourists in that fine harbour.

They had been compelled to bribe a fisherman to take them on this voyage. As they had to admit, it was scarcely to be expected that, after all the tomatoes that had gone from San José to La Paz that morning, yet more tomatoes would be departing for the same destination later in the same day. There must be a limit to the tomatoes which La Paz requires of San José in one day, and the English gathered, after much conversation of the misleading and optimistic type so freely practised by Mexicans, a courteous race and loath to disappoint, that this limit had been reached.

However, several vessels were placed at their disposal by their proprietors, and soon after noon they had embarked in one of these. They had believed that they would be deposited in La Paz late that night, not realising that their presence was in no way intended to interfere with the vessel's professional career, and that the night would be spent in fishing. It was not, in fact, until eleven o'clock in the morning that they rode into the bay, and saw before them the palm-lined harbour front of the Pacific's greatest pearl city.

They landed on one of the wharfs, and, after passport trouble still more heavy and protracted than that which they had suffered at San José, walked weakly about the harbour among oyster shells, dead turtles, diving suits, fishy warehouses, and pressing vendors of tortoise shell, ambergris and seed-pearls, looking for Julia and Mr. Phipps.

" Phipps is probably buying or selling pearls some-where," Benet said. " But whether he is doing it on the harbour from the oyster's mouth, or in the offices of some company up in the town, or in one of these warehouses that smell so strongly of oyster, I can't see how we can tell. It's not much use asking in La Paz for a small fat Americano ; there are probably hundreds, and all after pearls."

" Well," said Catherine, more zealous for experience, and less single-minded in pursuit, " as we are in La Paz, one of the world's greatest pearleries, I think we ought to go and see some pearl-diving, if we can."

" Really, Catherine," said Benet, becoming querulous, " this isn't an excursion of pleasure."

" It certainly isn't," said Catherine, becoming cross.

Both were feeling the effects of their day and night's trawling. Here they were, after it, wandering about a noisy harbour that smelt of oysters, and quite unde-cided as to what to do next.

" Well," said Benet, " let's have lunch. We'd better go into the town and look for the best restaurant, because that will be the one Phipps will lunch in, if he is still here."

Walking through the cheerful streets and plazas of La Paz, bordered with palms, flowering trees, low adobe houses, and shops which displayed tortoise-shell, ambergris, and pearls of all descriptions, they recovered good spirits.

The three hours devoted in Mexico to the mid-day meal had begun, and inside and outside every restaurant and café the citizens of the pearl city ate and drank. The menus posted outside usually indicated to Mr. Phipps's young friends whether or not Mr. Phipps would be satisfying his hunger there. If they were very Mexican, and mentioned little but chile con carne, huevos, frijoles, tortillas, shark's fin soup, goat cutlets, and the like, it did not seem to them that Mr. Phipps would be inside. When, on the other hand, they had a rather more cosmopolitan and less local touch, there, thought Benet and Catherine, Mr. Phipps might be found at food, probably with some pearl prince, the while he ably conducted some nefarious deal.

At the corner of the Jardin Velasco stands the Restaurant Porfirio Diaz, which has a certain appearance of luxury. Glancing into its so fragrant-with-food interior, they perceived among the loquacious and conversing crowd, Julia, lunching richly with a fine young man.

" She's got off with some one," the brother remarked. " I hope she hasn't been neglecting Phipps for him."

They entered the restaurant and approached the table where Julia and her gentleman friend were eating turtle cutlets, and conversing with mutual pleasure.

Julia looked up at them without surprise.

" Oh, there you are," she said, " at last. You *have* been a time coming over. This is Mr. James. Look, these are my brother and my cousin, Miss Gray."

Mr. James rose and extended his hand. He was a good-looking young man, with a soft check shirt, splendid shoulders, wide brown eyes and a cleft in his square chin. He beamed with a charming cordiality.

" Pleased to meet you, Miss Gray and Mr. Cradock. I hope you had a nice trip over from San José."

" No," said Benet.

" Are you taking dinner here ? Their *precio fijo* eat is right good to-day. We'll have the mozo lay two more places at our table."

While this was being had, Mr. James narrated to them how he had been so fortunate as to fall in with Julia on her arrival last night by fruit-boat, and to render her some little assistance with the immigration officials, since when, it seemed, they had kept in close touch.

" He's been helping me to watch Phipps," said Julia. " It was very useful, because, of course, Phipps didn't know him by sight, so he could follow him without being noticed, and he heard his plans."

" What are they ? "

" Your friend," said Mr. James, " seems at the moment highly interested in pearls. It seems he wants a pink pearl or two, and he's casting around for them.

Knows the game, too ; he can keep his end up among all the Jew buyers from Europe and the States. I guess he'll be around here a day or two longer. Then he's joining a Mex friend of his and driving up the Peninsula to the frontier. I heard him say he wanted to put in a day at the Tia Juana races, and they don't last after next week, so that means that he'll have to push off in a day or so."

" How far is it to Tia Juana ? "

" Eleven hundred odd miles of the world's worst roads. It'll take him about a week to make it. I know, because I've just done it. Driving along these Mexican roads is like going into battle. My car's been at the ambulance ever since I got here last week, being pieced together again before I drive her back. Say now, what I was saying to your sister was, I'm due to get back to my office in Santa Barbara, California (I'm a realtor there), so soon as I can get there, or rather sooner, and I'd be pleased to take you folks along with me. I had a pretty mean time driving down alone, with every Mex hiker in the peninsula cadging a ride, and I'd be right glad to have company going back. We'd push off early to-morrow morning, and so get ahead of your friend and wait for him at the frontier. We could even put in a day at the races, if we wanted. Does the scheme look good to you ? "

" Superb, if you're sure you don't mind."

" It's all right with me. I'd be right pleased." Mr. James looked at Julia. It seemed that they had made great friends in that short time. People from Santa Barbara often possess a kind of superhuman grace and charm, to which the English utterly succumb.

" I've been giving this God-forsaken peninsula a look-over," he went on, " with a view to real-estate development. There's a lot could be done, if one could get a chance on it. All that mountain land lying waste —it's a crime. Why don't they build ? Now in Southern California . . ."

When he had told them about Southern California, and they had eaten their *comida*, Benet said he would go and wire to the United States immigration authorities at Tia Juana to stop Mr. Van Tilden at the frontier.

" *That* won't be much use," said Julia. " He'll probably not be using either his Van Tilden or Phipps passports. We don't know what any of his other passports say, do we ? "

" I shall describe the man," said Benet. " In detail."

Mr. James said he would go and see about his car, and would be right pleased if Julia would accompany him and see some pearl-diving afterwards. Then they could all meet again in a few hours. Julia, also right pleased with this arrangement, went off with him.

Benet went to telegraph to Tia Juana about Mr. Phipps, and Catherine explored the town of La Paz by herself.

CHAPTER XIX

PRECEDING MR. PHIPPS

I

NINETEEN miles and a half from La Paz, the near front wheel of Mr. James's Essex car showed every symptom of insecurity, and Mr. James, slowing up, remarked that he would not be surprised if it had not shed at least three of its bolts. The only thing which, he said, did surprise him, was that, after a few miles on the main roads of Baja California, any part of his car should remain fixed.

" Should *not* remain fixed," suggested Julia, who, enraptured by her new friend's use of the double negative, wished to hear it again.

" Not it is," he agreed, willing to cede her any point of English grammar ; and they all got out of the car to inspect the damage.

"Well, there's only two gone after all," said Mr. James. " I'm surprised."

It had been, to the ingenuous family unacquainted with Mexican roads, a strange nineteen miles and a half. More like thirty-nine miles and three-quarters, it had seemed to them. And more still like a scenic railway at a fair. They had leaped and bounded along what their log-book described resignedly as " a good desert-type road, of sandy loam, rough going in parts, with some high centers, and broken by arroyos and deep washes." It had climbed up from La Paz, through cactus and mesquite scrub, to a high mesa. From this mesa, while the others dealt with the wheel, Catherine looked back along the road eastward, saw how it wound, a brown and dusty snake, down and down from the mesa to the plain, past the deep inlet of sea that thrust sharply into the land and formed La Paz harbour, to La Paz itself, the pale-coloured city lying proudly on its bay, backed by mountains of the soft morning blue of bonfire smoke, or of bluebells seen through a wood. And beyond the mountains, girdling the mountains on either side, before and behind, west and east, the deep purple-blue of the bay, the faint mauve-blue of the gulf beyond. And beyond the gulf, hovering on the horizon like a long, pearly wing, like the muted whisper of a dream, the ghostly hint of the Mexican mainland, of the shores of Sinaloa.

It was early. They had started at dawn, and even now the sun's golden rim was only just pushing up from the gulf. Soon those mysterious purple waters would be blue with day and flecked with the gold of morning. Soon it would grow hot and hotter, brilliant with the flare of noon. But now dawn lay coolly on the desert land, on the low grey-green forest of cactus and mesquite that grew densely to the road's edge, and on the silent mountains, that seemed to lie piled, colour on colour, fold on fold. Like fabrics in a draper's shop the mountains lay, and they were of all the soft and delicate and fashionable colours—oyster where the dawn-light paled their wan and barren slopes, soft mole in the shadowy clefts of canyon and creek, a

biege on the western peaks that was nearly pink where
the sunrise kissed it and a cold puce in shadow,
bright green patches and squares where maize or cane
decorated the lower slopes, and dark green for the
climbing forests ; and always the distant peaks
melting from indigo into that hazy blue of bluebells
or of smoke. Range beyond range they circled, silent,
brooding and barren, dotted with tiny villages and
ranches, grey with miles of cactus forests ; and, crossing
the peninsula from east to west, from the Gulf of
California to the Pacific Ocean, there undulated,
broken by its arroyos and deep washes, the good
desert-type road of sandy loam.

Across the road, just in front of the car, a wild-cat
slunk, coming stealthily out of the cactus scrub,
plunging into the cactus scrub again.

" Hullo," said Mr. James. looking up from his task.
" Bob-cat on its way to bed. Plenty of bob-cat all
around here. Deer, too. Next time I come to Baja
it's going to be in the hunting season. Well, I guess
we'll push on now. We'll be lucky if we don't lose
more than a couple of bolts every twenty miles, these
roads. Let's see what the log promises us between
here and Arroyo Seco, where we hit the Pacific.
' Poor going is had, due to rocky chuck-holes, and
deep ruts. The numerous washes are rock-filled.
Care needs be exercised, due to the extremely
high centers. Dust is hub-deep and as fine as
powder . . .' I remember those washes. I got some
in my magneto, coming down. Well, we should make
Arroyo Seco Ranch in another hour, bar accidents, and
El Refugio by one."

" Can we get lunch at El Refugio ? " Julia enquired, for her mind harped on food when she began the day early.

Mr. James regarded her with affectionate compassion as he started the engine.

" At El Refugio, sister," he replied, " there's a tiny ranch-hut where I tried for a drink of Mexicali and only got tepache. They might happen to sell a bar or two of musty chocolate, too. Nothing else. Not a guava or a banana. Not even gas or oil. Are you folks wise to the fact that on the main road of Baja California there are no meals, no gas, oil, or other supplies, to be gotten between La Paz and San Miguel, a village containing two hundred inhabitants, two hundred and thirty-five miles from it ? Yes ; that's the kind of country Baja California is. Not so much as a little store or a service station, along two hundred and thirty-five miles of its main road. If you run out of gas, you're stranded, and have to depend on charity from some other guys' car. . . . As to food, Miss Julia, I brought a basket along for the lot of us, and we can eat our dinner any place we fancy. As there's nowhere to sleep, by the way, before Mulege, a hundred miles beyond San Miguel, we shall have to camp out to-night, among the bob-cat and deer. Unless you ladies prefer to stay in the car."

2

They jerked ahead over the chucky road. Julia sat by Mr. James in front ; they loved one another, it

appeared, more and more each chucky mile. Mr.
James talked to them of California ; of development ;
of the sunshine in Santa Barbara county, which was,
it seemed, brilliant and profuse during all the months
of the year ; of the fruit in the same region, which was,
if possible, even more so, during even more months ;
of the cities which were springing up, and were shortly
to spring, all over Southern California ; of . . . but,
in brief, he talked like a Santa Barbara realtor.

Of this barren, desert, utterly forsaken and un-
attended to Mexican peninsula of Baja California he
also spoke, at length. He regarded it as merely the
raw material for a habitable land, perceiving in it as
many requirements before it should achieve that state
as the Lord had noticed in the world on the third day.
The trouble was that, in Baja California, there was no
one to set about the required work with the admirable
competence and briskness so noticeable in the other
and larger task. Now, said Mr. James, if only the
new president would allow some intelligent Californian
realtors to take it in hand, they would, very shortly,
show the world. Sign-boards, it needed ; advertise-
ments all along the road, making their witty boasts
of this and that, telling travellers about hotels and
auto-camps, about food and drink, about the next gas
and oil station, and the other amenities of life.
Which, added Mr. James, must, of course, be provided, so that the boasts should not be empty.

" You want to see our Camino Real," he told them.
" Not a dull mile, all the way down from Frisco to
San Diego. Every mile marked by a bronze bell, to
show the way these old Spanish missionaries hiked

along, and the space between each two bells as well
planted with cute ads. as a garden bed is with flowers.
Not a dull ten yards ; scarcely an empty tree trunk.
By the time you've travelled ten miles on the Real,
you'll know the name of every comestible and beverage
that you can consume in the State, and of every hotel
and camp where you can stay for fifty miles around.
Now, I ask you, look at this. Miles and miles of cactus
and that low-down mesquite, and not a board. Every
tree empty, supporting nothing, only its own thorns
and tree-frogs. Not a thing to look at to brisk up the
journey and distract the eye from these doggoned
roads." The Essex plunged hub-deep through a wash,
scrambled up a sharp grade beyond it, leaped some
boulders, and sank profoundly into sand. Mr. James
waited until she had been, not without heat and
dust, dragged out, before finishing his remark. " Not
a thing to look at, on this so-called road, only cactus
and chaparral and road-runners and those darned
flowering aloes, and here and there a low-down little
rancho with a mean-looking party of horses or cows.
Now, if we got a chance at it, first thing you know we'd
build us smart service stations all along the road.
Then we'd make the road a road, not a piece gotten
loose from one of those old-world torture-factories.
We'd lay concrete from Tia Juana to Cape San Lucas,
and have it paved for two miles each side of the towns.
Yes, there'd be towns all right, sure there'd be towns,
first thing you know. Towns spring up like flowers,
directly you lay a road down for them to grow on.
Then folks would start hotels and auto-camps, and the
tourists would commence to hustle through. And then

we'd get to work and stake out all this mean mountain and cactus country with cute fancy cities. Yes, sir, that's what California's done. We've dreamt swell new towns all over the State, and where we've not had the time to get them built yet, we've staked them out. You should see the town of San Clemente, between Los Angeles and San Diego. There it lies, situate on a green site above the ocean, like a child waiting to be born—if you'll pardon the expression, ladies—with all its streets named already, and the very recreation ground and lecture hall and church indicated by name, so that, though there's not a brick anywhere laid or a piece of turf dug into, you can see with the eye of the mind all those dandy streets and houses and plazas, all mighty pretty, built in the Spanish-Cuban style, like Santa Barbara, with patios and arcades and tiled roofs, and 'dobe walls painted right smart ; why, I tell you, sister, it's like a lovely dream." (When Mr. James got excited, he failed to remember to address anyone but Julia.) " Yes," he dreamily continued, as the Essex panted boiling up a steep grade, " yes, I certainly would like to lay out some of these cute dream towns among these mountains. . . . Boiling again. This peninsula would sure be good for making tea in. We're running right down to Arroyo Seco after this climb, and we can change water there."

The mountain road now zig-zagged down, and below it stretched the Pacific, luminous with the blue of morning. Arroyo Seco, consisting of a tiny ramshackle ranch-house, a few tumble-down huts of adobe and plaited twigs, a field or two of maize, and a few lean kine, was huddled on the cliff above the sea.

They had crossed the peninsula, from the Californian Gulf to the Pacific Ocean.

3

The day wore on. The sun, climbing to its noon height, blazed tremendously down. The soft pastel shades which had coloured the morning mountains faded like fadeless fabrics, drowned in sunlight. Gone was the deep vivid gentian blue, the soft indigo, the hazy smoke-blue as of bluebells in a wood, the pinks and beiges and greens. Sea and land paled and glittered, in a wan glare, drenched in light. The road, running for a while up the Pacific coast, bent inland through a level country, dusty and gray-green with cactus and mesquite. Other cars, gaunt, wild, bone-shaking things, each filled to the teeth with smarthy inhabitants of this peninsula, rattled by occasionally, enveloped in pale whorls of dust. Miles behind, miles ahead, they saw the dust-cloud that followed each car puffing along the road, as an engine is accompanied by its smoke. Often, in addition, there were clouds of steam. The Essex, too, every now and then threw up these, starting to boil like a kettle. On the mesa beyond El Refugio, in the hottest hour of afternoon, they took off the radiator cap and the water spurted up like a geyser.

"How," said Benet, "I should enjoy a nice cup of tea."

They got a change of water from a ranch, and jerked along the sandy track through a cactus forest.

They were still on this cactus mesa when the brief

twilight and swift purple darkness fell, and here where the stream of Pozo Grande washed across the road, they made their camp for the night, for, said Mr. James, he was blest if he was going to do any blind driving on these tracks in hell. So the ladies lay beneath a candelabra cactus on Mr. James's air cushions and waterproof sheet, and beneath Mr. James's mosquito netting, and the gentlemen reposed in the car.

"But I can't believe," said Catherine, "that Mr. Phipps, who is a luxurious man and loves comfort, will consent to spend a night like this."

"Your friend will likely drive right through to Mulege," Mr. James opined. "It's three hundred and thirty miles, and these Mex Fords would make it by midnight if they started early. They don't mind driving in the dark ; they're used to the road, and their cars don't suffer so as you'd notice. We'll have to make some pretty swell going to-morrow, or your friend will be catching us up. . . . Well, I certainly hope you ladies will be partially secluded under that net from insect life. Of course, we're high up here ; it's not like we were down on the coast."

It was high, and it was cold.

Julia moaned to Catherine that she would not sleep, she would be chilly, she would be bitten, she would be tousled, and would only have the cold stream to wash in in the morning, and that, in consequence, she would look plain.

"It will make no difference," said Catherine, kindly. "All of us here will love you just the same. He won't even notice it, Julia, believe me. He has

already, it seems, arrived at the stage when he sees
you through a golden mist, as he sees those Californian
dream cities he speaks of. He may think I look plain,
but never you."

" I hope you may be right," Julia said, with hope
and doubt. " For indeed, Catherine, I couldn't endure
to disgust Mr. James. Don't you think, Catherine, that
he is ravishing ? "

" Very ravishing."

They lay and watched the strange and lovely night,
how the rising moonlight drenched the grey chaparral
and cactus with its milky flood, and silvered the
distant sea ; how the dark and shadowy mountains
circled round above the mesa, range behind range,
against the stars.

The lights of the tiny ranch of Pozo Grande winked
and went out ; they saw far off among the mountains
other little lights that winked and went out too, till
there seemed no life left for miles around, except the
wild creatures that slunk or leaped or flew about the
cactus and sagebrush, the barking of coyotes, and ever
and anon a wild car that fled along the wild road in a
cloud of storming dust.

4

Soon after dawn, they took the road, which now
started to wind back again across the mountains from
the Pacific to the Gulf. It was a steep and rocky road,
zig-zagging over high grades ; the surface, and particularly at each hairpin bend, seemed to have been
prepared for a combination rockery and shingle beach.

In the Comondu Canyon the Essex attempted to take in her stride some loose boulders for which her clearance was too low, scraped her bottom and jarred a spring.

As they jolted, fortunately slowly, down the mountains above Concepcion Bay, a rear wheel came off, and Mr. James's denture was jerked out of his mouth.

By the time they got down to the shores of Concepcion Bay the carburettor was spitting, having inadvertently absorbed some water from the washes they had traversed.

At the charming little town of Mulege, in the late afternoon, they stopped for repairs and supplies.

Between Mulege and Santa Rosalia, forty-two miles further up the Gulf, the radiator was found to be leaking at the rate of about a pint per mile.

All these little mischances Mr. James took philosophically, as occurrences incidental to a business trip through Baja California.

They reached Santa Rosalia by daylight, but, since this town is one of the very few in Baja California that wears something of a cosmopolitan air, with its French copper mining company, its frame houses, its well-stocked store, two gas stations, garage and French hotel, they stayed there the night. The place, being full of the employees of the Boleo mine company, had that busy briskness to which Mexicans so seldom attain, and the crisp and business-like accents of France were heard in the streets and plaza.

" They sure are a great nation," Mr. James said, as they sat in the plaza and listened to the band, the damage inflicted by the road on their car and persons having been partially repaired. " There's something about these Dago and Indian races that makes one regard a bright quick people of business like the French with considerable pleasure. They mayn't have the amiable politeness of the Mexes—that comes down from old Spain, I guess—but they know what business is. That big store of theirs would do credit to our business block in Santa Barb. Of course they charge high, but that only shows their intelligence. Why, they say the peasant women charged our boys six cents for a mug of water, when they were over in France for that war. I'll say the French have the best business heads in Europe. If they were a more adventurous, buccaneering, romantic people, and had gotten about the world more in the past, they'd have had it all in their hands long ago. Darned good settlers, too. Mix better with blacks and browns than we do, or you folks either. And why, because they don't have such a sharp sense of smell. The Lord seems to have made them without it. That sense of smell we've gotten, I certainly think it's more a curse than a blessing, considering the strong odoriferousness of this world that we have to get about. The Spanish don't have it, either ; if they did, the great Mex nation would not have arisen. That's a nation that was born out of the unparticularity of the Spanish race. It's a peculiar reflection, that the very quality which has given us northern folks our sanitary plumbing has stood in the way of our founding great nations of half-castes all the world over. Good plumbers, but poor mixers ; that's what we are. Now the French, they don't get the hang of our colour problem at all ; it just looks silly to them. But you folks have gotten this smell-sense worse than us, I guess ; so you're worse mixers."

"We are shocking mixers," said Catherine. "But that is partly because we are frightened and shy."

"We are a very farouche people," said Benet. "Rather like squirrels. And we certainly don't care for seeing much of people whose smells displease us. That is the chief reason for our odd class barriers. The different ways we pronounce our words has much less to do with it than the different amounts of soap and water we use. Still, we don't talk about class much now ; we have settled that it's vulgar to dwell on it. I don't know why. I think different sections of people, with different habits and ways of talking, are rather an intriguing social study ; but I expect it's like theology, and prohibition, and the motor speed-limit, and not to be talked about for fear it should rouse bad passions. Human beings are so *human*, unfortunately, and get all worked up with pride and scorn towards one another instead of being dispassionate and polite."

"Yes ? " replied Mr. James, suddenly in an unexpected way he had seeming tired of the conversation. "Well, I guess if we're making another of these dawn starts of ours, we'd maybe better be going to bed."

He was melancholy now, and so was Julia, for another day was over, and they were pushing on so fast.

Never again, perhaps, would they be travelling together in Baja California, leaping up these fine mountains and down to those wild and lovely coasts, halting in these strange adobe villages and mountain towns ; and all they did with it, nearly all, was to jolt recklessly and continuously along roads full of chuck

holes and washes and hub-deep in dust, roads where
poor going was had for mile on mile, between cactus
and sage-brush and mesquite scrub, desert-type roads
which surely needed some work done on them, and
would never get it. No time for the amenities of travel
or companionship, while racing Mr. Phipps up Baja
California. Mr. James would have liked greatly to
have paused awhile on the broad and sandy shores of
Concepcion Bay, to have shot the duck and the goose
and the quail, to have fished for the clam, the crab,
the lobster, and the bonita, to have kissed Julia and
have struck camp awhile on one of the islands of the
bay. But no, it was not to be, since Julia and her
family had only one idea, to hurry on and on and reach
the border ahead of this Phipps. A very unromantic
people, the British. Nearly as unromantic, thought
Mr. James, as the French. They thought of nothing
but their stolen watches, snuff boxes, and other gew-
gaws.

5

They were off again next morning, jolting up the
Inferno Grade into the mountains in their shaken and
battered car, taking bends so acute that it was necessary
to back before getting round them, hanging over
ravines and chasms on one wheel.

On their right the Three Virgin volcanoes loomed,
blue as cornflowers, against the clear blue heavens,
and the deep blue Gulf sprang on to the horizon as the
road twisted north, and hid itself again beyond folds
of shadowed mountain as they bent sharply south
again.

The road all that day was full of burros ; long trains
of them, clip-clopping up and down the mountain
way, dragging carts of timber and loaded up with
dates. For miles around San Ignacio the mesa was
green with date gardens. For miles each side of the
village, burro trains trailed out from it, so that all the
way to San Ignacio the Essex met them, and all the
way beyond it passed them. At every bend of the
mountain track, when cars met or passed burros, it
seemed a question which would be precipitated over
the edge. Yet somehow all scrambled by, the burros,
the carts, the Essex, and the wild Fords full of Mexicans.
All day they scrambled by, crawling, beyond San
Ignacio, along a road all of which had been washed
away except a high centre between two deep gullies,
innumerable boulders, and about the same number
of holes. If only, as Mr. James remarked, someone
would put in a few days' work fitting some of the
bouledrs in to some of the holes, the road might not
be so bad.

Slowly anger grew in Catherine. She became full of
resentments, of little desires which she might not,
because of the Cradocks' obstinate covetousness and
firm vindictiveness, gratify. She wanted to stop for
the afternoon in the pleasant little town of San Ignacio,
eating dates in the plaza and seeing the eighteenth-
century mission church. She wanted to have a siesta
beneath the giant cactus trees at Mesquital Ranch ;
to make Sylvester Alverez, its owner, refuse to sell
them gas, so that they would have to cease this fierce
and senseless motion ; to get out at San Xavier Ranch
and sketch the view ; to wait and gather mussels and

abalones at low tide at Miller's Landing and then to sail across the Bay of Sebastian Vizcaino to the Island of Cedros ; to induce Mr. James to prefer her to Julia, so that he would perform her wishes ; to spend the summer in Baja California with loved ones ; or, alternatively, to leave it this moment in a boat and never return ; to pluck the creamy blossoms of the aloes, the scarlet blossoms of the poinsettias, the figs, the guavas and the dates from the ranch orchards ; to stay by the aloes that flowered (it was said) once only in each hundred years, and to all of which the exquisite centenary occasion appeared to have, by some divine coincidence, arrived during the present week ; to leave the Essex buried deep in the soft white dust in which it so frequently sank in the rutted road, and continue travelling to the United States frontier on burros ; to sleep in a soft, clean, white bed and be awakened by letters and tea ; to catch a mountain sheep ; to see a chaparral cock fighting a rattlesnake ; to converse with Mexicans about politics and with Yuma Indians about God.

But for none of these diversions was there opportunity, as they jogged, hurtled, scrambled and leaped along Lower California's main road, with short pauses to eat, to take in gas or water, and to patch up the continual damage inflicted on the car.

" Look," said Catherine, as they got stuck on a steep bridge, " wouldn't it really be better to give up Mr. Phipps, and take Lower California more slowly, so that we could see it properly, and not rush along so ? "

Mr. James, twisting fiercely at the wheel, glanced

enquiry at Julia. " That'd be all right with me," he
said.

" No," said Julia and Benet. " We want Phipps."

" Just as you say." Mr. James backed jerkily
down. " Can't make this durned bridge : go through
the river instead."

They were set on their prey. They had mean, small,
hard minds, thought Catherine ; obstinate, selfish,
materialistic and vengeful. She did not know why she
had found them charming. They were even stupid, to
be so oblivious of the amenities of travel, so set on
their small private ends ; so fatuously unaware, too,
that they would never, even if they should run up
and down Lower California for the rest of their days,
outwit Mr. Phipps.

6

Nor, indeed, did they. On the evening of the fourth
day they arrived at Harrison's Ranch. Standing among
hills above the Pacific, surrounded by mountains alive
with such wild creatures as sportsmen have agreed
to call " game," and a mile or two from an ocean shore
teeming with lobsters, clams, abalones and other sea
life suitable for taking, providing clean beds, baths,
excellent food and scenic surroundings, this admirable
hotel is the Mecca of travellers in this peninsula so,
for the most part, devoid of comfort.

They arrived on a sultry evening, after a desperate
day spent on a trail that wound for many miles deep
in soft volcanic dust through cactus-forested mountains,
then for many more miles across the Santa Maria

Lagoon plains, equally deep in soft grey mud. As they sat wearily in the veranda of the ranch after all this, and after dining, Mr. James remarked cheerfully that he would not be surprised if there were not a touch of storm before morning.

Soon after he had said this, a few large warm drops splashed lazily out of a hot purple sky.

" What I said," Mr. James observed. " If it goes on, we'll be corked up."

" Corked up ? "

" Sure we'll be corked up, brother. You'd be surprised. A night's rain, and the Lower Californian main road is washed clean off the map. As you may have observed, it isn't precisely a first-class paved automobile track even in fine weather. When it's wet, only Noah and his ark would stand a chance of fording the holes and gulches, and only a mud-turtle would make any way in the rest. As to trying to get around those hill-bends—well, there maybe are a few that have tried it too soon after rain ; you can see the hulks of their cars rotting at the bottom of the canyons all the way along. Why, yes, sure if it's going to rain any we're up against a few pleasant days in this agreeable spot. I'm certainly sorry if it's going to inconvenience you folks, but you'll admit the bad weather couldn't have come on at a better moment for us. We might have been lying out in the cactus, among the coyotes, or bracing up our minds to enter the beds in one of those miserable 'dobe Mex burgs we've been through. I'll certainly say we're lucky to have got to Harrison's. I'd as soon spend a few days here as anywhere, in nice company."

" It looks rather dull to me," said Benet, looking at the forested mountain shapes that towered blackly to right and left against the purple sky. " Countrified."

" It certainly does want developing," Mr. James admitted. " It's what I keep on saying—the Mexes don't *do* anything to their country. But it's good game country around here, and this is a fine cultivated ranch."

The western sky glimmered suddenly, revealing to them the Pacific Ocean, which lay, dark and quiet, at the foot of the mountain slopes. Thunder rolled gently round the world.

" What's that ? " Catherine asked, hearing through the growling of the heavens sounds of bustle and welcome in the house behind them.

' It sounds," said Benet, after a moment, " very like the arrival here of the man Phipps. Well, if we're corked up, so is he. I dare say he'll make our country house party more amusing. Look, the rain's coming in on us ; let's go in and welcome Phipps."

" Well, I'll say," said Mr. James, disgusted, " that I didn't calculate he'd have gotten up the peninsula so quick as this. What'd he been doing in La Paz that he had to make his getaway so sudden ? "

" I dare say," said Julia, " that heaven spread some pearls before his sight and that he used his opportunities."

They went out into the hall.

There all was bustle and genial arrival. Miss Olivier, their hostess, a tall, lounging, drawling, sweet-tempered and derisive Lousianian spinster, was making welcome three dripping gentlemen, of whom one showed signs of being a Mexican general, another of being an English clergyman, while a third was a small and plump American.

" Dear me," said Mr. Phipps, affably, as he shook the rain from his clothes, " my young friends from the Eugenia again, who insist so charmingly that I remind them of an old acquaintance back home. Well, well, isn't that nice. Miss Olivier's ranch, I am told, is the happy meeting place of travellers from all the world over. And as it seems to be settling down for a wet spell, we shall perhaps enjoy several days of each other's company here. Ladies and gentlemen, meet my friend, General Luiz Vegas, who kindly brought me along in his car, and the Reverend Prebendary Churton, of Ely, England, 'who joined us to-day. The Prebendary is researching among the peons and Yuma Indians of this peninsula for his book on Religion and Peasant Life. Unfortunately his car met with a mishap on the mountains while visiting the San Fernando Mission ruins, and General Vegas and I were fortunate enough to be able to assist him to pursue his journey. So here we all are together, and I don't see why we shouldn't have a real nice time in this romantic and commodious ranch, in spite of the mean weather."

" Personally," said Benet, " I prefer wet weather when I'm staying in the country. At least people don't take you for walks, or to look at the animals they keep. One is left in peace, to talk or read or do nothing."

" Ah," said Mr. Churton, " you're like me ; I am afraid I am an incurable loafer, and prefer to idle with a book and a pipe rather than to be taken out sight-seeing. It's a terribly reprehensible attitude, I fear, but there it is, we can't help it if we're made that way. What a night ! Will the storm last long, should you say ? " he enquired of Miss Olivier, since those who live in a place always know how long the weather there will last.

" Yes," said Miss Olivier, who was economical of speech.

CHAPTER XX

I

" It's curious," the prebendary was saying, " how few traces of the old Mexican religious cults I have been able to come across in Lower California. I had expected more from what I had read. The peons appear to attend church in a very ordinary manner, and those I have questioned don't appear to be familiar with the names of the ancient gods. What should you say, General ? "

General Vegas shrugged his shoulders. " Señor, our peones are much ignorant mans ; gente sin razon. They not know what they pray or why."

" In that they're only too like many Europeans, I'm afraid. You don't think then, that there is much cult of the old Mexican gods among the Yuman Indians ? "

" The Mexican gods, señor, not flourish, only in Mexico City, among the intelligentes. Our peones not hear of them. The Indios are Catholic, when they live near to a church. There are also, surely, much Indios in the montanes, who not go to a church. Who knows how they pray ? It is not of consequence."

" I'm afraid I'm too much interested in human beings to agree with you there, General. I'm insatiably curious about people and their ways of thought. And people's attitude towards religion always seems to me the most profoundly exciting thing about them. I've worked in several parts of the country in England, and I've usually succeeded in getting through the crust of reserve that the British labourer protects his soul with, to the real man. An extraordinarily interesting kind of excavation. I've been lucky, I suppose ; or perhaps I've been helped by having some sense of humour. The British working man resents any attempt to come the parson over him, but he appreciates a joke, and I'm afraid I'm an incorrigible jester. But it's far more difficult among foreigners, of course, especially as my Spanish isn't strong, and my Indian *non est*. I haven't, for instance, been able to make out whether the spirit of scepticism has made any way among the country people of Lower California. In England it's a very serious obstacle in the Church's way. The agricultural labourers of Norfolk, for instance, where I had a parish once, had great difficulties with the Old Testament stories. One had to explain them away. Fortunately, the Anglican Church is modernist in these days, and can explain its faith in terms comprehensible to the modern mind. There, if you'll forgive my saying so, General, we have the advantage over your great Church. But possibly you'd call it a weakness in us, not a strength. Our poor old Ecclesia Anglicana comes in for a lot of contempt, I'm afraid, from her more uncompromising and fundamentalist sisters. Yet somehow she muddles along."

" Sure, señor," General Vegas politely agreed, and added, to show interest (though religion was not really

his subject, and indeed, he could think of little but
how eager he was to get on to Mexicali, where he was
hoping for some political trouble), "is it Catholic,
your English Church, or Protestant ? "

" Ah," the prebendary smiled on the company,
" now you raise a very vexed question. Which indeed ?
Both, I fear, is the only answer. We are a strange, but,
I think, rather gallant compromise, and nothing like
us is to be found in any other country, I'm quite sure."

Perceiving that the General was little the wiser as
to the nature of the Anglican Church, Miss Olivier,
who was rubbing a dog dry, explained, " They're
P.E. I had English friends in New Orleans, and it was
to the P.E. Church they went. Protestant Episcopal,
if you understand me, General."

" Ah, Protestant." General Vegas nodded. He had
heard of Protestants. " The churches," he added, " are
troublesome ; perigulosas to the government and sure
greedy to the peoples. In Mexico we 'ave to be much
severe with the Church. The priests—carramba, que tan
greedy hombres ! they would rob us of all and rule
the peoples. Not "—he bowed politely to the prebendary—" same as in your country."

" Conditions are very difficult," the prebendary
agreed. " And as to ruling the people, on the contrary,
we are ruled by them. They won't even allow us to
modernise our seventeenth-century prayer book.
Though I must admit that the majority of my
parishioners in Norfolk were inclined to welcome that.
They seemed, in fact, to feel a little tired of the old
prayer book. But our House of Commons decided
against change. Our dissenters felt particularly

strongly on the matter. Yes; we are a very curious nation in many ways. I'm afraid we have a world-wide reputation for being rather mad."

" Why, no," said the courteous General; but Miss Olivier who had had English friends, and knew what they liked to believe about themselves, said, absently but kindly, " You-all sure have," in the admirably hospitable spirit in which she offered her English guests water to bath in and the other comforts they enjoyed.

They were sitting in the large living room of the ranch, watching the deluge that had descended all day, a grey lashing torrent, on the soaked mountains and woods. It was a groaning, hissing, moaning world of beaten trees and rushing water. Mr. James, who had made an expedition of exploration in the morning, reported the road flooded out, and the sea so wild that no boats would sail. They were marooned at Harrison's, and had to endure it as best they might.

Indeed, they were, for the most part, not displeased. Mr. James had at last the chance he desired of dalliance with his adorable Julia. He wired to his office in Santa Barbara and explained about the rain. Julia too was pleased, since she had now the company both of Mr, James and Mr. Phipps. Catherine was relieved at the break in their hurrying career ; she hoped that it would soon be fine enough to go out, but not to take the road. Benet accepted the situation with resignation, since he had, anyhow, Mr. Phipps under his eye. Mr. Churton, the prebendary, was quite happy writing up his notes on Peasant Religion in Lower California, and con-versing with anyone who would listen. The two who were a little worried by the delay were, apparently,

Mr. Phipps and General Vegas, for the General was
in great haste to reach Mexicali in time to assist in
the trouble brewing there and to run his own friend
for the presidency in case some accident should overtake the extant president; and as to Mr. Phipps, he
also, presumably, had his plans, for his was a well-
organised life. However, since he was delayed, he
accepted it, and proceeded to make himself as agreeable
as usual.

Perceiving that the English prebendary was interested in speaking of religion, Mr. Phipps contributed
that for his part he was a minister in the Christian
Science Church in Oshkosh.

"That explains Phipps," Benet, in the verandah
outside, said to Catherine. "No doubt he doesn't
even know when he is stealing. They say Mrs. Eddy
scarcely did. I believe that's about the only true thing
Phipps has ever told us about himself."

But Catherine was listening to the General, who was
telling the prebendary that the peons of Mexico felt
no desire for a new or revised prayer-book, and that
men of education would like, naturally, to be rid of
the Church altogether, but that it helped to keep the
pigs of peons quiet.

In return, the prebendary told the General that
Berkshire was riddled with both Protestantism and
doubt, that in Cornwall they were somewhat sullen,
Celtic, and incomprehensible, that Anglo-Catholicism
made little headway among agricultural labourers in
Sussex, that many of the Moujiks of the province of
Kharkov had not yet heard of the revolution, still
looked to the Little Father as the head of the Church,

and, unaware that the national attitude towards Judaism had undergone a change, still held village pogroms at suitable intervals as of old. As to the shepherds and farmers in the vale of Tempe on the Thessaly hills, their use of the Greek tongue was so unlike that of the prebendary, and their dogs had barked so loudly, that he had not been able clearly to understand their thoughts on the topics he had endeavoured to broach with them, but they had seemed to show little sign of familiarity with the Anglican Church, or of interest in those steps towards union with it which many Anglicans think it would be desirable to take.

" You has sure rambled all the earth, señor," the General politely told him.

" Not quite that, General ; but I admit I am an incurable vagabond : I have Danish blood in me ; perhaps that is partly to blame. We English are a restless people. Now you Latins are more inclined to stay put ; to remain, I mean, where you are. Perhaps it is that you have so much more natural liveliness that you don't need to move about to stimulate yourselves."

General Vegas bowed, pleased with the word Latins, to which not all his ancestors could have laid claim.

" Todavia," he said ; " I would sure move about now, if it made not so much rain. Will it rain much time more, Señorita ? "

" Yes, I guess," said Miss Olivier, and left the room with the dog.

2

Mr. Phipps, tiring of religious discussion, came out to the verandah and sat down between Catherine and Benet.

"Well," said he, making genial conversation, "I'll say it's raining. Yes, I certainly will admit we've gotten a kind of moist day in B. C. at last. Mighty good for the crops, I dare say. Vegetation looked kind of dry as I came along. You'll join me in a drink, won't you?"

"No, thanks," said Benet, coldly.

"What about you, Miss Gray?"

"No, thank you, Mr. Phipps; I'm not thirsty."

"Why, that is certainly a mighty peculiar reason to give for not having a drink on a wet morning in the only decent hotel in B. C. Just the same I shall have a Mexicali myself while we chat. Where's that lazy mozo?" He tinkled a grass bell, and settled himself comfortably in his cane chair. "No reason," said he, "why we shouldn't all be friends together, that I can see. I observe that you continue to call me Phipps. Well, since you insist on it, I will admit that that is one of the names to which I am entitled. In any case, what's in a name? Say, I know that you folks are mad with me for that little joke I played on you in order to recover the trifles put by for me by my grandfather. But, after all, since you've gotten them off me, can't we bury the hatchet and be friends?"

"No," said Benet. "Because of the other trifles we've not gotten off you yet, that you took from our house. My snuff-box, for instance."

" My dear sir ! I don't have your snuff-box. I didn't
take a thing from your house. Why, do you mean to
tell me that's what's biting you all this time ? Well,
now, doesn't that beat the band ! All these weeks
you've been thinking me a thief ! And you too, Miss
Gray, I presume ? "

" Why yes," Catherine admitted.

" Well, well, I'll admit that peeves me considerably.
I'll say right out that hurts me where I live. Because I
never have been a thief. Perhaps you heard me say
in there that I was a Christian Science minister in
Oshkosh. Well, so I was. And I simply don't believe
in evil. No, sirs, I just can't believe evil is true.
Dishonesty "—Mr. Phipps took a long drink and
put down his glass with a bang on the table at his
side—" that's a thing that simply does not exist to
me. Do you suppose the Lord knows anything about
dishonesty ? No, sirs, he does not. He passes it by,
knowing it doesn't exist, that it's just a piece of mortal
mind. And what the Lord gives the go-by to, believe
me, there's no necessity for you and me to worry over.
No ; I just don't believe in dishonesty, let alone
practise it. Well, well, well, so you thought I had made
off with your things. That'll never do at all. Now
don't you really think it more probable that that
little preacher, Jacinto, took the objects ? "

Benet shook his head.

" We know more or less what he took. Your servant
said you kept bringing things back with you when you
came to see us, and went off with all of them when you
left. So, you see, we know you had them. What we
don't know, is whether you still have them. We've

been following you about to get them back, and to get
you arrested at the frontier."

Mr. Phipps sighed. " Well now, isn't that vindictive
and persevering of you. And I dare say the objects
are of no great value either, if you come to think of it.
Just the same, you feel affection for them and you
want them back, and I don't blame you. But, lordy,
you'd never have me arrested at the frontier ? Not
for a snuff-box and a trinket or two, or whatever it
may be you think I've gotten of yours ? "

" Yes, we would," said Benet. " We would like you
to go to prison, in the States. Not in Mexico, but in
the States. You deserve to go to prison."

The blood of a judge flowed in Benet's veins, Catherine
reflected. That was the sort of insulting remark that
judges make.

" Well, well," Mr. Phipps gently countered. " We'll
have to see. Yes, we will certainly have to reflect on
what is to be done, about all this ill-feeling. No one
regrets ill-feeling more than I do : you see, it's nothing
but mortal mind, and the Lord is entirely unaware
of it. I don't believe in it either : it's not real, it's just
a bad dream we'll all wake up from soon. One day
you'll understand that. You must come to Oshkosh
and attend our church there. You'd be surprised . . .
Dear, dear, what weather. My friend the General is
getting quite peeved at being delayed like this. He's
afraid the trouble he hopes to be involved in in
Mexicali will be over before he gets there. Still, he may
be on time for the next. There's always something, in
Mexicali. Now, won't you join me in another drink ? "

" Yes, I think I will," said Catherine, who hated to

hurt people's feelings, or seem churlish, and was getting
sick of the deplorable weather. " I think I'll have a
Bronx."

Benet, who disliked cocktails, had indigestion, and
did not in the least object to seeming churlish, opened
the nineteenth-century Spanish love-story he had
found in Miss Olivier's small but miscellaneous library,
which consisted mostly of the leavings of travellers,
and read.

Melancholy was submerging Benet. He was weary
of this desolate peninsula, of its so-called roads, its
eternal cactus, its yucca, its miserable ranches and
pueblos, its awful mountain peaks and barren wastes,
the hot and lashing violence of this unnatural storm.
So much natural grandeur, so little architectured
elegance, oppressed him. He wished he were in Europe.

3

Julia and Mr. James were looking at the weather
from the arcade that ran round the patio at the back
of the house. They sat in cane chairs, drawn close
together, and, while they watched the heavy rain lashing
the orange trees and date palms in the patio, and
sluicing on the ground with a sound as of many waterfalls, they spoke of love. Yes ; at last they eased
themselves of the weight of affection which had been
mounting up for five long days, and showed one another
their hearts. Julia felt that she had been waiting for
one-and-twenty years for a young realtor from Santa
Barbara with brown eyes and a square, cleft chin and
a Southern Californian accent to take her into his

arms and his home town. She loved excessively and
delightedly, with the affection at once passionate and
enduring that was natural to her monogamous soul.
He no less, since for nine-and-twenty years he had been
waiting (he now perceived) for a slim young English
nymph, just so blonde, fragile and pale, with just
such large and rolling blue eyes, such sleek, fair,
banded hair, and just such absurdities babbled gently
in the falling cadences of a soft English voice.

" I want to have you marry me right quick, Julia,"
he said, dwelling with a tender drawl on her name.

" Oh, yes," she breathed. " Right quick. Very
nearly at once."

" What about if you stayed with us—mother and
Viney and me—in Santa Barb for a few weeks, just
to give us time to get a home ready, and then we
got married right off ? Why, Julia, I know the very
house for us ; it's situated on Mountain Drive, above
the town, among the olive trees, looking down on the
ocean, with a cute garden, and two cypresses at the
gate. It's kind of honey-coloured 'dobe, picked out
with blue doors and windows and all. Spanish style
architecture, of course, with tiled roof and arcades
and the cunningest patio with palms and orange trees
and a well. I'll say it's a dandy home for a swell girl.
And a real high-class view, the ocean in front and the
mountains behind, and the blue sky overhead, and only
ten minutes in the automobile down to Hernando
Street, where my office is situated. What about it,
honey ? Does that sound good to you ? "

Julia conveyed that it did.

" You don't think, do you," she added, " that I'd

better go home to England first, to get some things I
left there, and you come over and us be married from
my home, with my family and friends looking on ? "

" Do you ? " he asked.

" No, Buck," she answered (for Buck was Mr.
James's name. Julia loved it ; it was like a name in a
film).

" Well, then, forget it. We'll pay England a
visit together, after we're married and settled down.
Because I sure don't want to wait any more, after
waiting for you close on thirty years. Oh, my
honey . . ."

After an interval Mr. James spoke of religion.

" We're Methodist Episcopal. I guess you're Protestant Episcopal ; the English visitors all seem to be
that. There's a mighty fine Protestant Episcopal
church in Santa Barb, too. I guess if you're set on it
I'll have to come along to it with you and desert the
old ship, though mother'll be sorry. But what I say
is, we're all Christians together, whether we're Catholics,
or Methodists or Baptists or Protestant Episcopals,
so what's the odds ? "

" But, Buck, darling, I don't think I'm a Protestant
Episcopal. It sounds extraordinary ; what is it ?
I mean, what do they worship, and how ? "

" Well, I don't know, baby, but the English that
come to Santa Barb say it's their church, and I suppose
they ought to know. I guess it's the likest thing to
their church at home that they find over this side.
Just the same, if you don't feel strongly about it, so
much the better. You can come along to church with
me and the rest ; that'll be fine."

" Yes, darling Buck. I'm a Quaker in England, but I expect I can soon pick up yours."

" A Quaker, are you, sugar ? Are all your family Quaker church members ? "

" Oh, no, Buck, honey. Papa's an Anglican, and goes to the Temple with the other judges. My little sister at school is Church of England too, and rather High for her age. My eldest sister isn't anything particular, nor is Benet. I became a Quaker last year. They make quite the best chocolate, you know, and are very thoughtful and wealthy and good."

" Well, candy-stick, you sure don't have to quit being Quaker if you don't want. But ours is a mighty nice church with a mighty nice lots of folks, all friendly together, and a right smart preacher, and I'd like to have you join it if you feel you can. But what does it matter about church ? I'll say, if men and women are white, and lead straight, clean lives, and try to do their duty, they can pray just how they want, and it's all right with me."

" Yes, Buck, syrup. And can they if they're not ? if they don't I mean ? "

" Well, I guess you and me don't need to worry about that, baby."

" Oh, Buck darling ! Are you white and straight and clean ? How too marvellous ! How I wish I was ! Does it feel lovely, like a shirt fresh from the laundry ? Do you feel you couldn't ever even dream of doing a black, crooked, dirty action ? "

" Now you're kidding me, toffee. I guess I'd do a hundred crooked acts to get you, if I couldn't have you any other way. Well, after all, I'm just an ordinary man, I don't set up to be an angel. But I'm straight in business ; I never would do a man or woman down on a deal, even though I'm a realtor. I won't stand for graft."

"Well, Buck darling, I do hope we'll be able to afford the cute house on Mountain Drive, all the same. Do you know, chocolate, I never heard before of a man that sold estate property who wouldn't stand for graft, or do men and women down on a deal. I suppose you're sure you're quite wise to take that line ? "

"Why, yes, strawberry. Sure I'm right. Look at that little cuss Phipps ; he's played crooked, and look at him chasing up this doggoned country like a hunted rabbit with a pack of dogs after him."

But Julia rejected Mr. Phipps as a protagonist of a cautionary tale.

"Phipps won't come to any harm," she said. " I feel that Phipps will always make good."

4

Through the day the storm rolled away westward, dying with soft and lingering growls, like a dog tired with his own anger, until, when the sudden night swallowed the grey end of day, there was heard only the beating of the rain on the drowned green valley and purple mountain crags. And that grew lighter, gentler, less determined, through the night, till by midnight there was only the heavy dripping from the soaked trees, a quick, clumsy pattering as of feet at a country dance.

The steam rose from the warm soft, beaten, hissing earth, into an air growing quickly colder and more clear. By two o'clock a few stars had pricked out, tiny candles shaking between the drifting gloom of clouds.

A droning hum filled the night, approaching Harrison's ranch from the north-east, like the sound of a swarming hive. An aeroplane bumped through the clouds, swooped about, looking for its direction, descended in a level field half a mile behind the ranch, where two signalling gentlemen awaited it, picked them up, and lurched up among the clouds again, heading north-east. Through the dark dawn it droned, over the barren mountains and desolate cactus-grown deserts, the fierce northern spurs of the Sierra San Pedro Martin, the wild southern spurs of the Sierra de Juarez, the hot springs of the Arroyo Agua Caliente, and the flat lagoon country south of Mexicali, Yuma, and the border.

Julia was right ; Mr. Phipps, assisted by his friend the General and the General's political allies, had made good once more.

5

" I'm glad Phipps has gone," Catherine said. " Now we can think about something else."

" A rather curious, secretive departure," said the prebendary, who felt left in the lurch. " I suppose they had no room in their machine for any of the rest of us. Is there any chance of the roads being passable in a day or two, Miss Olivier ? "

" No," said Miss Olivier.

" Well, one must enquire about steamers, and meanwhile make the best of this really enchanting spot. . . . I can't help feeling it a little odd that neither Mr. Phipps nor General Vegas said a word about their departure to me."

" Did they pay their bills ? " asked Benet.

" No," said Miss Olivier.

CHAPTER XXI

GOING HOME

I

Two days later a steamer from Port San Quintin carried the travellers and their car to San Diego, California, U.S.A. There they met the Rickabys, and enjoyed an agreeable stay, visiting the new Agua Caliente racecourse on the last two days of the races. Or rather, most of the party visited it on one day only, but Catherine on both, for she was a confirmed and persevering gambler, and, throughout her career, alternately lost more than she ever earned, and won more than such skill as she possessed deserved. On this occasion she was not fortunate, and lost. She was left with a banker's draft for a hundred dollars to arm her against that sea of debt which beat noisily and angrily against the doors of her London flat, and from which last autumn she had fled. A hundred dollars, relations from whom to borrow provenance and a ticket home, and, in England, a long-suffering but long-since exasperated parent, a lover worse off than herself, and a novel which could not come out till next spring. Impatient and bored, Catherine turned aside from a visit so unpromising to consider again, with interested attention, her relations.

2

"Listen, Adrian," Isie said. "This place is getting hellish. It's just crawling with people, and it's hot as hell. I want to go up to San Bernardino right at once. To-morrow, I mean."

"Just as you say," Adrian agreed.

They lay on the Santa Barbara beach in bathing suits, half in the shade of the cliff, Isie, Adrian, Catherine, and Benet. Julia was staying in Santa Barbara with the family of Mr. James. The beach, this hot Sunday afternoon, was alive with people, Californians, Europeans and Mexicans, disporting themselves in the shimmering Pacific or roasting themselves at its edge.

"Look at them," Isie requested, carefully restoring to her lips the desirable vermilion hue which the Pacific had dimmed. "I ask you! Just crawling. What a sight! And what figures!"

"Why, then, do you ask me to look at them? Adrian enquired. He did not, in fact, do so : he looked instead at Isie, who lay on her side, her head on her golden-brown arm, her smooth golden brown thigh from the edge of the wet scarlet bathing-suit down, roasting in the sun like a nice joint of meat. Adrian wanted to stroke or to slap it.

His young wife was the most beautiful human creature (not that this is to say much) that he had ever seen. You could not look on Isie's beauty and remain unmoved. No one did. Most beauty is debatable, much exists only in the eyes of lovers, but Isie's in

the eyes of practically all human beings of her own
hemisphere, whatever might be thought of it by
Ethiopians, Mongols or Papuans, whose ideas are so
different. Curious, thought Catherine, how we have
agreed, however roughly, to agree about human
beauty. What is it, this fortuitous, chance arrangement
and proportion of features, limbs, and colour, that
appeals so strongly, so strangely, to the human eye?
Watching Adrian's brooding gaze on Isie, Catherine
saw his conscious surrender, his deliberate enchainment
by his senses to desire. With a shock of surprise she
had seen it when first they had met again in San Diego,
a fortnight ago. They had left a sullen and weary
husband, brooding over his lost love, wincing from
the crudities and tempers of his schoolgirl wife ;
they found a lover surrendering, if half-ironically, to
the beauty of a youthful mistress. The admiring
glances of other men fanned in the husband a proud,
possessive flame. She was, after all, his. Few men
had such a handsome young creature to wife. No need
to listen to what she said, in that loud clear voice of
hers ; talk was, anyhow, a bore. She was like a lovely
animal, stretched, lithe and golden, beneath the Californian sun. You wanted to stroke or pat her.

Another surprise, thought Catherine. Here was a
thing one had not thought would happen, and, as
usual, it was happening.

" There's a woman exactly like a whale," said Isie,
still finding painful pleasure in the sight of her fellow
bathers. " Oh, Adrian, do look ! Isn't she just terribly
like a whale ? "

" Very like a whale," Adrian answered without

looking, dribbling the hot sand through his fingers over Isie's leg.

" I can't think what you see in them," Benet said. " I mean, why you find them so intriguing."

Isie yawned and stretched.

" I don't. I think they're just too terribly discouraging. Well, then, is that fixed ? We all go right up to San Bernardino to-morrow. I'm crazy to get into the mountains."

" I shan't go to San Bernardino," said Benet. " I've got to sail from New York in a month, and I've too many cities to see to waste time on mountains and canyons and rims of the world. I shall get on to the Southern Pacific and make my way east."

" I think I will come with you," said Catherine, " if you don't mind, that is, and if someone can lend me the fare. I must get home and try and get hold of some money to settle some of my more clamorous creditors."

" Why," said Isie, " I call that just silly, running right into trouble that way. Listen, Catherine, you'd much better stop with us a while longer, as our guest. Hadn't she, Adrian ? Aren't you crazy for the Rim of the World this weather ? I am."

But Catherine, who knew the Rim of the World already, was crazier to get back to Europe, despite her clamorous creditors, for she would fain meet again her lover. Such is the folly and the force of love, which persuades lovers against all reason that the beloved is a finer spectacle than mountains, a stronger attraction than the Pacific Ocean.

" I must go back," said Catherine. Besides, she

thought, these two will be better on the Rim of the World by themselves, since that is the way they will have to be when they come down from it again. They must learn, like other couples, to live alone together.

" Well, I'm going to have another ocean ride," said Isie. " Come on, Adrian."

" No."

" Oh, you're lazy as hell. All you Britishers, you're slack as hell."

She stood up, dropped her white bathing wrap over her husband's head, and walked down the burning sands to the Pacific, in shape and stride a young goddess, a cigarette between her scarlet lips.

Adrian, disentangling himself from the bath robe, watched her, with impassive, expressionless face.

Benet, tired of lying undressed in the heat, perhaps an over-rated diversion, went to a tent to assume a costume in which he might go up to Santa Barbara.

2

" I suppose it's all right for Isie, all this exercise," Catherine tentatively said.

Adrian watched Isie mounting her board, being drawn rapidly by a motor-boat over the surfing ocean, like Venus in a cockle-shell.

" Why not ? " he returned. " Oh, I see, you're thinking about that baby. You needn't worry. There's no baby at present. It was a mistake. Didn't we tell you ? "

" No," said Catherine.

" Oh, well," he said, vaguely. " It's all for the best," he added. " She can enjoy herself better without it."

Catherine could not read his face. Was he cynical, bitter, resigned ? Had he been angry at this ancient snare ? Had he ever been deceived by it ?

" Better without it," he repeated, and watched Isie pitching headlong from her chariot into the Santa Barbara Channel, as her speed-boat sharply turned.

" Perhaps," Catherine doubtfully agreed. " She's not the mother type, exactly, I suppose. Not yet, at least."

" Oh, type. That's all nonsense about types, surely. I mean, an accident as common as parenthood, it may happen to anyone ; it does. And no one is fit for it ; no one carries it off particularly well."

" Still, Julia and Buck James will enjoy it. I call Buck a father type."

" You call everyone a type. That's where you're hopelessly out. There are no types, and no groups. Only a haphazard crowd of eccentrics, each odder than the next. We can't even understand or classify ourselves and our own reactions, let alone anyone else's. . . . Well, it doesn't matter."

He subsided into listlessness, his chin on his arm, his eyes staring at the blue bay of Santa Barbara and the slim scarlet figure that scrambled again on to a board and stood balanced like Phæton holding the reins of his rushing chariot. So lovely a sight was the poised, balancing and laughing figure against the deep blue sea and the clear blue sky, that Catherine smiled in pleasure.

Adrian did not smile, but stared with brooding eyes narrowed against the sun.

" How beautiful," Catherine exclaimed.

" Isie ? " he said, half absently. " Yes, she's beautiful . . ."

So, thought Catherine, might a man speak who wakes from a long night of dreaming, and, putting behind him his dreams, too exquisite and frail for possession, turns with a welcome half cynical, half greedy to the brilliant yet storm-ridden day that burns upon his eyes. Is this, then, what he has, for his long, wistful, unhappy dreams of a joy he could not grasp ? This, then, is what he has ; broad daylight and hot beauty and thunder quivering in the air. Not peace, and not what he has for too long known as love, but a bright, turbulent, electric day of easily snatched pleasures, of luxury, of nagging angers and pains.

Catherine thought, one day he may kill Isie, or Isie may kill him, they will both quarrel so often. That is, if they are together long enough. But how should they be ? Isie, exuberantly young, lavishly beautiful, stormily loving and extravagantly rich, was, surely, not a wife who would for ever tarry by one husband. Adrian, accepting now her youth, love, beauty and wealth, as a man disappointed with life turns with deliberate self-consolation to gratifying food and drink, had already shown himself a husband too impatient and too nerve-ridden to endure for long so much irrational excitement at his side. By mutual agreement they would surely fly asunder, as, in these days of brevity and fatigue, so many better lovers do. On the other hand, even in these days of fatigue and brevity, so many worse lovers stay, for one reason and another, together, through years and years and years.

So, thought Catherine, you never know. She became aware that Adrian was watching her, having turned his mocking eyes from the ocean to her face.

" You're interested in us, aren't you ? " he said. " You want to get it right, for your next novel. Perhaps, then, you'd care to hear the latest news of Claudia. I heard from her at San Diego. She said she had got engaged to a rich widower with three children—or is it five ? He's been asking her ever since his last wife died, and now she's accepted him, mainly to gratify her maternal instincts, so she says. And so much for your mother types. You didn't guess Claudia was one, did you ? "

" No," said Catherine. But she was hurt by his manner and his malicious attack on her, and said no more.

" Well," he said, sombrely and with spite, " she is. She wants to vent her instincts on a widower's five children, and doubtless five more of her own as soon as she can come by them. Do you find that odd ? Probably you do ; you seem to find such a number of things odd. But I'll tell you for your information that Claudia's a sentimentalist. She doesn't really love ; she only plays about with nice little feelings. . . . Oh, damn, what do you pry on us like this ? I don't want to tell you anything. Haven't you affairs of your own to attend to ? I could pry into them, I suppose, and worm them out of you, but I don't want to, I don't want to know them. Leave ours alone, then."

He fell silent and ashamed, after the longest speech

he had ever addressed to Catherine Grey. He lay with his chin on his arm, and said listlessly. " I'm sorry. The sun's too hot."

" I'm sorry, too," said Catherine, her voice trembling with hurt and affront, " if I have seemed to pry. It's not been deliberate, I assure you. And I didn't ask you to tell me anything."

A tear of mortification dropped from her eye and dented the hot sand with a dark spot. Adrian, observing it, marked that though she presented such a calm, controlled exterior, she was not calm or controlled at all, but as upset and weak as anyone else. No doubt her soul was a seething storm of hysterical passions, like everyone else's. Yes, everyone's; unless they merely played about with nice little feelings and married widowers for their children.

" Well, I beg your pardon," said Adrian, tired. " I apologise. Let's forget it.'

" All right," said Catherine. " Anyhow we part to-morrow, so you won't be bothered with me much more."

There she went, thought Adrian. Going on, like a woman. When he said let's forget it, why *not* forget it, and be done ?

" Well," said he, formal and polite. " It's been charming to see something of you. We must meet again in London. Are you bringing out another book soon ? "

" I always am," said Catherine, crossly. " It's my trade. Do people keep asking you, are you designing another house soon, and Uncle Dickie, is he hearing another case soon ? "

" I beg your pardon," said Adrian again, still more distant. " I dare say they do. Anyhow I don't suppose we should either of us object to answering if we were asked. I merely asked out of politeness, not inquisitiveness. Writers seem rather self-conscious people."

Benet came back from the tent, dressed in white flannels, looking fair and frail and rather charming, though badly burnt.

" I'm going back to Santa Barbara," he said, " to see about my ticket."

Catherine scrambled up.

" If you'll wait ten minutes, I'll come with you, to see about mine."

She went off to her tent to dress.

" I've been hurting Catherine's feelings," said Adrian.

" Well," said Benet, calmly, " that's no great feat. It's quite easy. She's sensitive."

" Yes, I didn't know before. I supposed she was as tough and placid as she looks and sounds."

" Is anyone ? "

" Probably not."

" What did you say to her ? "

" I suppose I rather accused her of peeping and prying into other people's concerns. It wasn't quite fair, because she's really always the lady, though she *is* damned inquisitive and interested. As a matter of fact, I like Catherine very much. You'd never suspect her of all that turbulent and disorderly private history she seems to have—all those debts and love and what not, I mean."

" My dear, why on earth not ? Surely practically
everyone has some turbulent and disorderly private
history. Though plenty of people keep it pretty well
corked down ; fortunately, since it's usually the least
amusing thing about them. Turbulence, excitement,
mess—no one seems to escape these dreadful things,
any more than they escape colds in the head. All one
can hope is that they won't sneeze much in one's
company. I must say, Catherine doesn't. I shall
quite like her as a travelling companion. She looks
cool and clean in trains, too."

Catherine here strolled up to them, clad. She was
done to a pleasant brown. Adrian and Benet, on the
other hand, being incorrectly pigmented for the sun,
were burnt in scarlet patches.

3

Benet complimented Catherine on the difference, as
they walked up to the Coast Hiway, through the green
plaza of a phantom city-to-be. The city was called
Santa Juana, and its plaza was Plaza de Los Toros,
and was surrounded by signboards indicating the City
Lecture Hall, the Methodist Episcopal Church, the
Public Library, the Theatre, the Real Estate Office
and the Business Block.

" YOUR HOME TOWN IS RIGHT HERE.
SEE IT GROW.
ROME WASN'T BUILT IN A DAY
GIVE US FIVE MINUTES."

the largest sign hopefully and politely requested.

Catherine, with equal politeness and hope, was prepared
to give them all the minutes they required. When she
went through Santa Juana, her American blood
stirred in her, till she heard up and down those empty
grassy thoroughfares with Spanish names (Calle
Naranjas, Camino Viejo, and the like) the hurrying of
busy feet on pavements by the Business Block, saw
the crowds trooping out of the Lecture Hall with the
blank, dazed, replete faces of those who have attended
lectures, the merrier crowds queuing up for a talkie
at the Theatre, the Episcopal Methodists, hymn-books
in hand, shaking hands with their minister at the
porch of their church, and, all about the Real Estate
Office, business men surging over one another in their
eagerness to purchase lots. A beautiful city it was to
be, built, like Santa Barbara itself, of softly-coloured
adobe, with arcades and courtyards and orange-
gardens, and it lay there on the green sward above
Santa Barbara's blue bay, already, to the eyes of
faith, hope, charity and Californians, blooming like a
nosegay of bright flowers.

" I always get quite a kick out of Santa Juana,"
Catherine said, hoisting the stars and stripes after her
encounter with the sardonic British Adrian.

They stopped in the Rambla, Santa Juana's main
thoroughfare, and looked back from the city of dreams
to the smooth white beach and the sparkling deep blue
channel, where, far out, the islands rode like a flotilla
of ships, dimly, deeply, hazily blue, Santa Cruz
leading, the nearest, clearest, and longest, Santa Rosa
sailing behind, and little San Miguel coming out of
the west like a small boat trailing in their wake.

"Adrian's water-sporting, too, now," said Benet; and, sure enough, there was the thin, blue and white form of Adrian being rushed over the sea on a board behind the motor-boat, while the lithe scarlet and brown form of his wife sat in the boat's edge and jeered.

"So long as they can play together, they'll be all right," said Catherine, prying again into what did not concern her. "It's when they're not playing and not lovering, and Isie talks, that the trouble sets in. Adrian's so irritable, and poor Isie's irritable too, and has silly little faults that will always annoy him . . ."

"My dear, hasn't everyone? We're a more or less silly little race, if you come to think of it. 'Marriage is not commonly unhappy, otherwise than as life is unhappy,' or so Dr. Johnson said. Still, as he also said, he often spoke very laxly, so I dare say he was quite wrong. Anyhow, though, of course, I should be sorry if Adrian and Isie weren't to be at all happy, I can't feel it matters excessively to me, can you? I mean, not in the way my own happiness does."

"Well, no, quite a different way, of course. Still, one's interested."

"I'm not," said Benet, "particularly. I haven't, actually, much time to think about it; I'm too busy arranging my own affairs. Look, there's our tram."

They boarded it, and jingled along the hiway into Santa Barbara, which, lovely city of delicately-hued Moorish-Spanish arcades, and plazas green and gold with palms and oranges, bloomed like a town in fairyland between the mountains and the sea.

" What," Catherine kindly asked, " are you going to do when you get back to England ? "

" Go into Laver's and sell soap."

" Sell soap ? Dear me, how surprising of you ! "

" My dear, why ? You're so easily surprised. Soap is sold, you know, in considerable quantities. As a matter of fact, it's a rather promising job. I may die a soap king."

" That would be nice, of course. Still, I can't help feeling it a rather unexpected kind of job for you to be doing."

" Well," Benet admitted justly, after reflection, " perhaps you are right. Perhaps life *is* unexpected. Though, as to that, it all depends, naturally, on what one expects. . . . By the way, would you have expected that prebendary of being the Churton who knows all there is to know about Maya buildings, and discovered that temple buried in the Honduras jungles from an aeroplane last year ? I wouldn't. Well, I mean, he seemed so silly. And really he must be all that there is of the most highbrow. Anyhow about archæology, though of course one thing doesn't seem to go with another in the brain. . . . Look, here's the railway station."

And the end of my stay with my relations, thought Catherine. On the whole, it has been a very agreeable visit, though rather peculiar in some ways. But then, most visits are that, I think.